KERRIN WILLIS

Strange Arithmetic

D1260500

KERRIN WILLIS
AUTHOR

WEST BRIDGEWATER PUBLIC LIBRARY

First published by Kerrin Willis 2023

Copyright © 2023 by Kerrin Willis

All rights reserved. No part of this publication may be reproduced, stored or transmitted in any form or by any means, electronic, mechanical, photocopying, recording, scanning, or otherwise without written permission from the publisher. It is illegal to copy this book, post it to a website, or distribute it by any other means without permission.

This novel is entirely a work of fiction. The names, characters and incidents portrayed in it are the work of the author's imagination. Any resemblance to actual persons, living or dead, events or localities is entirely coincidental.

First edition

ISBN: 979-8-9861325-0-1

This book was professionally typeset on Reedsy.
Find out more at reedsy.com

To my girls, Charlotte and Georgia

&

To my crazy, sometimes emotionally stunted, always hilarious, and fiercely loyal Irish Catholic family. I love you — now let's not talk about it.

Acknowledgement

When I was growing up, I loved listening to my dad and my uncles tell stories about life during World War II. My grandfather, like Maggie's father, owned a market in town. Like Maggie, he worked in a laundry facility at Camp. Like Maggie, he saw thousands of men and women pass through the camp on their way to and from Europe. I grew up on stories of Taunton in the 1940s — blackout drills, the news on the radio, and, of course, Italian co-belligerents. Thanks Dad, Uncle Paul, and Uncle Joe for passing down the stories to the next generation.

Many, many thanks to the amazing editors at The History Quill, especially Rachel Smith and Cecily Blench. Without your assistance, Leo would have had about six different birth dates. Thanks to Brigitta Larson, whose copyediting and proofreading skills are beyond compare. The student has become the master.

I couldn't possibly do what I do without my amazing writing students, both past and present, at BFHS. From the alumi who beta read the story for me to the students who listened to me kvetch, you've all been instrumental in bringing Maggie, Leo, and Niamh to life.

Thank you so much to my amazing support system. I'm beyond lucky to call Dr. Rebecca Dedrick my best friend, not least of all because she has always been there to answer my

i

frantic medical texts, such as "how would someone have lost an arm in WWII?" and "talk to me about rubella....what do you know?" Thanks for always being there and believing in me, Bex. Thanks to Rachel Murphy for talking me off multiple ledges and reminding me that I do not, in fact, suck at writing. Thanks for being there through thick and thin for decades.

Jules – I won't say it, because as this entire book just proved, Irish Catholic families don't do mushy stuff. But thanks for being my person, and for being the other half of my weird, dysfunctional brain. Thanks for listening to me go on and on about Maggie and Leo for a year, and for helping me work through plot problems and character issues.

And lastly, to my girls — Charlotte and Georgia. I can't say you helped with this book much at all. In fact, you hindered it at every possible point. But I love you more than I could ever express, and I'm beyond grateful to be your mom.

Chapter 1

Maggie — 1944

"I don't need to wear stockings," Maggie grumbled from her seat at the end of her best friend's bed, where she was busy getting ready for the local Catholic Youth Organization dance to celebrate the end of summer. "My socks and shoes will be fine."

"Don't be ridiculous, Mags. You are not walking into the dance in ankle socks like a twelve-year-old. Take a pair of my stockings; top drawer on the left." Betty's voice wafted in from her bathroom, where she was teasing her blonde hair into perfect victory rolls. Maggie sighed with a smile, shaking her head before opening the aforementioned drawer. This was Betty; generous to a fault, but still insisting that fashion standards be upheld, even in the middle of a war.

Maggie's eyes widened in amazement at the sight of twenty pairs of brand-new stockings, most still in their packages, all neatly rolled up and ready to wear in Betty's bureau.

"Elisabeth Curran," she gasped, "how did you ever get all these? You have more pairs than Jordan-Marsh!"

"I don't know; my daddy just brings them home." Betty stuck her head out of the bathroom and fixed Maggie with a stare. "Socks and saddle shoes are for schoolgirls and we, darling, are women of the world."

"Are we now?" Maggie grinned, goading her. "I read in *Laff* that Judy Garland has given up wearing stockings to support the war effort. There is a war on, you know, even for socialites like us. Isn't wearing socks and shoes just being patriotic?"

Betty stomped her foot in childish irritation, and Maggie grinned.

"Margaret Veronica, I simply will not allow it." Betty pouted. "Not when there are plenty of stockings here to go around."

"Thanks for the offer, love. You're a gem. I don't suppose it could hurt to wear one little pair." Maggie grabbed a pair of nude hose from the drawer and slid into the bathroom with her friend, taking a seat on the edge of the pretty pink bathtub. There was twitch in her belly — guilt for giving in to the luxury of stockings when her brother Owen was God knows where fighting God knows who tonight. Then again, she rationalized, it wasn't like she was taking the nylon stockings away from someone who needed them; they were already bought and paid for. Betty's status as an only child meant that her parents spoiled her rotten; that wasn't Betty's fault. She had been Maggie's best friend since they were in diapers and was always generous to a fault in sharing what she had. She could be petulant at times, and rather insistent on getting her way, but always had the best of intentions, and that was what mattered.

"So, do you think there will be anyone worth dancing with

2

tonight?" Betty asked in the mirror, securing a roll of hair with a bobby pin and spraying it in place.

"I'd imagine there won't be many. Plus, shouldn't you be saving your dancing feet for one Billy Morris?" Maggie asked. She rolled the brand-new stockings up her legs, reveling in the feel of the diaphanous fabric against her skin. She hadn't had a new pair of stockings since last Christmas, and these felt decadent.

"Billy's in Europe," Betty replied with a wave of her hand. "I don't intend to let anyone kiss me tonight, but a few little dances never hurt anybody."

"Is that what you'd say if Billy was the one out dancing with a beautiful French girl?" Maggie let the question hang in the air, concentrating on the seams of her stockings and intentionally avoiding eye contact.

"Billy wouldn't dare," Betty declared, scandalized, and Maggie raised one manicured eyebrow in response. Point made. "Dancing with a few boys before they go off to war is harmless," Betty sniffed. "I'm doing my patriotic duty, and I don't want to hear another word about it." She left the bathroom in a cloud of indignation and *Evening in Paris* perfume, and Maggie couldn't help but laugh. The war might be on the forefront of everyone's mind, but even that couldn't prevent Elisabeth Curran from being herself.

"Bets?" Maggie asked, following Betty into the bedroom and taking her burgundy dress off its hanger on the closet door. "What do you suppose the boys are up to right now? Billy, Charlie, and Owen?"

"Since they're on the other side of the world, I'd imagine they're sleeping. It's the middle of the night in Europe, and I think it's tomorrow out in the Pacific. Can you see my slip at all?" Betty twisted from side to side in the full-length mirror.

"Nope; you look fine," Maggie replied automatically. Billy was infantry, so he was somewhere in Europe, most likely in France. Charlie and Owen, however, were Navy boys. That meant that they could be anywhere in the world on their respective ships, facing all manner of enemy attack at this very moment, a thought that made Maggie feel as if she needed to be sick.

"Are you worried Charlie's going to find someone else, you silly girl?"Betty asked, looking up from her purse to fix Maggie with a stern look. "That boy is mad about you. You have nothing at all to worry about."

Maggie coughed to cover the snort she felt rising in her nose. She prayed every morning and evening that Charlie would come home safe and sound, but never once did she worry that he wasn't serious about her. Ever since he had deployed, his letters had become more and more alarming by the day. "When I get home, Mags," and "In our future, Mags," She wasn't exactly sure how she should react to these statements, but she knew that an urge to run and hide under her bed wasn't terrific.

The day Charlie had enlisted was a blur for Maggie.

He'd knocked on the kitchen door at three pm on a Tuesday. Charlie was never available at three on Tuesdays — that was when he had his Western Civ class with Brother Maurice at Providence College. Sometimes he'd come by afterwards and take Maggie on a walk, regaling her with what he'd learned about Greek democracy, but never until at least five-thirty.

As soon as Maggie had let him into the kitchen, she knew. He was wearing his church suit, and his hair was slicked to the side with Brylcreem. This wasn't weekday Charlie. This was serious Charlie.

"I signed up," he said, voice cracking on the last word. "I ship out on Friday."

Maggie had wiped her hands on her apron, and looked to her mother with a question in her eyes.

"Go," Mam replied with a sigh. "But don't be takin' too long, now." Within minutes, Maggie had removed her apron and was out the door with Charlie. They headed towards the Green at the center of the city, matching each other step for step, her arm tucked neatly into his elbow.

"Can I buy you a soda?" he'd asked, and Maggie dimly recognized those as the same words he had used when he had first asked her to go out with him three years before. She nodded and allowed him to lead her through the doors of Woolworths and over to the soda fountain.

"You enlisted," she said finally, once they were settled on their stools, cream sodas fizzing in front of them. "In...?"

"The Navy," he grinned, showing off the dimples that she had always found so charming. "I don't know where I'll be sent, but I'm hoping for the South Pacific."

"You'll burn." Maggie barely realized that she was speaking out loud. Her voice sounded tinny, far away. "Make sure you wear your hat when you're on deck."

"I'll be swell." He grabbed her hand and squeezed in reassurance. "I won't be staying in one place long enough to get a burn."

Maggie opened her mouth to scold him about the ridiculous nature of that sentiment, but thought better of it. Charlie would need to start fending for himself soon — she wouldn't be in the Navy with him to see to it that he was safe.

When Maggie had first set eyes on Charlie, the ganglier of

5

a gangly set of redheaded twins from down the street, she instantly felt the need to mother the poor boy. His father had left when he and his brother were babies, and his mother worked long hours at the silver factory. He needed her. And he loved her. And—

"I hope you're not going to be a drip tonight, Maggie." Betty's voice broke through the reverie. She was standing just outside the bedroom door, ready to head downstairs and out the door. "I know you miss Charlie, but we are about to be surrounded by dreamboats in uniform who ship out any minute — let's cut a rug, Cookie!"

Shaking her curls to clear her mind of Seaman Charles Morris of the United States Navy, Maggie pasted a smile on her face and hurried after Betty, determined to have a good night.

Chapter 2

Niamh — 2015

" Why is it that doctors can run two hours late, but if I waltzed into work at ten o'clock in the morning without a call, I'd be out on my ass?" Niamh Reilly asked her wife. The ass in question was starting to go numb from sitting on the hard plastic chair in the waiting room of the Massachusetts General Hospital fertility clinic. "It's like they don't care that we both took the morning off for this."

Her wife Christine was, as usual, serenity personified. She placed a hand on Niamh's knee to stop it from bouncing, and replied, "We'll see Dr. Bennett, no matter how long it takes, love. We've been the ones in there getting bad news before — sometimes appointments take longer than planned."

"I know," Niamh grumbled with a sheepish half-smile. God, Christine was the picture of cool composure. They'd been together for seven years, and Niamh still had no idea how her wife always managed to look so put together. In contrast, Niamh was a spiky little ball of nerves, ready to climb out of her own skin if the doctor didn't call her name soon. Today was their third attempt at insemination, and the last of the sperm they had purchased from donor CA41222GV. If Niamh's body didn't cooperate today, then all the time, money, and worry they'd spent over the past six months would be for nothing.

"I'd tell you not to worry, but I know that wouldn't do any good. May I offer a distraction?" Christine raised one perfectly arched eyebrow and gestured to a stack of magazines on the side table.

"There's no way I could focus on anything," Niamh sighed. "Aren't you nervous?"

"Of course. I've been nervous every time." Christine's coffee-brown eyes softened as she put an arm around Niamh's shoulders and squeezed.

"What if it doesn't work, Chris?"

"If it doesn't work, we'll figure it out. We can look into IVF, and I know you want to carry, but I'd be happy to do it if for some reason you can't."

Niamh snuggled into Christine's side, letting her head melt into her wife's shoulder and willing the nervous energy coursing through her body to subside. Christine wanted to be a mom just as badly as she did, but Christine hadn't spent her whole life longing for the day that she'd hold her biological child in her arms. Niamh had. Christine had family — a mother, father, and brother who had the same wide smile and lanky build as she did. Niamh could see her wife in her in-laws, and they in her, but she had no one in her life that reflected her looks back to her in the same way. Her dark hair and freckle-prone complexion, her stormy green eyes and diminutive stature, came from ancestors who were as mysterious to her as Santa Claus and the tooth fairy. For as long as Niamh could remember, she had dreamed of a child who was tied to her through genetics and DNA, and she wasn't ready to give up on that yet.

"I know, baby," Christine whispered into Niamh's hair, her breath warm and ticklish. "One step at a time. We'll get there."

A young man in scrubs came through the door that led back to the doctors' offices, carrying a stack of files and scanning the expectant faces in the waiting room. Niamh's heart picked up speed again.

"Nee-amm-ah Reilly?"

Niamh jumped to her feet, gathering her things and brushing past the nurse without so much as a "hello." She felt a twinge of guilt for her rudeness when she heard Christine's quiet voice correcting the man.

"It's Niamh, like *NEEVE*."

No matter. Niamh didn't care what the hell they called her. She had a doctor to see.

Chapter 3

Maggie — 1944

Downtown Taunton, Massachusetts shimmered with excitement every Saturday night during the summer. All of the local teens and twenty-somethings were out in their best glad rags, crowding the ice cream parlors, movie theaters, and restaurants in town. Music poured out of the open windows along Broadway and Main Street — Bing Crosby, Glenn Miller, the Andrews Sisters — inspiring Betty to grab Maggie by the hand and pull her into a jitterbug in front of Durand's Ice Cream Parlor. Maggie laughed, playing along and enjoying the chance to let all the worries of the world wait for a few moments.

"Careful," Maggie gasped through a twirl, "or my hair will look like a fallen cake by the time we get to the dance."

"You look fantastic, doll. And so do I, if I do say so myself." Betty twirled again with a grin and a wink, before dropping

Maggie's hand and continuing her progress down Main Street, her pretty face flushed from the activity. Betty stopped at the top of the street and gave a low wolf whistle; Maggie scrambled to catch up.

"What's going on?"

"Just appreciating the view." Betty turned to Maggie with a wicked grin. "I love a man in uniform." Across the street from the church where the dance was being held stood the Officers' Club, a function hall exclusively for higher-ranking military officials and whichever girls were lucky enough to be on their arms for the evening. Maggie followed Betty's gaze to a group of men standing outside the club with their dates, laughing and swapping stories in their official-looking uniforms. "I can't get enough of Billy in his uniform."

"I imagine he looks exactly the same as Charlie." Maggie wondered again where the boys were at this exact moment and she prayed that they were safe. The Morris twins were raised on Randall Street right alongside the Currans and the O'Callaghans, and Maggie couldn't remember a time when it wasn't understood that she and Charlie were an item, or that Betty and Billy were the same. All their lives, the older boys on the street had teased the girls mercilessly, even going so far as to break the china tea set Mrs. Curran had ordered for Betty out of the Sears & Roebuck catalog. It always went the same way: Betty would cry, and Maggie would go chasing the older boys up the street to tell their mothers on them. Then Charlie and Billy would inevitably swoop in, setting the tea table to rights again, or getting down on their hands and knees to help locate missing jacks or marbles under the front porch. The four of them were a team. It was natural that they'd end up together.

"Devilishly handsome," Betty said with a sigh. "Maybe the boys will move up in the ranks and take us to the Officers' Club one day."

"One day," Maggie repeated, taking Betty's hand to lead her across the street to the church. "But tonight, my friend, it's the CYO, stale cookies, and Sister Mary Elizabeth watching everyone to make sure they're leaving enough room between them for the Holy Ghost." Maggie gave a meaningful look towards the entrance to the church basement, where four boys of perhaps fifteen or sixteen stood, coated in acne and enough Brylcreem to grease the wheels of the entire United States Air Force. She groaned as the boys caught sight of them and stood tall, tucking their combs into their back pockets and licking their lips.

"Trust me, Mags," Betty said with a grimace, "keeping distance between me and those little boys will *not* be an issue."

* * *

Maggie had never seen the dance halls in Boston or New York, but as she descended into the church basement behind Betty that evening, she felt certain that the leaders of the Taunton Catholic Youth Organization fell a bit short of the real thing in their design. She wrinkled her nose and stepped into the room, which smelled precisely how she'd imagined a room crowded with over one hundred sweaty teenagers would smell. A band was set up just off the dance floor, and a crooner she didn't recognize belted out a Bing Crosby number as couples twirled around the floor or stood by the lemonade tables. Betty turned and called something over her shoulder, but whatever it was got swallowed up by the cacophony of sounds around them.

"What?" Maggie yelled, grabbing her friend by the arm and pointing to her ear to indicate that she hadn't heard.

"I said," Betty yelled over the noise, "that all the men here are practically children!"

She wasn't incorrect. There were several boys from the parish who couldn't have been more than fifteen or sixteen, and the oldest person Maggie could age with certainty was Marshall Boyland, who was seventeen and the son of her mother's hairdresser.

She wilted in relief when she spotted two of her girlfriends, Nadine and Susan, waving at her from across the crowded room by the lemonade table. Taking Betty's hand, she forged a path through the crowd towards them. Before they made it, however, Betty was pulled away to dance by a tall fellow with straw-colored hair and chin acne. Maggie reached for her friend, but Betty just gave her a shrug and took the boy's proffered arm.

"Traitor," Maggie muttered. Without Betty behind her, she was suddenly swarmed with sweaty boys asking her to dance — at least two of whom she had once babysat before they grew facial hair. She politely declined, missing Charlie if for no other reason than that other boys left her alone when she was with him. She pushed on, murmuring "excuse me" and "pardon me," keeping her eyes trained on the lemonade table, until she finally arrived next to Nadine in a rush of relief.

"It's a jungle out there," Maggie stated the obvious, grabbing a paper cup and swallowing its sticky sweet contents in one gulp.

"Yes, it is," Nadine replied, shrewdly perusing the dance floor through her tortoiseshell glasses. "And these fools think we're the prey."

"They'll be heading off to the front soon enough," said Susan, always the placater of the group. She rarely had anything bad to say about anybody. With her brown hair, big gray eyes, and nervous demeanor, Susan had always reminded Maggie of a bunny rabbit. "The least you can do is dance with them before they go."

"The least *we* can do?" Maggie asked, dabbing at the perspiration on the back of her neck with a paper napkin. "You don't intend to dance with any of these fine young men before they ship out, do you?" Susan's eyes widened in terror, but softened as Maggie handed her a cup of lemonade as a peace offering. "I'm just teasing and you know it, Susie-Q. Us wallflowers have to stick together." Susan lips twitched in a nervous approximation of a smile, but her eyes still swept the dance floor for danger.

"Ugh," Nadine exclaimed, crushing her paper cup in her palm before tossing it into a trashcan under the table. "Doesn't being here make you feel like you never left high school?"

Maggie surveyed the room, from the handmade decor to the exuberant dancers to the nuns guarding the snack table, and nodded in agreement. "It does. But what else are we supposed to do on a Saturday night?"

"My gran asked me to play bridge with her and her sisters tonight, but I'd already promised Nadine I'd come," Susan said, stepping back to avoid a group of kids grabbing a drink.

"What is this world coming to when a night with Susan's grandmother sounds like a hoot in comparison to this?" Nadine asked with a wry smile and a raised eyebrow. "It would certainly smell better."

Susan wrinkled her brow in confusion. "My gran's house

smells like mothballs and old pot roast."

"I said what I said," Nadine smirked, eliciting a laugh from Maggie. The dance might be a bit beneath them, but Maggie was enjoying the opportunity to spend time with her friends. Ever since graduating from St.Mary's High in the spring, the girls had struggled to find times when they could all get together. Nadine was training to be a nurse, and Susan had taken a job doing the books in her father's office. Between that, Maggie helping her dad in the market, and the fact that they lived on opposite sides of town, it hadn't been easy. Thank goodness for Betty, who lived right next door on Randall Street and was always happy to chew the fat over a cup of tea or an ice cream.

"My sister says that all the good boys have enlisted, and that what's left in Taunton is the dregs," Susan said offhand. "Do you think that's true?"

"I think," Maggie grabbed Susan's hand and spun her around in a circle, laughing at the terror on the other girl's face, "that I promised Betty I'd have a good time tonight, and that's what I intend to do."

Chapter 4

Maggie — 1944

By around nine o'clock, Maggie had had enough of declining the increasingly insistent requests to dance. One look at Nadine and Susan confirmed that they were ready to leave as well. Betty, however, was having a ball, and after confirming that she didn't mind, the other three girls made their apologies and headed out into the night.

The muggy air outside the dance was only a degree or two cooler than it had been inside, and it hung heavy with moisture and the smell of gardenias. Maggie lifted her long dark hair to fan the back of her neck. At least there was a slight breeze, and she sighed with audible relief as the air brushed across her sweaty skin.

"Do I have mascara puddles under my eyes? I feel like I have mascara puddles under my eyes," Nadine lamented as the girls crossed over Main Street and walked toward the Strand

Theater and Dunnington's Ice Cream shop. The downtown area was still bustling with Saturday-night energy, but it was somehow quieter than it had been a few hours before, like the citizens of Taunton had settled in for a night of recreation.

"It's too dark to see, Nadine," Maggie assured her. "Plus, your glasses would hide most of it if you did."

"Boys don't make passes at girls who wear glasses," Susan sing-songed. She stopped when she saw the looks of mutual horror on her friends' faces, and then her mouth opened into a shocked "O." "Sorry," she muttered, cheeks aflame. "I didn't think that was out loud."

"Clearly," Nadine huffed, adjusting the offending glasses with one hand. "Would you like us to walk you home, Mags?" They had reached the Taunton Green; Maggie's house lay roughly a half mile to the east, up Broadway, while Nadine and Susan lived in the opposite direction, near the Weir.

"No, I can make it. I don't mind my own company." Maggie waved off the offer and gave her friends a quick hug before turning for home. It would be nice to be alone with her thoughts, a luxury she didn't often get as the only daughter in a family of seven. As she strolled up Broadway, Maggie allowed herself to think about how the night would be different if Charlie was home. He'd have spent the entire night on the dance floor, and then she'd likely have had to bat away his wandering hands on the walk home. *Can't fault a fella for trying*, he'd always say with a shrug.

"Well, hello there, gorgeous."

Maggie stumbled in surprise at the voice behind her, a bolt of pain shooting up the side of her calf as her ankle rolled. Righting herself, Maggie readjusted her shaking grip on her handbag, and kept walking. She was in a quieter part of the

17

city now, the bustle of the Green fading behind her, and the lights of St. Mary's Square shining like a beacon ahead. Here, however, it was dark, and there was none of the commotion she had been surrounded by moments earlier.

"Hey, lady, my friend here said you're gorgeous. It's rude to ignore him." The owner of the second voice came up on Maggie's left, and she could just make out a lanky figure in dungarees and a dark coat out of the corner of her eye. He wasn't much taller than she was, but as he wasn't alone, his short stature didn't give her much comfort.

"I think the proper thing to say here is 'Thank you, Jack.' Isn't that right, Bob?" The first man was on her right flank now, and Maggie concentrated on slowing her breathing and keeping her eyes straight ahead while they closed in on either side of her. Maybe if she didn't look at them, they'd give up and go away.

They did not.

"Lady, did you hear what my friend said?" The man called Bob inched closer, keeping pace with her long strides, a menacing tone creeping into his voice. "He wants you to say thank you."

Maggie clenched her teeth until her jaw ached. Why hadn't she accepted Nadine's offer to walk her home? Just a bit further now; Maggie could see the lights of the square in front of her, and beyond that, the sign for Randall Street.

"I said" — the man on her right grabbed her roughly by the arm, and Maggie shrieked in pain and terror at the contact — "say thank you, lady." His fingers dug into the flesh of her upper arm, and she could smell stale cigarette smoke and the sour reek of his sweat. She bit back a whimper as his fingers dug into her skin, and turned to look at her would-be assailant.

18

With shock, Maggie registered that the lanky stranger was no more than sixteen or seventeen years old, and before she could stop it, a bubble of nervous laughter emerged from her throat.

Thinking quickly, Maggie asked, "Does your mother know you're out this late?" doing her best impression of Sister Dorothy, her senior physics teacher from St. Mary's High School.

"Aw, don't be like that, sweetheart." The second boy came up behind Maggie, grabbing her left arm in a vise with one hand, and planting the other hand firmly on her rear end. "We're just passing through town, after all, and we'll be fighting Hitler by next week. How's about you show us a good time before we go?"

Panic settled in Maggie's belly, and she opened her mouth to emit a bloodcurdling scream. Suddenly, she felt a rush of relief in her arm as Jack let go and blood was able to circulate to her bicep once more. Almost before she could register what was happening, she heard the dull thud of a fist making contact with an eye socket. Frozen to the sidewalk with fear, Maggie wanted to run but she couldn't seem to get that message to her feet. She turned her head to see one of her attackers slumped to the ground, and the other running away without a thought for his friend.

"Filthy dog," a heavily accented voice spat, and Maggie dimly recognized that a third man had arrived on the scene. He was tall, with dark hair and an expression bordering on murderous. Maggie watched, stunned, as he reached down and pulled her much smaller attacker up by the front of his shirt, until they were nose to nose. "You are a coward and a *bastardo*, treating a woman like this. And if I ever see your face again, I will kill you." With that, he all but threw the terrified boy onto the street and watched as he scrambled to his feet and ran off in the same direction as his friend.

"And you, *bella*?" He turned to look at Maggie, eyes glowing emerald green in the dim light. "Are you alright? He did not—"

"I'm fine," Maggie interrupted with a curt confidence she did not feel. "He did not." She smoothed her skirt and turned in the direction of home, but stumbled when she discovered that the heel of her shoe had broken off in the scuffle.

"I have you." The man's voice was suddenly gentle, completely different from the infuriated tone he had used on her would-be assailants, and he placed a hand under her arm to steady her. The contrast between the boy's hard grasp and this man's steadying hand brought Maggie back to the reality of the situation, and the very real danger she had only barely escaped.

"Wait, please. I need..." she trailed off, surveying the damage to her person. Other than her heel, the only real harm done was a tear in the seam of her sweater, and of course the bruises that would surely be visible on her arms tomorrow.

"You need a moment, yes?" He offered a reassuring smile, and Maggie found herself giving him a small, albeit tentative, one in response.

"Thank you," she managed. "How did you...?"

"I heard you scream, and I think the only reason for a scream like that is fear. So, I ran." He shrugged, as if his timely arrival was merely an everyday matter, but Maggie could still see the fury burning behind his green eyes. Those boys, and what they would have done to her... Maggie shivered in spite of the warm summer night, and the man took off his army-issue khaki coat to settle it around her shoulders. It smelled faintly of tobacco and Old Spice, and the assurance of safety.

"I should go. That is—" Maggie stuttered, "my parents will worry if I'm not home soon."

"Then I will walk you." He offered her his elbow, but Maggie simply stared, too overcome by the events of the past few minutes to be sure how to react.

"No, I couldn't—" she began.

"Because I am a stranger?" He cocked his head to one side, and his smile widened, revealing dimples on both cheeks that gave him the appearance of a small boy in a man's body. "I am *Caporale* Leonardo Castiglione, *Italiano* Service Unit, Camp Myles Standish. And you are?"

He raised an eyebrow, and Maggie's cheeks burned. He was a POW, one of the Italians who were no longer considered a threat by the Allies but were still kept in detention camps around the US. She had seen them moving about the city for the past year or so, and despite her father's ranting and railing to the contrary, had always found them to be polite and well mannered.

"Pleased to meet you, Corporal. I'm Maggie."

"And you may call me Leo. We are no more strangers." He gave an exaggerated bow, making her laugh, and it was then that she noticed the left sleeve of his uniform shirt, pinned up at the shoulder. So, he'd been wounded then. As the corporal lifted his head, he caught Maggie staring at the place where his arm should have been, and visibly shifted so that it was behind him. He again offered Maggie his right elbow, and this time she took it, albeit cautiously.

"I don't live far — it's just up ahead," she said as they began to walk, slowly to allow for her broken shoe and sore ankle.

"If it is all the same to you, *signorina*, I would still feel more comfortable if I deliver you to your door."

Maggie nodded, trying to reconcile the warmth settling in her chest with the adrenaline that still surged through her veins from the attempted assault. Within minutes, they had turned onto Randall Street and arrived at the front door of the house Maggie shared with her father, mother, and brothers. She reluctantly shrugged off the corporal's coat and handed it back to him with a grateful smile.

"Thank you," she said, wincing at the woeful inadequacy of the expression. "If you hadn't been there, Corporal—"

"—but I was," he interrupted, "and I do not think my rank matters here in America. Please call me Leo."

"Leo," she repeated, trying the name on for size. It fit with his boyish smile and flashing eyes, and something inside her shifted as he grinned at the sound of his name on her lips.

"Margaret?" The front door swung open, and Annie O'Callaghan, Maggie's mother, stood silhouetted in the light from the living room. Maggie jumped at the sound of her mother's voice, and after thanking Leo one final time, scurried up the steps and past her mother into the house.

Chapter 5

Maggie — 1944

After slipping out of her broken shoes before anyone could ask about them, Maggie followed her mother into the front parlor. It was a room confused about its purpose, centered around stiff, formal furniture, hobnail lamps, and numerous framed portraits of Jesus Christ at different stages of his life and death. Counting the multiple statues of the Virgin Mary and the enormous and lifelike painting of the Immaculate Heart of Jesus, there must have been a dozen pieces of iconography in the little room. Maggie couldn't know for sure exactly how many there were, though, because her mother was constantly rearranging and adding to the collection whenever the mood struck.

Mr. O'Callaghan's corner of the room was the only section not taken up by a brocade sofa or a piece of religious art. Instead it was occupied by both Da's cozy armchair and the prized family radio, a purchase Mam had only approved of once her children promised to listen along with the guided Rosary program put on by the Archdiocese of Boston each week. This evening, however, the radio was turned to the Jack Benny show, and Maggie's three younger brothers were all sitting on the floor in front of their father's chair, listening to the program while Da read his newspaper.

"Who was that young man, Margaret? He wasn't anyone I've seen before." Mrs. O'Callaghan spoke with the soft brogue of her native Ireland, but her voice held an undertone of accusation. Da lowered his newspaper, waiting for an answer from his only daughter. Although Ambrose O'Callaghan had long ago accepted the presence of Charlie Morris in his daughter's life, he was still suspicious of any man who looked at his daughter for longer than was strictly necessary.

Maggie perched on the edge of the gold brocade sofa with a sigh, accepting that she wouldn't be allowed to go to her bedroom until her mother's questions had been answered. "Corporal Castiglione, Mam."

"Is he one of the Castigliones over on Linden Street? The brickyard?" Da asked, newspaper forgotten in his lap.

"No, Da."

Maggie shifted in her seat, one of the clips on her garter belt digging into the back of her thigh. She made an effort to keep her tone light, and to keep the crushing exhaustion of the night's events from showing on her face. "He's one of the men from Camp Myles Standish, from the Italian Service Unit."

"A prisoner of war?" Fourteen-year-old Frankie turned and stared at his sister, Jack Benny forgotten in light of this interesting development...

"Jaysus, Mary, and Joseph," Mam muttered, crossing herself as if Maggie had been seen with Mussolini himself. "What was he doing out? Should we call down to the camp, Ambrose?" Maggie's stomach froze into ice at the idea that Leo could get in trouble simply for having helped her.

"Hush, Annie. All those Italians need to get passes into the city these days is a heartbeat and a promise not to support Hitler." Ambrose sighed. "Soon we'll be overrun with them, out carousing while our Owen is God knows where fighting those fascist bastards."

Mam bowed her head in response and made the sign of the cross again, no doubt praying for her eldest child. It was a bone of contention in the city that the Italian POWs were safe and well fed on American soil while Taunton's own sons were off in harm's way.

"He wasn't breaking any rules," Maggie assured her parents. "He just saw me walking alone and offered to see me home safely, that's all."

Frankie, clearly disappointed that the story wasn't more interesting, turned his attention back to the radio.

"And why were you alone? Where was Elisabeth?" Mam's eagle eyes bored into the side of Maggie's head, making her squirm. In another life, her mother would have made an excellent police dog.

"Betty was having fun with some of the other kids — I wanted to go home, but there was no need to ruin her fun."

"Margaret Veronica O'Callaghan," Annie began, and Maggie knew by the use of her full name that she was about to hear a lecture on safety and personal responsibility. "Do you have any idea what could happen to a young girl walking alone at night?" Yes, Maggie had a pretty good idea, and a shiver went up her spine at the thought of the awful young men who had tried to assault her, with their filthy hands and their filthier intentions.

"Yes, Ma. I know."

"Well then, what were you thinking, then, making your guardian angel work overtime when he has others in far more peril to look out for?" Annie shook her head with a *tsk tsk tsk* sound that made Maggie feel roughly four years old instead of nineteen.

Maggie took a deep breath and forced her voice to remain steady. Calm. "Corporal Castiglione made sure I arrived in one piece."

"I'm sure getting you home safely wasn't all he had in mind," Annie sniffed.

"Mam, it's not a big deal—" Maggie protested, but her father chose that moment to add his perspective.

"You think that, Margaret, but you don't know men, and you don't know what men are after," he said, his stern voice leaving no room for argument.

It's thanks to Corporal Castiglione that I didn't have to find out first hand, Maggie thought, but she knew that revealing the close call to her parents would only make things worse. They'd probably never let her leave the house again.

"And the Italians are the worst of the lot," Ambrose continued. "All that Mediterranean blood in them. There's a reason all those poets and playwrights are from Italy, my dear. And now they're here in Taunton; 'co-belligerents,' they call them, while our boys are facing God only knows what tortures at the hands of the Huns." Maggie watched her mother make the sign of the cross for the third time in the past few minutes, and she realized that the best course of action was to agree with her father, placate her mother, and escape up to her bedroom with her book.

"I understand, and I'm sorry."

After Maggie kissed her mother and father goodnight, Ambrose made one final point to his daughter. "This Italian corporal may seem kind, Maggie, but he's a prisoner of war. Is it fair that he gets to walk a pretty girl home from a dance tonight, while your brother and Charlie might be shivering in the cold?"

Maggie nodded and started upstairs, but she couldn't help but think that this Italian corporal, this Leo, had made her feel more alive in five minutes of acquaintance than Charlie Morris had in the past nineteen years of her life.

Chapter 6

Niamh — 2015

"You make us sit in these chairs on purpose, to let us know who's the boss — don't you, Ms. Reilly?"

Niamh watched Tommy Marchetti's father make an exaggerated attempt to fold himself into a chair built for a five-year-old, eyes darting between Niamh and his wife, clearly waiting for one of them to laugh at his genius physical comedy. Niamh rubbed her thumb and middle finger across her forehead, trying in vain to keep the headache at bay, and gave him a thin smile. "It's Mrs. Reilly, and no, sir, these are just the chairs that we have in the classroom."

Kane Elementary School's spring parent/teacher conferences were moving into their third hour, and Niamh wanted nothing more than to go home, put on her sweats, and watch *Criminal Minds* with Christine. Unfortunately, she still had to meet with four more sets of parents before she could do so.

"Right then," Mrs. Marchetti began with a huff, ignoring her husband and opening a small wire-bound notebook, pen at the ready. She looked like a Senator preparing to grill Niamh during a confirmation hearing. "How is Tommy progressing with his phonetic recognition?"

Niamh would never understand why so many parents were obsessed with their children's academic progress, to the point where they forgot to let them be children. Poor Tommy liked trains and playing tag with his friends at recess. He wasn't quite ready for Harvard Law School.

"We are working on reading, Mrs. Marchetti," she began, choosing her words carefully, "but kindergarten is also about developing social skills, and learning how to succeed in a classroom."

"Tommy is *very* bright," Mrs. Marchetti reminded her.

Niamh made a herculean effort not to laugh at this, and she wondered how Mrs. Marchetti would react to the news that her genius son had stuck his finger so far up his nose this morning that he gave himself a nosebleed. One glance at Mr. Marchetti, who was currently making a valiant attempt to wedge both of his knees under the teeny tiny desk, confirmed which parent Tommy took after.

"He'll be transferring to the Marshall School for first grade," Tommy's mother continued, "where they are better set up to challenge a student with his intellect."

"Of course, of course," Niamh nodded, trying to maintain the picture of sympathetic agreement, while inwardly rolling her mind's eye. Had this woman met her son? And how did she end up with Tommy's dad, who was clearly more interested in having a laugh than he was in hearing about his son's academic achievements?

"My husband is the CEO of Landon-March Investments in Boston," Mrs. Marchetti informed Niamh with a warm look towards Tommy's dad, who smiled as if on cue. "If we can afford a better education for our boy, then we really ought to take it."

"Naturally." Niamh pulled her lips together in a tight approximation of a smile. She'd miss Tommy next year, but if she never saw his simpering, elitist mother again, she'd sleep just fine.

"Are those... *tattoos*... Ms. Reilly?"

Damnit.

Niamh noticed too late that the sleeve of her slouchy teacher cardigan had ridden up, exposing several inches of tattooed skin. There was nothing in the teacher handbook that expressly forbade her from having visible tattoos, but leave it to a judgey mom like Mrs. Marchetti to notice them and get that rule changed lest Niamh pollute her young son's mind with the intricate Celtic symbols on her arm. She pulled her sleeve down over her wrist and changed the subject.

"As I was saying, kindergarten is just as much about social skills as it is about academics. Tommy is working on learning how to wait his turn, and how to be a good friend, and I see him making real progress."

Mrs. Marchetti scribbled down every word Niamh said as if she would be quizzed on it later. Her eyes crinkled at the corners when she was concentrating, just like her son's did. Niamh's heart clutched painfully in her chest, and she wondered for at least the billionth time that day whether she'd ever get to see her own features on a little face.

The Marchettis' conference wrapped up, followed by Katie Petrillo's parents, and then Rohit Singh's. After the last parent finally left her classroom, Niamh put her head down on the desk and closed her eyes. Going through life and pretending that everything was normal when it wasn't was exhausting.

"Oh no, Niamh, did the Petrillos do you in? Whose ass do I need to kick?"

She raised her head from her desk at the sound of her friend Marcos's voice from the doorway, and gave him a wicked grin.

"No, but Tommy Marchetti's mom could use a reality check. You up for that?"

"Only if you can assure me I never have to deal with her kid in my class."

"Done. He's transferring to Marshall at the end of the year." Niamh waved finger guns in the air and blew imaginary smoke from the barrels for effect.

"Damn girl, you good. You don't need my help." Marcos looked her up and down and gave a long, low whistle. "You know what you do need? Tequila shots. On me."

The offer was tempting, but she couldn't accept it.

"No, thanks, Marcos. I still haven't taken the test yet, so—"

"So, there might be a bun in that cute little oven of yours. Got it." His face turned serious. Marcos had been Niamh's best work-friend for three years. He'd talked her down from throttling more than a few children, and he had slept on her couch countless Friday nights after *let's just get one drink* turned into eight or nine. He knew how much this meant to her. "How are you feeling?"

"Well, I was a little nauseated this morning, but that could have been the sausage, egg, and cheese I got from Dunkin' on the way in. And my boobs hurt, but if I'm not pregnant then I'm PMSing, so that explains it." She shrugged. "So, I have no fucking idea if I'm pregnant or not."

"I'm thinking pregnant thoughts for you, baby. Text me?" He held an imaginary phone to his ear and winked.

"I'll tell you what," Niamh said, pushing back in her chair and looking around for the keys she lost at least ten times per day. "If it's positive, I will call you screaming, crying, and completely unable to form a sentence. If not, I'm ghosting the fuck out of everyone and staying in bed for the weekend." She shrugged her way into her coat, and shut off the overhead classroom lights on her way out the door. "Walk out with me?"

"You got it."

Marcos and Niamh headed for the parking lot, and when they stopped behind her green CR-V, he wrapped his arms around her and squeezed. Niamh allowed herself to lean against him for just a moment, absorbing the care that came solely out of concern. She always leaned on Christine, but Christine was just as invested in Niamh being pregnant with their baby as Niamh herself was. She'd be devastated if it failed again. Marcos would be too, but he'd be sad for them, not for himself at all. For the moment, that felt nice.

"You're taking it tonight?" he asked, still holding her tight.

"Yep," Niamh answered into his chest. "I've got a hot date with the pee stick as soon as I get home."

"You got this, girl. Call me if you need anything."

"I will," she promised, stepping back and unlocking her car. But deep down, she knew that what she needed was to be pregnant, and that if she wasn't, all the friends in the world weren't going to be able to help her.

Chapter 7

Maggie — 1944

By the time she finished getting ready for nine o'clock Mass the following morning, Maggie had almost stopped buzzing from the events of the night before. She was eager to fill Betty in, however, and to find out if anything exciting had happened after she left the dance.

The O'Callaghans and the Currans had sat together in church since long before Maggie or Betty had been born. Every week, the families would arrive to Mass at precisely eight fifty-three — any later would be tardy by St. Mary's standards, and any earlier would just be silly. The mothers, Annie O'Callaghan and Ethel Curran, entered the church first. Maggie, Francis, Paul, and Joseph O'Callaghan and Elisabeth Curran followed their mothers, and then the last to proceed down the center aisle and into the twelfth pew from the back on the righthand side were the fathers, Ambrose O'Callaghan and Patrick Curran. It had been the same every Sunday, week after week, for as far back as Maggie could remember. This week, though, when she caught sight of Leo Castiglione sitting among several other foreign-looking men in a pew down front, she let out an audible gasp.

"What?" Betty whispered from over the head of nine-year-old Joseph, who sat between them. She followed Maggie's gaze across the aisle and up to the front left of the church, and then turned to Maggie with pursed lips. "They're handsome, I'll give you that," she hissed, "but I think it's disgraceful that they're allowed to socialize with decent Americans." Betty sniffed, and turned her face back towards the altar where the deacon was preparing for Mass, the pretty picture of piety.

Is it unfair? Maggie wondered as she sat between her two youngest brothers and willed herself to pay attention to the Mass. She would give anything for her brother Owen to be here beside her right now, shooting his no-nonsense glare at Joe and Paul when they began to wiggle, or catching Maggie's eye and trying not to laugh when the elderly woman in front of them fell asleep by the second reading and began to snore. And Charlie, too — as conflicted as her feelings might be about their future together, Maggie prayed every night for Charlie's safe return home from the war. Didn't that mean that somewhere, Corporal Leo's family was praying for him? God wasn't Irish — as much as her mother and father might argue that he was — and he wasn't Italian either. Surely he heard all of their prayers the same. Did the safety of Italian POWs have to mean the suffering of Americans in Europe? Or were they all just men, wanting to beat back Hitler and the Japanese and return home to their families?

By the time the congregation rose to its feet for the *Pater Noster*, Maggie was so deep in thought that she didn't realize she was the only one still sitting until Paul poked her in the shoulder. She leapt to her feet, guilt warming her cheeks, joining in with the Latin prayer before her mother could notice that she hadn't been paying attention: "...*et ne nos inducas in tentationem sed libera nos a malo.*"

"I heard that some of them go home with the Italian American families for dinner after Mass," Betty whispered over Joe's head during the Sign of Peace. "I wouldn't want them in my house."

Maggie wrinkled her nose in response. Surely Betty would want her Billy to be taken in by some family in France and given a slight reprieve from the war, no matter how brief? Besides, she thought, looking back across the aisle at where the Italian servicemen sat, they weren't the enemy, and they hadn't been since Italy had surrendered the previous fall. Regardless of their country, weren't they using the same words to worship the same god? Weren't they all just people, after all?

* * *

After Sunday Mass, the most important event of the week for the O'Callaghan family was Sunday dinner. The entire family would gather in the dining room, where Mam would set the second-hand table with her precious Irish linen tablecloth and "the good china." Each week, they ate the same meal whether it was January or July — pot roast with potatoes, onions, carrots, and celery, and sliced bread from McCaffrey's bakery with a thin coating of margarine. After dinner, the remaining pot roast would be saved, placed between two slices of leftover bread, and served as lunch to the O'Callaghan children on Monday, Tuesday, Wednesday, and sometimes even Thursday if Mam could stretch it that far. The boys often said that by Thursday, their lunch resembled a baseball glove served between two hockey pucks.

That afternoon, however, the roast was still fresh, and it smelled delicious when Mam called the family to the dining room. Maggie braced herself against the sound of three hungry boys pushing each other in their rush to get downstairs. Frankie, who was clearly Mam's favorite to feed if the size of his waist was any indication, arrived first and took his seat at the table, followed by Paul, and finally Joe, the baby. Maggie rolled her eyes at her brothers' antics and hurried to help her mother bring things in from the kitchen.

Once everyone had taken their seats and said the Grace, with a special prayer for Owen's health and safety, Maggie looked up to see her father watching her with a peculiar expression on his weathered face. She self-consciously checked her teeth and wiped her face with her napkin to make sure that an errant piece of pot roast wasn't the reason for her father's attention.

"Maggie, I ran into Mr. Clark when I went in to get the paper this morning. He tells me that they're hiring girls over at the camp, to help with the war effort."

Maggie stared at her father, bemused. What did this have to do with her?

"How would you feel about working at the camp? You haven't had a good way to fill your days since Charlie left and you graduated from school."

Every eye at the table swung from Ambrose to Maggie, awaiting her response. Maggie felt lightheaded as the idea spun around in her mind like a playground toy gone out of control. Working at the camp? Her? Going to work every day... at least until Charlie got home... and they got married was what Da meant. But what if that wasn't what she wanted? What if she didn't know? Maggie supposed she could do it for now... it would be a nice way to keep busy, and help with the war effort, and not be under Mam's feet all day or working at the market. She opened her mouth to respond, but her mother beat her to it.

"Ambrose, I don't know. I don't like the idea of Maggie being around all those soldiers all day. Is it safe?" Annie's face took on a pinched expression, as if she had smelled something foul. Women weren't meant to work outside the home, in Annie O'Callaghan's opinion. Women were meant to cook and clean and look after their families as God intended.

"Safe as houses, my dear," Ambrose replied with a wink for Maggie. "They need the help — it doesn't look like we'll be getting more Italians to help in the camp, and word is that more men will be coming through to train for the Pacific. They need our Maggie."

Again, Maggie opened her mouth to reply, this time to ask her father what it was she'd be doing in the camp.

Again, her mother cut her off.

"And how will she get there, Ambrose?"

Dad's smile faltered a bit, and his shoulders dropped, his wife having stolen some of the wind from his sails. "I thought you would approve of this, Annie. It will help her to feel as if she is doing something of value."

"Perhaps," Mam shrugged, sawing into a piece of pot roast with her knife and fork. "But I do have concerns for her safety, Ambrose."

Maggie knew that Mam's overly casual demeanor and decision not to meet her husband's eyes was a trick. Annie was a master hand at making her husband think he was in charge, while really she was skillfully manipulating everything that happened under the roof of number 14 Randall Street.

"She will be under the protection of the United States military. What more assurance of her safety would you like?" Da removed his glasses and began to rub his eyes with the forefinger and thumb of his right hand.

"I'm simply of the opinion that a nineteen-year-old girl has no business in a military embarkation camp." Mam rested her fork and knife on the rim of her dinner plate, adjusted the folds of the napkin on her lap, and turned her gaze towards her husband. "Perhaps I'm old-fashioned, but that is the way my mother taught me, and the way her mother taught her, all the way back to the Virgin Mother herself."

Paul rolled his eyes, and said in a whisper loud enough to be heard a block away, "Are you supposin' Mam believes herself related to Jesus then?" Frankie and Joe each choked on their bites of supper, faces turning red in an effort to keep from laughing out loud. Mam glared at her sons from her side of the table, and even Maggie had to fake a cough to cover up her own laughter.

"I don't think the Blessed Virgin has made her feelings known on this specific matter, my dear." Da placed his glasses back onto his nose and met his wife's glare head on. "But as she chose women as the recipients of her message at Lourdes, at Fatima, and even at our own village of Knock, I think we can assume she'd agree with our Margaret taking on some light duties to help with the war effort."

A tense silence filled the room as everyone waited, barely willing to breathe, for Mam's response. The room didn't come to life again until she emitted a curt, "Well, you'll be driving her then. I don't want her takin' the bus."

And that was that.

The remainder of Sunday dinner passed as it always did, in occasional bouts of conversation interspersed with long moments of quiet chewing. And through it all, Maggie felt a shimmer of excitement running through her — she was going to take a job at the Camp.

Chapter 8

Niamh — 2015

There were two bottles resting on the black granite countertop when Niamh walked through the door of the townhouse she shared with her wife, right next to a Clear Blue Easy box from CVS. Christine was sitting at the kitchen island, flipping through a Viking River Cruise catalog without actually looking at it.

"Hey there," Niamh said, tossing her keys onto the counter with an ease she did not feel.

"Hey." Christine smiled warmly, and Niamh was reminded yet again of how lucky she was to have her. Christine untangled her long legs from behind the island and came over to greet her.

"Are we doing this right away?" Niamh asked with a nod toward where the test lay screaming on the counter.

"Hello, Christine," Christine intoned with an exaggerated

eye roll. "My beloved wife. I've missed you all day."

"Oh, shut up." Niamh went up on tiptoes to kiss her. Christine stood nine inches taller than her wife, and although Niamh's head fit just perfectly into the curve of Christine's neck, it did mean that she had to reach up every time she wanted a kiss.

"I got sparkling cider and wine for after," Christine said, giving away her nerves by fiddling with the ends of her hair. "Let's see which one we're going to have." She handed the box to Niamh, who marched to the bathroom without even taking off her coat. She'd been waiting for this, and she wasn't about to wait a moment longer.

Niamh pulled down her leggings, took her seat on the throne, and waited. She'd taken enough of these to know that she was supposed to catch the pee mid-stream, so she waited to get started before reaching in with the little test strip.

"How's it going?" Christine leaned against the door frame, watching intently while chewing on one fingernail.

"It'd be going a lot better if you'd stop staring at me," Niamh replied, annoyed. "Can you pee with an audience?"

"How do I count as an audience?"

"You're watching me and waiting for me to perform like a circus monkey."

"When was the last time you watched monkeys pee at the circus?" Christine

asked, settling into their easy banter.

"Never, but I also don't know how hard circus monkeys have to try to get pregnant. Get out!" Niamh leaned forward and kicked the door shut with her foot. Thank goodness for small bathrooms.

Left alone with her goals and her stick, Niamh was finally

able to pee on the little strip, although her hands were shaking so bad that she got pee all over her fingers. Gross. She put the cap on the stick, washed her hands twice, and set the timer on her phone for four minutes.

Four minutes until she knew if she was going to be someone's mother. Or not.

"Now can I come in? I heard you flush." Christine's voice was muffled by the door, and Niamh swung it open to face her.

"Let's wait in the living room," Niamh said, her back to the stick. She could feel it staring at her, laughing manically while it decided her fate.

"Sure thing." Christine let Niamh take her hand and lead her into the living room, where they sat criss-cross apple sauce next to each other on the couch. Niamh stared at Christine. Christine stared back. Fuck, this was going to be the longest four minutes of their lives.

"How were the conferences?" Christine asked.

"Fine." What was it now? Three minutes and thirty seconds?

"Oh, good. I know you don't love them."

"They're a necessary evil." Three minutes and fifteen seconds? Had time actually slowed down, like when Niamh accidentally set the playback speed on an audiobook to .5x, and everything sounded like Alan Rickman after he'd smoked a LOT of weed?

"What the hell; this is crazy! I feel like we're on our first date," Christine sighed, throwing her head back in frustration.

"And we're already waiting to see if you got me pregnant." Niamh raised an eyebrow. "Fast work there, cowgirl."

"There's my girl; I knew you were in there somewhere under those nerves." Christine reached around to ruffle Niamh's short black hair, and Niamh ducked out the way, scowling.

"When we do have a baby, the poor thing doesn't stand a chance at avoiding anxiety, does it?" Niamh had been taking Zoloft since high school, and Christine had finally broken down and gotten on medication after accepting her first job with a hot shot law firm.

"Forget nature vs. nurture," she winced. "How about nature *and* nurture?"

"At least we're keeping the pharmaceutical companies in business."

"They really do owe us a thank you note."

"You, me, and every other Xellenial, baby." Niamh lay her head on Christine's shoulder, and Christine pulled her in, allowing her to melt into her side. Some people say that petting a cat or a dog can lower your blood pressure — that's the reaction Niamh had to Christine. She was just so capable; Niamh got the feeling that whatever went wrong, her wife would be able to handle it and make sure they both came out ahead.

And she was hot. Which didn't hurt.

The *Harry Potter* movie theme song chimed from Niamh's iPhone, and she felt Christine's whole body tense. It was time.

"Do you want me to go look?" Christine asked, and Niamh did. She really did.

"No." Niamh sat up, squaring her shoulders and trying to remember that she was a fully grown adult, and that the test already said whatever it said. Going in and looking at it wasn't going to change anything — but somehow, while the test was in the bathroom and the women were out here, it was Schrodinger's pregnancy test. Niamh wasn't sure she was ready to give up the hope of not knowing.

"Niamh? You in there?" Christine waved a hand in front

of Niamh's eyes, breaking both her train of thought and her thousand-yard stare.

"Yeah — I'm ready. Let's go." Niamh stood up, wiped her palms on her leggings, and walked over to the bathroom. Christine was half a step behind. They opened the bathroom door, turned on the light, and leaned forward.

It was negative.

Chapter 9

Maggie — 1944

" Do you have any experience with laundry?"

The harried-looking private who was tasked with introducing Maggie to the duties of her new job glanced up from his clipboard with tired eyes.

Was this a serious question?

"I do most of the laundry at home for my family, if that's what you mean," Maggie replied, willing her voice not to tremble and reveal her nerves.

"And you've used a machine with a wringer before?" He made a little check with his pencil, and Maggie couldn't help but wonder what exactly was on the sheet of paper attached to his clipboard. *Subject is an American female. Seems capable of running a simple appliance.*

"All of our machines are Maytags," he informed her. Maggie was unsure if she was supposed to respond or not, so she settled for a simple nod, which seemed to satisfy the private. "And what about tumble dryers? Have you used those before?" Maggie shook her head. Her father had wanted to buy a tumble dryer with his bonus several years back, but Mam had forbidden it, saying it was an extravagance. "You can learn." The private checked one last box on his mysterious clipboard before turning on his heel and marching out of the Civilian office. It took Maggie several seconds to snap to and realize she was meant to follow him.

She hurried out the door of the office and into the bright sunshine, letting the screen door slam behind her. The private — what was his name? Jones? Jonas? — was already halfway across the lawn with no idea that Maggie wasn't following close behind him like a baby duck. Clearly people in the armed forces were used to everyone and everything falling in line exactly as it should. Well, Maggie thought, I was raised by an Irish Catholic mother who considers herself a drill sergeant for the Almighty. I can handle the armed forces any day.

By the time she caught up to the private — my goodness, what was his name?— Maggie was breathing heavily, and she could feel the telltale prickle of perspiration on her forehead. She forced herself to take slow, steady breaths in through her nose, and she hoped that wherever the private was taking her, it was somewhere cooler than this exposed block of asphalt baking in the summer sun.

It was not.

Maggie's first thought upon entering the Camp Myles Standish Laundry and Dry-Cleaners #4 was that this must be how it feels to be roasted alive. A wall of hot air met them at the door, and the fans — which had obviously been set up to alleviate some of the heat from the dryers — did nothing whatsoever besides blow the hot air around. A girl Maggie had never seen before stood behind the counter at an ironing board, hard at work pressing creases into khaki shirts.

"Marshall? This is O'Callaghan. She'll be taking on the open shifts," Private whatever-his-name-was barked, and the girl set down the iron, wiped her hands on her apron, and came around the counter to shake Maggie's hand. Maggie recognized that, unlike the majority of the people she had seen since her father had dropped her off at the camp that morning, this girl was wearing civilian clothing.

"Call me Sadie," she said, her deep, gravelly voice at odds with her petite, almost child-like appearance. "Welcome to Midway."

"Midway?" Maggie repeated dumbly.

"Sure, that's what they call us in here. We're just about in the middle of the camp, it's hot as Hades in here, and we're essential to an Allied victory." Sadie laughed at her own cleverness as she led Maggie around the counter and to the back of the building. "I've got this, Private Johansen," she called. Johansen — that was it. "You can go back to saving the world."

Maggie heard the telltale slap of the screen door against its frame, and by the time she turned to look, Private Johansen was already halfway across the yard on his way back to his office.

"Don't take it personal, kid." Sadie indicated the private's retreating back. "Women make him nervous. Before the war, I don't think he'd ever spoken to one who wasn't his mother. Let's get you an apron and I'll show you the ropes."

As Sadie showed her around the back room, which was lined with washers, wringers, tumble dryers, and dry-cleaners,

Maggie began to relax and settle into her new job as a civilian assistant. Anything beat being under the judgmental eye of her mother, but this seemed like it might be genuinely fun. The work was solid, she was helping out with the war effort, and Sadie had the makings of a real friend.

Chapter 10

Maggie — 1944

Maggie arrived for her second day of work with a spring in her step. Finally, she felt like she was doing something useful, and no amount of sighs or eye rolls from her mother could stop that.

"I'm fairly sure someone died in this one," Sadie said by way of greeting, her face a mask of disgust as she removed a soiled uniform from its bag. Maggie grabbed her apron from its hook by the door and stepped closer to investigate. The stench of blood, shit, and something Maggie assumed must be decomposition hit her while she was still several feet away from the stained and fetid wool, and she recoiled several feet.

"I think they may have been left in it for several days *after* they died," Maggie added, making a concerted effort not to gag. "Do we just throw that in the bin?"

"Oh, no, Uncle Sam wouldn't have that." Sadie tossed the

offensive uniform into a pile in the corner, which did nothing but spread the stench. "Waste not, want not. I think some borax should help with the stains, and hopefully the smell." Military Laundress may be a useful job, Maggie thought with a grimace, but that didn't mean it was going to be pleasant all the time.

"The machine seems to be working again, *signorina*."

A tall, dark-haired man emerged from the back room with a toolbox, causing Maggie to stop where she stood, her fingers and toes buzzing from adrenaline as she recognized the man who had rescued her the weekend before. "Thanks, Leo," Sadie called, not even looking up from the slip she was filling out. "This is Maggie, by the way."

"I have met this Maggie," Leo said, voice low as he placed his toolbox on the floor and crossed the room, his right hand extended for her to shake. His warm smile did something to Maggie's insides that she found both intoxicating and concerning, and that feeling only intensified as he took her hand in his large warm one.

"It's lovely to see you again, Corporal," Maggie replied, more stiffly than she had intended.

"And how do you two know each other?" Sadie's interest was piqued, one eyebrow raised in question as she turned her head back and forth between the two of them.

"We met in the downtown a few days ago," Leo explained.

At the same time, Maggie blurted, "The corporal was my knight in shining armor a few nights ago." As soon as the words were out of Maggie's mouth, she wanted to snatch them back in mortification. Knight in shining armor? Who did she think she was, Snow White? He must think she was ridiculous.

"Here I am not a *caporale*, Maggie. Here I am just Leo." His words danced in their softly accented syllables, *I am-a just-a Leo*, and through her embarrassment, Maggie noted that his emerald eyes had not left her since he had emerged from the back.

"Sounds like there's a doozy of a story there," Sadie whistled, eyebrows rising to her hairline, "and I'm going to need to hear it, perhaps when Leo finally brings me the part for my broken dryer. But now that the washer is fixed, can you go put some of the underthings back there through the wringer?" She addressed the question to Maggie, and her message was clear. They were friendly here, and they might even be real friends one day, but they had a job to do.

After nodding a reluctant goodbye to Leo and heading back to the washer room, Maggie could hear Sadie's tinkling laughter as she teased Leo.

"You've got the hots for our new civie, Leo. It's written all over your face."

"And how would you know what these hots look like, *Signorina* Sadie?" Leo replied, the sound of a smile evident in his deep voice.

"Because that's the same look Guillermo gets whenever I walk into a room, of course," Sadie replied. "You look like you can't decide if you want to worship her or devour her."

"Perhaps I want to do both," Leo laughed, and soon after came the sound of the screen door slapping against the frame to indicate that Corporal Castiglione had left the building.

You look like you can't decide if you want to worship her or devour her. Maggie replayed Sadie's words over and over in her mind and she ran piece after piece of flannel underwear through the automatic wringer. *Perhaps I want to do both.* She wasn't quite sure what either Sadie or Leo had meant, but she wouldn't have to wait long to find out.

* * *

It was late in the afternoon, long after Sadie had gone home for the day, when Leo returned with the part for the broken dryer. As he stepped through the door and into the laundry, Maggie silently thanked her guardian angels for the fact that she had managed to get most of the foul odor out of the uniform from earlier in the day. Thanks to open windows and a nice breeze, the building wasn't as offensive as it could have been. She finished folding a stack of shirts and followed Leo into the back room, which was lined with washing machines and automatic dryers.

"It looks like you're in high demand around here," she began, watching as Leo took out a screwdriver and began removing a panel from the back of a tumble dryer. "Can I... do you need help?" Maggie asked. Leo was quick and agile working with his right hand, but surely he must feel some hindrance from his missing left?

"You can help by talking to me," Leo said, flashing his dimples at her before lifting the panel on the Maytag and fiddling with something in the interior of the machine.

"What would you like me to talk about?" Maggie asked, feeling very much out of her depth in this moment. Was she flirting with him? Was that what she wanted to do? She wasn't sure.

"We can start with you, Maggie O'Callaghan." Leo turned his head to wink at her, and a flush began in her toes and raced all the way up to the top of her head. "To start, where did you get those *bellisima* blue eyes?"

"You, sir, are a flirt," Maggie laughed, and Leo shrugged as he continued to fiddle with the dryer.

"You are not the first to tell me that. Hand me the wrench, *per favore*?"

"Oh, really?" Maggie asked, settling into the rhythm of their banter. "And how many girls have had cause to call you a flirt?" She handed him the wrench from his toolkit, making sure to hold it by the very end so that there was no chance of their fingers touching.

"Well, there's you, and then there is—" he broke off, searching for the right word.

"Your girlfriend?" Maggie asked, feeling a thrill at her own boldness.

"My old lady. That is, my mother." Leo returned the wrench, grinning at Maggie. "Now tell me, where did you get those eyes?"

"As far as I know, I was born with them, but my father would say I got them from his mother, my gran, Honoria."

"Your gran, Honoria, must be a very beautiful woman." Leo's voice was low, and only a hair above a whisper. What was happening here?

"My gran is eighty-two, lives in Ireland, and writes long letters to my parents about her gout."

Leo threw back his head in laughter, and Maggie flushed crimson. Why in the world had she said that? Leo didn't seem to mind, though, and he was doing an expert job at splitting his attention between fixing the dryer and looking at Maggie in a way that made her belly do somersaults. "You are a funny young woman, *Margherita*."

"Margherita?" She scrunched up her nose.

"*Margherita* is your name in *Italiano*."

Maggie rolled the word silently around on her tongue, and discovered she liked the feel of it. It was different, exotic, somehow.

"It is also the name of my favorite kind of pizza," Leo laughed. Maggie, feigning indignation, slapped him playfully on the leg. "Hey now. *Margherita*, that is the best thing I could say about you. I love nothing so well as I like pizza."

"Not even your mother?" She raised an eyebrow, and Leo's eyes softened, taking on a far-away expression of longing.

"Well, my mother is the one who makes the pizza, so she must be first." Leo lapsed into silence again, his attention focused on the doohickey he was installing.

He must miss home, Maggie realized with a start. For all his jovial smiles, she knew that Leo was still a prisoner of war. He could go into the city with a pass, but he couldn't go home, and that had to chafe at him. She wondered how old he was, and how long he'd been in the camp.

"Leo." Maggie took a breath and fiddled with the contents of the toolbox before asking, "How did your English get so good?"

He ducked his head out of the dryer to look at her, and raised an eyebrow. "You have to make a promise to me that you will not laugh."

"Of course I won't laugh," she declared, wondering what on earth would prompt him to say that. Leo sat back from his work, leaning against the wall, his one arm draped over his knees, and Maggie couldn't help but admire how handsome he was. His army-issue olive drab pants and button-down shirt fit him well and clung to the muscles of his thighs and chest.

"Do you know the American soap opera, A *Light in the Darkness*?" he asked. "It is on the radio each day."

A laugh threatened to bubble up in her throat at the idea of this man, this corporal in the Italian Army, listening to soap operas, but she managed to stop it in time and arrange her face into a careful expression of neutrality. "I do. My mam listens to it religiously."

"Well, after I was captured, they sent us to *Nuova* York, and then on a train to a camp somewhere — they didn't say where it was. The guard, he was a sergeant in the Great War, and he listened to A *Light in the Darkness* every day in the mess hall while we ate our lunch." Leo shrugged. "I liked to hear about the Nortons and the Bethelridges, and the sergeant said that I needed to learn to speak more English, so I listened and studied. By the time the postman returned Mrs. Bethelridge's stolen baby, I was hooked, and my English was much better."

"You learned English by listening to soap operas," Maggie repeated.

"And you promised that you would not laugh — remember that." He cocked his head to the side with a grin that left Maggie weak at the knees. In her whole life, no one had ever once had that effect on her — including Charlie. The thought of Charlie landed on Maggie's head like a bucket of cold water. Here she was, flirting with a POW, while Charlie might be fighting for his life somewhere in the Pacific. She was disgusted with herself — she'd known Leo for a week, while she'd been going with Charlie for years. Maybe her father was right about Mediterranean men and all that hot blood.

Leo interrupted Maggie's guilt. "Now, will you hand me the socket wrench, *bella*, so that I can finish my work and you can go home?"

55

Chapter 11

Maggie — 1944

"For the last time, Betty, I barely interact with the soldiers at all. They bring by their clothes for cleaning, and I hand them a ticket. Then when they come back, they hand me the ticket and I give them their clothes. We're not getting to know one another."

Maggie was helping out in Da's store for the afternoon, stocking shelves and ringing up customers while her father took a rare Saturday afternoon off. Betty had offered to keep her company, but it didn't take long for Maggie to figure out that what Betty really wanted to do was hound her for gossip from the camp.

"You can be such a drip sometimes," Betty pouted as Maggie organized cans of stewed tomatoes on the shelf. "You're surrounded by dreamboats in uniform every day, and you can't even take a photograph with your mind so that you can describe it to me."

"Bets, you have gone completely khaki wacky, I swear." Maggie placed the last can on the shelf and turned to her friend, hand on her hip. "I'm *working* at the camp, cleaning blood and dirt and heaven knows what else off the clothes, and the men are getting ready to ship out. They're there for three days, maybe four, before they're sent off to Boston and put on a ship. They don't have time to socialize."

"Oh, I could make them want to socialize," Betty purred suggestively, and Maggie slapped her friend playfully on the arm.

"Billy Morris? Tall boy, freckles, sandy hair, love of your life? Or have you forgotten?"

"I have *not* forgotten," Betty replied, injured. "I love Billy and I'll be faithful to him till the day I die, but it doesn't hurt to look, does it?"

"Like I said," Maggie turned, smoothing out her skirt, "khaki wacky."

"You take that back, Margaret," Betty commanded, following Maggie up the aisle and back behind the counter and the till. "You take that back right now."

"OK, OK, I take it back." Maggie held up her hands in surrender, recognizing the clear signs of Betty headed for a temper tantrum. "You're wonderful and I love you."

"I love you too," Betty grumbled, lower lip stuck out in a pout that Maggie knew from experience was intentional. "But are you really going to tell me that no one is there for more than a few days?"

"Well," Maggie began, dragging out the word, "there are men who work there, mostly veterans, but probably a few hundred enlisted men and women who keep things running.

And then there are men in the Italian Service Unit."

Betty wrinkled her pretty little nose in disgust. "Maybe, but who'd want to look at them?"

"Betty, in the 4th grade you informed the whole class, including Sister James Winifred, that you were going to marry Anthony Liotti."

"So?"

"So," Maggie threw up her arms in exasperation, "you clearly don't mind looking at Italian boys."

"First of all, Margaret, I was nine." Betty tilted her nose in the air when she was being supercilious, and Maggie had to resist the very real urge to slap her. "And secondly, I think Anthony's mother is Irish — or maybe Polish? Either way, it's completely different."

"There is a very nice Italian mechanic who comes in to fix the washing machines and the tumble dryers all the time. His name is Leo, and he is my friend." The words came out in a rush, and Maggie tingled in relief to be rid of the secret. Betty's jaw dropped open, and her perfectly manicured eyebrows shot up to her hairline. "Margaret Veronica O'Callaghan, how *could you?*"

"How could I what?"

"How could you do that to your brother? To Charlie? To *me?*"

"I beg your pardon?" Maggie drew back from her friend, confusion coloring her response. All she had done was mention that one of the ISU men was nice, and that she considered him a friend. Italy had switched sides — they were co-belligerents, not even really considered enemies anymore.

"That man might have shot and killed some of our boys," Betty hissed, glancing around as if she didn't want anyone in the empty store to hear her.

"But he didn't," Maggie protested. "He was in North Africa when he was captured. Billy's in Europe, and Owen and Charlie are in the Pacific somewhere. Plus, the Italians are on our side now."

"Sure, now that it's convenient for them, they are." Betty was growing more heated by the moment. "But before that, they were in league with Hitler. Why do you think President Roosevelt isn't sending them all home now, if Italy is so harmless?"

Maggie didn't have a response for that, and Betty took the opportunity to cement her point. "They're enemies, Mags, and they're being treated too well as it is. Do you think our boys go out drinking and dancing in Berlin or Tokyo? No. And are they getting three squares and bed? I doubt it."

Maggie remained silent. She knew Betty's information wasn't exactly right — but she wasn't exactly wrong either. Was it a betrayal of her country to offer Leo her friendship?

"Let him fix the machines, Mags, that's his job. But you don't need to be his friend. What would Charlie think?"

Maggie's face grew warm. She didn't want to admit that when she was with Leo, Charlie was the last thing she wanted to think about. Guilt washed over her, reminding her that Charlie was out there, facing God knows what, and the only thing keeping him going was the thought of coming home to her... and here she was, flirting with an enemy POW.

"You're right, I guess," she sighed, resigned.

"I'm glad you see it," Betty said, pursing her lips with a curt nod. "I'd hate to have to tell your mother."

Good Lord, Mam would have kittens at the idea of Maggie fraternizing with any boy, never mind an Italian POW.

"Don't you dare."

"I won't," Betty replied. "I'm glad you see it my way."

But as the conversation turned to lighter topics, and the afternoon turned into night, Maggie couldn't let go of the nagging feeling that she didn't see it Betty's way, at least not entirely.

Chapter 12

Niamh — 2015

Later that night, as Niamh tossed and turned for the third hour, she couldn't stop thinking about her failed attempts at motherhood.

They were out of sperm from the donor they had decided on, so whatever they chose to do, they'd have to buy more. Was she ready to try in vitro, with all the hormones and the shots and the egg harvesting? What if she went through all that, and her body still wouldn't cooperate? Christine had said she was happy to carry the baby, and they could try inseminating her next, but Niamh just didn't know if she was ready to give up the dream of having her own biological child.

It wasn't that Niamh didn't think she could love a child who wasn't connected to her by DNA — she knew that she would. She'd adore a little boy or girl with Christine's deep brown skin and wide smile just as much as she'd adore a scrappy little nugget who came out of her own body — but that was the thing. Niamh knew what Christine's genes produced; she knew and loved Christine's parents, her brother, and her niece and nephews. Niamh, on the other hand, had never known anyone biologically related to her except her mother, and she died when Niamh was seven. She had longed for that connection to another human being for as long as she could remember — had envied her foster siblings for all sharing the same nose, and felt a pang in her chest each time a sitcom dad referred to his kid as a "chip off the old block." Her need to know what that felt like was primal, and it defied both logic and fertility.

Why was it that when the alarm went off in the morning, Niamh wondered, her bed felt positively decadent, but at two twenty-eight in the morning, it was a hot, stagnant morass of sheets? And as God was her witness, she loved her wife, but that woman snored like a foghorn. By quarter of three, Niamh gave up on the idea of sleep altogether. She swung her legs out of bed, and after grabbing her bathrobe from its hook by the door — courtesy of Christine, as Niamh had almost certainly left it on the bathroom floor again — she padded downstairs to make herself some cocoa and watch infomercials.

An hour and two different rotisserie cookers later, Niamh heard the telltale sound of Christine's feet on the stairs, coming down to check on her. Walking around the side of the couch, Christine plunked down next to where Niamh was lying and lifted her feet into her lap.

"We'll keep trying, honey. This is another setback, but we're not out of options." Her raspy voice broke through the drone of QVC and the stillness of the pre-dawn hours, and Niamh sighed.

"I just don't know what to do next."

"And you don't need to know tonight." Christine rubbed Niamh's toes. "Your feet are freezing, woman. Come back to bed."

"Am I being stupid and selfish?" Niamh asked, the words rushing out as she turned to look up at her wife's face in the near dark.

"What? No! Of course not." Christine grabbed Niamh's arm and tugged her up so that Niamh was almost sitting in her lap. Christine smelled like sleep and nighttime moisturizer, a comforting combination. "Honey, I know how badly you want this, and I know why."

"But?"

"But it hurts me to see you so broken. I want to fix it, and I can't." She ran her nails up the back of Niamh's neck, swirling them around in the short hair at the base of her skull. "I wish I knew you when you were little. It breaks my heart to think of you so alone." She sighed, hesitating, and Niamh could tell her wife was about to say something she wouldn't like. "Did you ever wonder if maybe you're so focused on looking forward that you're not thinking about looking back?"

Niamh sat up and stared at her, perplexed. "Que?"

"So, I went out on a limb," Christine rushed, not meeting Niamh's eyes, "and I got you one of those DNA kits they're always advertising. I thought maybe if you took it, you might find some relatives who want to meet you."

Niamh sat frozen, a million thoughts running through her head at once, and a few of them even shivering down her spine like ice. DNA? Relatives out there somewhere? The ones who had never bothered to look for her before, when her mom had died. When she had no one?

"But DNA is so — so scientific?"

"And two lesbians buying sperm to make a baby isn't?"

"Touché." Niamh stuck out her tongue, but she remained serious.

"I don't want you to joke your way out of this, Niamh. There's hurt in you that needs healing, and it's a part of you I can't touch. Since the baby thing isn't happening as easily as we'd hoped, would taking the DNA test really be such a terrible idea?"

"If I promise to think about it, will you let me go back to bed?" Niamh asked with what she hoped was a light and flirty smile.

"Will I let you?" Christine's neck snapped to the side, and her eyebrows flew up. "You're the one who was up! I just came down to check on you."

"That's not how I remember it." Niamh stood up, leading her wife towards the stairs by the hand. Christine followed, amusement playing on her tired face.

"I'm not going to win this one, am I?"

"Not tonight," Niamh replied, heading back up to bed.

Chapter 13

Maggie — 1944

Sweat ran in rivulets down Maggie's back, leaving behind sticky trails of moisture that reached her blouse and made it cling to her skin in patches. She was never going to get it all done in time.

Sadie was home sick for the day, citing "female problems," and a whole platoon of new recruits had arrived at the camp the day before, all carrying laundry that needed to be cleaned, dried, ironed, and folded before they shipped out tomorrow. Maggie was busier than she'd ever been in three weeks at the camp, and she knew that it would take a miracle to get everything done before the end of the day.

Luckily, that miracle came in the six-foot form of Leo Castiglione.

Maggie was ironing her way through an interminable pile of white Navy shirts like an automaton when Leo came through the screen door with his toolbox. "Do you need me for anything today, *Margherita*? Everything is working as it should?"

"I think so," Maggie replied, wiping the sweat from her brow with the back of her arm like a fishwife and barely looking up. "I haven't stopped long enough to check."

"Where is Sadie?" Leo asked, placing his toolbox on the counter and coming around to stand next to Maggie, a concerned expression on his handsome face.

"Sick," she replied succinctly, her tone conveying that she had no time for conversation. Betty's words from the weekend played over and over in her head like a radio broadcast: *They're enemies, Mags. It's not fair to Charlie.*

Leo surveyed the workspace, with its piles and piles of uniforms, shirts, ties, socks, and underthings. "This would be too much work, even with Sadie to help," he determined. "I will help you."

"What? No," Maggie protested, torn between not wanting to accept his help and desperately needing it nonetheless. "Don't you have things to do?"

"Those other things can wait," he shrugged. "When do these need to be ready?"

"The men ship out tomorrow, so I can't go home tonight until it's all finished," Maggie admitted without looking up from the ironing board, defeat in her voice.

"Well then, if the United States of America needs these to be ready, we will be sure they are ready." Leo's tone was simple; determined. A job needed to be done, and he was going to do it. Maggie looked up and watched in stunned silence as Leo reached down and deftly lifted a basket filled with pants with his good arm and marched into the machine room, presumably to put them in the washing machine.

"Make sure you separate the colors," she called after him, needing to say something and therefore stating the obvious. She was rewarded with one of Leo's knee-weakening grins before the door swung shut behind him, leaving her alone in the front room once more.

"*Si, Bella.*"

* * *

As it turned out, Maggie and Leo made a good team. He did all the heavy lifting — loading the washing machines, feeding everything through the automatic wringer, loading and unloading the tumble dryers, and even operating the dry-cleaning machines for the innumerable pairs of wool pants and jackets that needed to be done.

Meanwhile, Maggie handled the tasks that required two arms — shaking out the clothes, ironing them, and then either folding them neatly into identical rectangles or hanging them up on wire hangers.

Just after they finished a hasty lunch of pot roast sandwiches and milk, Maggie shook out a standard-issue khaki shirt that gave her pause. One of the arms had been tacked neatly onto the shoulder seam of the shirt, indicating that it belonged to an amputee. Maggie was still staring at the shirt in puzzlement, trying to determine how best to iron it, when Leo emerged from the back with a load of dry socks.

"That is a smart idea," he commented, startling her, "sewing the cuff to the shoulder like that. I often have trouble finding someone to pin mine for me."

Well, it was now or never, Maggie decided. "How did you

lose your arm, Leo?"

"I don't agree with the way that sounds — I lose my arm — like I put it down somewhere and I cannot remember where I left it. I know exactly where I left it. In Morocco." Leo was quiet, his eyes focused on his right hand, which was fiddling with the buttons on a jacket Maggie had just hung up. She wanted to ask questions, wanted to know more, but she didn't want to push him, so she just waited and hoped that her silence conveyed empathy.

"We landed in Africa in '42," he began after a minute or so. "Right away, the British began shooting at us. We were not prepared — sent off to fight for the greatness of Italy, armed with our weapons and the clothes on our backs. It was all a lie. We had guns. The British had tanks."

A tightness pulled in Maggie's chest at the bleak look in Leo's green eyes. "It was hotter than hell itself, and nothing but sand as far as we could see. I was hit in the arm on the second day, just before we surrendered." He turned to face Maggie with a rueful smile and a shrug, and she could see the boy he had been looking through the eyes of the man he was. "It hurt like a *bastardo*, but the *medico* said it was clean and that I would heal with a scar to show off my bravery at home." Leo was far away now, lost in the memory. "I did not heal; bits of the bullet remained in my arm. We surrendered to the British, they loaded us onto a train, and my arm began to swell. I was hot and cold, and at times I did not know where I was. The British doctor at Casablanca said I was septic and that I was going to die."

"But you didn't," Maggie reminded him, her voice soft against his ragged one. She raised a tentative hand towards Leo, before dropping it to her side and clutching her skirt. She wanted to touch him and comfort him, but was unsure if she had the right.

"I did not, no. Another doctor took my arm off with a saw, and he sewed my skin closed where the bone used to be... but you are correct. I did not die."

"And then you came here." It was more of a statement than a question, but now that she had him talking about his experience, Maggie didn't want him to stop. Something in Leo had broken open, and she was desperate to see what was inside.

"After crossing an ocean and making a few stops, yes. I came here, and I met you." The corner of his mouth tugged up in a smile, and Maggie felt a flush creep across her cheeks at his words — it was clear that Leo didn't often share the story of how he lost his arm, and it meant a lot that he shared it with her.

"This is the last bit here." He indicated the basket of socks at his feet, grounding them back into the present. "If I match them, will you fold them into pairs, and then we will be finished?"

"Absolutely," Maggie agreed too quickly, wiping her sweaty hands on her skirt, placing the one-armed jacket on a hanger, and unplugging the flat iron.

Maggie and Leo worked in companionable silence through the ten minutes that it took to match and fold all the socks. Something had changed between them that afternoon, and Maggie doubted she was the only one who noticed.

Leo had rearranged his day to help her meet her deadline, and then he had shared something extremely personal with her. Maggie just wished she had something to offer him in return.

Chapter 14

Maggie — 1944

"Where on earth did you find that?"

Maggie and Sadie were hard at work the next morning — Sadie appeared to be feeling much better — when the screen door opened and Leo backed into the room ahead of a large radio on a wheeled dolly. At the other end of the dolly was a handsome, stocky man about Leo's age with olive skin and a wide smile that was directed right at Sadie.

"What have you two gone and done?" Sadie asked in a stern voice that was completely undone by the wide smile spreading across her features.

"We have brought you an elephant," Leo declared with a straight face, causing the other man to let out an undignified snort.

"We bring you a radio," the other man announced in a heavy accent, "so we can dance with the pretty girls."

"Oh, you wonderful man, you," Sadie cried, and she danced around the counter and right into his arms, planting a firm kiss right on his mouth. Maggie blushed crimson and looked at Leo, who grinned at her.

"*Margherita*, this is Guillermo. Guillermo and Sadie are..." he trailed off.

"We're best buddies," Sadie said with a whoop as Guillermo wrapped an

arm around her waist.

They were clearly more than that, and Maggie, who had been raised in a community where physical affection simply *was not shown*, wasn't sure where to look or how to react.

"Wowie, I had no idea." Maggie choked out an awkward laugh. "How long have you two been going together?"

"Since about the first day I started working here," Sadie grinned. "Guillermo wouldn't leave me alone, so I eventually gave in and let him kiss me." She rested her head on Guillermo's shoulder in a gesture of affection that seemed as natural as breathing. Maggie felt a tug in her belly that she dimly recognized as longing.

"And I have not stopped kissing her since that day." Guillermo looked so *happy* standing next to Sadie that Maggie couldn't help but share in their happiness. She wanted to ask Sadie if her parents knew she was seeing an Italian co-belligerent, and what their reaction was, but that was a conversation for another day.

While Guillermo and Sadie enjoyed one another's company, Leo wheeled the radio into the back room, and plugged it in next to one of the dry-cleaning machines. After a few moments of fiddling with the dials, the sounds of "Aurora" by the Andrews Sisters joined the soft whirring noises of the

WEST BRIDGEWATER PUBLIC LIBRARY

laundry machines. Guillermo and Sadie didn't wait for an invitation, and began dancing to the upbeat medley. Maggie laughed with delight to see her friend being whirled around the makeshift dance floor, beaming as if she and Guillermo were dancing to a live band on a Saturday night in front of the whole world, instead of the backroom of a military laundry at an embarkation camp.

"May I have the pleasure of a dance?" Maggie was startled to see Leo standing in front of her, holding out his hand, a tentative grin on his handsome features. His emerald eyes twinkled, and suddenly Maggie felt as if she too were in an upscale dance hall, dressed to the nines. A big band number blared from the speakers — "In the Mood," if Maggie's guess was correct. She took Leo's hand and allowed him to lead her onto the makeshift dance floor.

He really knew what he was doing, Maggie realized in surprise as Leo pulled her against him and swung her around with the finesse of a professional. She didn't have a moment to feel self-conscious as he made sure she could match his fancy footwork, twirls, and rhythm in time to the horns, trombones, and bass. Maggie found herself laughing and feeling lighter than she had in years, or at least since before the war started. The song ended with a flourish, and Leo dropped her into a low dip, her brown hair flying out behind her and grazing the floor. Maggie gasped, but Leo just grinned and held her tighter.

"I have you," he said, and Maggie's mind swam with the realization that he did. He had her, and he didn't seem to be letting go.

As some point in the last few weeks, she had begun falling for this Italian POW in a way that she'd never fallen for anyone else before. Her parents would be furious, her best friend would be gobsmacked, and Charlie Morris would be...

Maggie's stomach dropped to her feet at the thought of Charlie, manning a destroyer on the other side of the world. He was risking his life for the sake of a future with her, and here she was, dancing with *Caporale* Castiglione as if she didn't have a care in the world.

As if it wouldn't break Charlie's heart.

Leo guided Maggie back to her feet, and every nerve in her body felt the length of his arm encircling her waist, pulling her towards him as the music slowed and "Besame Mucho" by Jimmy Dorsey and his Orchestra filled the air. "This is Spanish, but do you know what *bésame* means in English, *Margherita*?" Leo's voice was low, hardly more than a whisper, and yet Maggie could feel it moving through her like warm chocolate, melting her worries and making her long to forget that there was anything whatsoever going on outside the backroom of the laundry, let alone a world war.

"It means," Maggie forced herself to step back, resisting the overwhelming urge to melt into him, "it means that I have work to do, and so do you, *Caporale*." She turned, deliberately picturing Charlie in her mind, and scurried through the door into the front room just in time to help a uniformed customer.

It was several minutes before the sounds of the radio dimmed to silence and Leo emerged from the back, toolbox in hand.

"I give them some privacy," he said, inclining his head toward the room where he'd left Guillermo and Sadie. "Thank you for the dance, *signorina*."

Despite herself, Maggie smiled back. "You're welcome, Leo. You're quite the dancer."

"I had quite the partner." Leo dazzled her with a grin, and

73

Maggie knew beyond a shadow of a doubt that she was going to have a problem on her hands with Leo Castiglione.

* * *

"Margaret, there's a letter for you on the table. It's from Charlie."

Maggie had hardly made it through the front door before she was bombarded with news of the mail from her brother Joe. To him, and to Frankie and Paul as well, Charlie was an American warrior, a real-life hero like "The Shadow" from their favorite radio program. Charlie, Owen, and Billy were out saving the world from Axis powers, and the O'Callaghan boys looked up to them with unquestioned devotion. They wanted to know every detail of every letter Maggie received from Charlie, no matter how personal.

"It's right here, Maggie. Open it." Frankie came running in from the kitchen, the letter in one hand and a cookie in the other.

Maggie groaned inwardly, knowing before she opened it that the letter would contain stories about life on board a destroyer, how thoughts of her were the only things that comforted him, and how he longed to return home and make an honest woman out of her. Not that she *wasn't* an honest woman; she and Charlie had never even come close to endangering her virtue. He was too much of a choir boy for that.

"Would you give me a moment to get a cup of tea before accosting me with the mail," Maggie grumbled, pushing past her brothers and grabbing the envelope from Frank's hand. She proceeded to the kitchen, where she turned on the heat under the kettle and spooned a tiny ration of tea leaves into a cup before sitting down to open the letter.

Dear Maggie,

Hello from the middle of nowhere! They won't let me tell you where I am, but that's OK because I haven't the foggiest idea anyhow. There's just ocean in every direction. There's a lot of downtime aboard ship, Mags. We all have our jobs to do, and the Navy works us all to the bone from time to time, but in between there's a lot of waiting around and staring out into the open ocean. I shouldn't complain, not when we might find ourselves at battle stations at a moment's notice, and sure as heck not when my brother could be anywhere right now fighting for his life. But the downtime gives me time to think of you, Maggie, and wonder what you're doing at this very moment. Are you with Betty, organizing a supplies drive to help the war effort? Or are you in church, praying for our safe return? Or are you tucked up into bed, sleeping like an angel? I can't wait until this gosh darn war is over and I'll never have to wonder where you are and what you're up to again. I just want everything to go back to how it was before Pearl Harbor. I miss you, Maggie. Send me a photograph? Lots of other sailors have photos of their girls pinned up in their bunks. I'm worried some of the boys will think I made you up if you don't send one!

Yours always,

Charlie

The sharp whine of the tea kettle yanked Maggie from her letter just as she reached the end. She turned off the gas on the stove, and returned to stare at the letter, and if she concentrated hard enough, she could will Charlie's hasty scrawl to make her feel something she just... didn't. She should be overjoyed to hear from Charlie. A letter from him should set her heart pounding in her chest, leading her to analyze and memorize every syllable he wrote, but instead his words made her feel hollow inside. The letter didn't make her heart swell with anything other than relief in the knowledge that he was alive and unharmed.

Maggie set the pages down on the counter and poured water into her cup, watching the tea leaves swirl around and struggle to make a decent brew out of the pitiful ration she was allowed. She would need to let Charlie down. She knew it, as sure as she knew that he would be devastated. She couldn't do it in a letter, of course — the poor man was at war, and she didn't want anything to distract him from returning home safe and sound. When he returned home, though, she would need to tell Charlie that her feelings for him were those of friendship. They were warm and comforting, but they didn't make her go dizzy in the head or weak in the knees.

And this didn't have to be about Leo Castiglione at all, Maggie reminded herself. It wasn't as though she thought she could do better than Charlie. If nothing else, her feelings for Leo had simply illuminated what she no longer felt for Charlie, and what she suspected she never had. She couldn't pinpoint the moment that she decided she was Charlie's girl; had she ever? Or had it just been determined by the neighborhood that the O'Callaghan girl and one of the Morris twins would make a good Irish Catholic couple? She hadn't fallen for Charlie so much as ended up with him, unlike with Leo...

...But this wasn't about Leo, she reminded herself for the umpteenth time. She would end things with Charlie when she could, she thought as she sipped her tea, and see where things led with Leo. She wasn't about to go looking for trouble. But, Maggie thought as she heard her brothers whispering in the hallway and waiting for her to tell them about the contents of her letter, she had a feeling trouble might find her.

* * *

Several nights later, Maggie was tidying up the laundry after closing. Sadie had gone home for the night, and Da would be waiting to pick Maggie up at the front gate in a few minutes, yet somehow she wasn't at all surprised when she heard the front door open and close, followed by Leo's deep baritone wishing her a "*buona serata, bellisima.*"

"Hi yourself, handsome," Maggie responded, placing the last of the cleaning supplies under the counter for tomorrow, and blushing at her own boldness. Her mother would flip her wig if she found out that her only daughter was alone with an Italian soldier, and with dark approaching to boot.

And yet Maggie found it increasingly difficult to care what her mother would think under Leo's gaze.

"I came by to see if I could have a dance before you went home for the night." Leo's smile was almost shy, and Maggie felt an answering pull in her belly. She was getting used to Leo giving her butterflies, but tonight the butterflies were dancing the jitterbug.

"I think that can be arranged." She took him by the hand and led him into the back room, where the radio had taken up permanent residence. Leo loved to eat his lunch there, cross-legged in front of the radio and listening to the latest episode of *A Light in the Darkness.* Initially Maggie had teased him about it, until she too was drawn into the drama of the Norton and Bethelridge families, and found herself watching the clock each day and waiting until the show began. Maggie and Sadie both agreed, however, that their favorite part of having the radio was using it to dance with their fellas.

Maggie turned the dial and an upbeat Bing Crosby song filled the room, surprisingly loud without the accompanying hum of the laundry machines. She stepped into Leo's embrace, and the world fell away as they twirled around the room. It was so easy to forget about Leo's amputation now. At first, Maggie had noticed the absence of a hand to hold on that side, but he had soon shown her how to place her hand on his shoulder, and he used his other arm wrap around her waist and press his fingers into the small of her back. They just seemed to *fit* this way, and now it felt as natural as breathing.

The song came to an end, and Maggie assumed Leo would help her lock up and walk her as far as the guard tower, but then the soft strains of "Fools Rush In" by Frank Sinatra filled the room. Leo tightened his arm around her waist, and Maggie melted against him, resting her head on his chest and swaying in time to the music.

She felt Leo's soft chuckle under her cheek, and his breath tickled her hair. "Do you know the Altieri family? They were the family that first signed me out to go to church with them?"

Maggie nodded against his chest, inhaling his scent of Old Spice and tobacco. She couldn't imagine a combination that suited him better.

"Mario and Tony Altieri are in school with my brothers."

"Well," the chuckle rumbled through his chest again, "Signora Altieri has a framed photograph of Frankie Sinatra hanging in her living room, right next to a painting of the *Vergine Maria*. Her husband says that in her eyes, Sinatra comes second only to Jesus Christ himself."

Maggie grinned against Leo's chest. "Well, he is quite

78

handsome."

"Are you admitting that you find Italian men handsome, *signorina*?" There was laughter in his tone, but something else too, something serious. Maggie felt his heartbeat pick up speed under her cheek, his skin separated from hers by only a few thin layers of army-issue fabric.

"Perhaps," she pulled her head back enough to look up at him, "but I prefer green eyes to Sinatra blue any day."

As if it were a choreographed part of the dance, Leo bent his head to hers, never breaking eye contact until she felt the softness of his lips against her own. They kissed, hesitantly at first, then deepening as they barely swayed in time to the music. Maggie put everything she had into that kiss. Leo's lips, his tongue, the feel of his arm around her waist, and his heart beating against hers — it was almost too much for her to take in at once. And it was certainly more than she had ever felt before with—

Maggie broke away first, putting a hand to her mouth and trying to steady her breath. Leo looked down at her, his emerald eyes hooded and searching.

"Was that... do I need to say that I am sorry?"

"Don't you dare apologize," she warned him, standing on tiptoe to kiss him once again but this time not allowing herself to get swept up in him. "It's just that my father will be here soon, and—"

"—and I will walk you as far as I am able."

Maggie's hands shook as she switched off the radio, and then the lights in the back room, and let Leo help her on with her lightweight coat. After she locked the door and stowed the key safely in her handbag, Leo threaded the fingers of his hand through hers and gave a gentle squeeze.

"Could we get in trouble for this?" she asked. "I don't want you to face any... difficulty."

"Do you mean is there a rule against a co-belligerent walking with a *bella signorina* on a well-lit path surrounded by the United States Military? No, there is not. As long as I do my job and do not make trouble, I am left alone."

"And is that what you do?" she asked, her tone teasing but her question conveying a need to know more about him, and what he was doing when he

wasn't with her.

"Of course," he replied. "When we were asked to join the Italian Service Unit and help the Americans win the war, I said yes right away. The sooner the Americans win, the sooner I can see my family again."

The sooner I can go home.

The unspoken words fell between them, weighing on their entwined fingers, but Maggie shook them off. The world might be on the brink of disaster, but tonight Leo was here, and he had kissed her, and that was enough.

Enough for now.

Before long, they reached the guard tower, where Leo would say goodbye and leave Maggie to walk the last two hundred feet to the gate and, beyond that, her father's Packard. He squeezed her hand, and although she wanted to kiss him again, she didn't want to push their luck.

"*Buona notte, Margherita*," he said with a smile that was just for her.

"Good night, Leo." She squeezed back before letting go and walking

towards the gate. "See you tomorrow."

Chapter 15

Niamh — 2015

" Hey, Deon, look! Mine has a ginger penis!"

"Mine does too!" Niamh and Christine's youngest nephew, age six, responded to his brother, molding the appendage in question out of cookie dough.

"Can mine have a ginger penis, Andrew?" four-year-old Camryn asked her eldest brother.

"Nope, stupid. Yours needs a ginger vagina," Andrew replied with absolute superiority, no doubt earned through his seven long years on earth.

"But I don't want a ginger fagina!" Camryn wailed, tantrum imminent. "I want a ginger penis. Auntie Niamh, I want a penis!"

"Freud says we all do, sweetie pie, but I've always found that theory pretty silly," Niamh replied, sweeping in to bop the little girl on the nose with a flour-covered finger. She and

Christine were watching the kidlets for the afternoon, and Niamh had come up with the bright idea to make Christmas cookies. Suddenly, she had another flash of genius, and blurted out, "Oo, Cam, you can make ginger boobs."

"Yay! Ginger boobies!" Camryn cried, sticking her tongue out at her older brothers and grabbing some dough to create her ginger masterpiece.

"What is Auntie Niamh teaching you?" Christine asked, coming into the kitchen to refill her water bottle, and raising an eyebrow in the direction of the children and their anatomically correct Christmas cookies.

"I'm merely inspiring a love of biology," Niamh shrugged. "I'm sure Craig and Tori will thank me when their children go to medical school."

"Somehow I doubt that." Christine looked down at the cookies over the children's little heads. She reached down and removed both ginger penises in one pinch, eliciting cries of protest from the peanut gallery. "I don't want to deal with the fallout when my brother kills my wife. Sorry, guys."

The kids, who had been bickering only moments before, joined forces to fix their Auntie Christine with three sets of liquid brown eyes and puffed out bottom lips.

"Oh, come on, honey," Niamh cried, the kids' well-crafted pathos kicking her right in the ovaries. "Who is it going to hurt? They're just parts like arms and legs — you don't want the kids to think there's something wrong with their bodies, do you?"

"Yeah," Andrew nodded. "Mom says that all bodies are beautiful."

"She also tells you not to play with your penis in the kitchen," Camryn added helpfully. Niamh tried to hide her laugh with a sip of coffee, but ended up snorting it out of her nose, resulting in tears from her and hysterical laughter from all three kids and Christine.

"OK, why don't we make gingerbread Christmas trees instead?" Christine asked as Niamh ran into the bathroom to snarf the rest of the coffee out of her sinus cavity in private. When she came back into the kitchen, Christine had taken a seat at the table with the kids, and she took a moment to lean against the granite island and watch them.

Four dark heads bent over their task in concentration. Four high foreheads and eight expressive dark eyes, all courtesy of Christine and Craig's father, Roy. Two sets of dimples, inherited from Christine and Craig's mother, Lela. And on all three kids' noses, freckles that they got from their mother. The scene in front of Niamh looked like a Super Bowl-level advertisement for heredity, and she felt the angst of her own childhood and the grief and frustration at her own inability to conceive wash over her again.

"Andrew — you ruined my treeeeeee!" Camryn shrieked, her already high voice rising in both pitch and volume, destroying her aunt's idyllic family vision.

"It wasn't me," Andrew sputtered, pointing an accusing finger at Deon. "He did it! He's got her icing on his hand!"

"It's green icing," Deon exclaimed. "We've all got green icing; how do you know it wasn't mine?"

Christine looked like she was about to cry, so it was Auntie Niamh to the rescue. She glided across the room, reached in front of Camryn, snatched her cookie and shoved it in her own mouth. Cam's eyes grew round and her mouth formed a perfect O.

"Delicious," Niamh said truthfully around a mouthful of

83

buttery crumbs and royal icing. Crumbs sprayed out of her mouth and down the front of her shirt, earning her a giggle from Camryn. The giggling soon turned to belly laughter, which moved on to Camryn's brothers and effectively diffused what could have been an epic sibling battle. "What?" Niamh asked. "Do I have something on my face?"

"Auntie Niamh," Deon giggled, "you're more fun than other grownups." Niamh grinned in victory at Christine, who made her middle and forefinger into a V and gave Deon the "I'm watching you, kid" gesture.

"I'm more fun than anyone," Niamh agreed with a nod. "You're just finally noticing it."

"Why do you act like a big kid all the time?" Camryn turned to ask. Now it was Christine's turn to snort cookies up her nose, which Niamh chose to ignore as she stuck her nose in the air.

"Well, honey, I didn't have fabulous aunties like you do, and my mom went to heaven when I was really little, so I had to learn to make my own fun." Niamh shrugged, pinching Cam's cheeks to make her giggle and chase away the sad feelings at the mention of Niamh's mother.

"All grownups should be as fun as Auntie Niamh," Andrew declared. "Oh, and you too, Auntie Christine."

"Thanks for remembering me, kid," Christine said with a smile and an eye roll before pushing herself to her feet. "Now the fun aunties need to feed you three some dinner. What should we have — spaghetti, pizza, or nuggets?"

"Ice cream and brownies?" Deon tried to use his puppy dog technique again, but with no success this time.

"Great idea, buddy," Niamh tweaked him in the nose, "but fun Auntie Niamh is not in the mood for three kids with a double sugar high."

"And I'm just a little bit scared of your mom," Christine admitted with a wink.

The kids finally agreed on spaghetti, and as Niamh moved around the kitchen with Christine, defrosting sauce, boiling water, and broiling frozen garlic bread, it struck her how *good* at this they were. They moved like dancers in a well-choreographed performance, cooking, cleaning, and distracting the kids when necessary. Niamh looked at her wife, head bent over Camryn's in rapt attention to what the little girl was showing her, and she had to swallow around the lump in her throat. They were going to be great moms.

She just hoped it wouldn't be too long until they were.

Chapter 16

Maggie — 1944

" He's coming home! Maggie, get down here — Billy's coming home!"

Maggie was sprawled across her bed, enjoying a rare moment of peace and quiet with her brand-new copy of *A Tree Grows in Brooklyn*, when she heard the front door crash open, followed by the sound of Betty's voice yelling loud enough to wake the dead. She scrambled to her feet, hastily grabbing a bookmark to mark her page, before scurrying down the stairs.

Betty stood in front of the open door, arms flung wide and an enormous grin taking up her entire pretty face. "He's coming home, Mags!"

"So I heard," Maggie laughed as Betty grabbed her in a hug and danced her around the living room. "When? How?"

"What in the name of all that is holy is going on out here?" Mam grumbled as she came in from the kitchen, wiping her hands on a dishtowel. "Oh." She stopped when she saw Betty. "I'm sorry, Elisabeth, I thought the boys were destroying something again."

"No, Mam, the boys went to the park. Billy Morris is coming home."

Annie's face was expressionless, but Maggie could see the gears turning behind her mother's carefully curated mask. If Billy was coming home, then Charlie might not be far behind, and she could have her daughter married off to a good Irish Catholic boy from the neighborhood by Christmas.

"That's lovely, Elisabeth. When does he arrive? No, wait, let me get you a cup of tea and you can tell me the whole story." Annie bustled back into the kitchen to put the kettle on, and Betty turned a confused look to Maggie.

"What's gotten into your mother? She's an eager beaver this morning."

"I think she caught a whiff of a potential son-in-law in your news." Maggie rolled her eyes and led her friend over to the couch. "Did Billy mention his brother at all?"

"He didn't." Betty fiddled with the tassels on the couch's throw pillows. "But it was just a telegram. *Leave in Taunton. Sept 8-11. Love you.*" Betty looked fit to burst at the news, and Maggie listened happily as her best friend went on and on about all the things she was going to show him, say to him, and do with him during his three-day leave.

"I'm sure his mam will want to see him as well, Elisabeth." Mrs. O'Callaghan came back into the room with two steaming mugs of tea. She handed one to Betty and took a sip of the other as she settled on the edge of her husband's chair. "Will his brother Charlie be coming home as well?"

Maggie felt the blood drain from her face. Could he be

coming home as well? What were the odds they'd be given leave at the same time? Maggie wiped her hands, suddenly slick with a cold sweat, down the front of her skirt and willed her face not to show her panic.

"No, Mrs. O'Callaghan, I don't think Charlie is coming home this time — at least, Billy didn't mention it. But I'm sure he'll be home soon, and you know he can't wait to see our Maggie." Betty gave Annie an angelic smile over the rim of her teacup — butter wouldn't met in her mouth. "Speaking of Maggie, did she not want a cup of tea?"

"Margaret isn't a guest in this house," Annie sniffed. "If she wants tea, she knows where the kettle is."

Maggie emitted a delicate cough to cover her sigh of relief. Leave it to her mother to be so utterly predictable.

"You'll come to the USO with us on Friday night, right, Mags?" Betty turned that sweet smile towards Maggie.

"Who do you think you're turning those baby blues on, Betty Boop? I'm not Billy and I'm not your daddy." But she'd go; of course she'd go. She'd hug the lemonade table again, and probably leave early, but she'd go. She'd just make sure that she stayed with the group this time.

* * *

"Leo, you said you'd been to Casablanca, right?"

It was late the following afternoon, and in what had become routine in the week since their first kiss, Leo came by the laundry after finishing his work for the day and helped Maggie close up. Today he was shaking out whites that had just come out of the tumble dryer, while Maggie folded them into a neat pile to be ironed in the morning.

"I have been to Casablanca; why do you ask?" And then, before Maggie could answer, he shook his head. "*Mio Dio*, Margherita, are you going to ask me if I've been to Rick's?"

Maggie grinned. "Maybe."

"I was in a military hospital in Casablanca for five days. There was no gambling, no piano, and no letters of transit." He paused, considering. "There was some drinking, though."

"I would imagine there was," Maggie smiled as she folded yet another white cotton undershirt. "How did you see the film?"

"I saw it *in* Casablanca, as a matter of fact. They showed the film at the base there to the British soldiers, so some of us were allowed to attend."

Maggie turned to him, eyes wide with amazement, the shirt forgotten in her hands.

"You saw *Casablanca*, my favorite film ever in the history of the entire world, while you were actually *in* Casablanca?"

"Well, I had just had my arm hacked off, I was burning with fever, and I only understood maybe half of the picture because my English wasn't very good yet — but yes, I did."

Maggie sighed. "I love going to the pictures. I used to go with my brother when we were younger, but now—" she trailed off.

"But now?"

"Now he's in the Navy. And I'm here. And I haven't been to the pictures since he shipped out. It doesn't seem right, you know, to enjoy one of his favorite things when he can't."

"I would like to meet your brother," Leo said, almost wistfully. Maggie pictured it — her fair-haired, freckle-faced Owen meeting this tall, handsome Italian man. They had a lot in common — their quickness to find the humor in any situation, their cleverness, their willingness to do what needed to be done, no matter the cost, their over-protectiveness when it came to her. In another life, they'd have been pals, Maggie was sure of it. In this one, however, would Owen see Leo as an enemy? And not just because Italy had once fought for the Axis powers, but because he had won Maggie's heart?

"Well, I have three more brothers at home," Maggie transitioned to a lighter subject. "Or, as I like to call them, the three stooges."

Leo threw back his head in laughter, and Maggie couldn't help but admire the lines of his neck, his Adam's apple, and the sharp angle where his jaw met his throat. She had an overwhelming urge to place a kiss just there, and see if she could feel his pulse on her lips.

"Tell me about these stooges," Leo prompted, breaking her reverie.

"Frankie is the oldest, after me. He's fourteen. Then there's Beansie, who's twelve, and Joe is eight."

"Beansie? This is an American word I do not know?" Leo scrunched his eyebrows together, making Maggie laugh.

"We've been calling him that for so long that I don't even realize how it sounds anymore," she chuckled. "When the boys were little, they used to go across the street to the fire station all the time. They thought the firemen were as close to the *Superman* comics that they were going to get in Taunton. Anyway," she continued, "my brother Frank was a chubby little guy, so the firemen took to calling him Porky. That meant that my brother Paul became Beans, or Beansie."

"And the youngest brother? Joe?"

"Oh, Joe never left Mam's side long enough to go to the fire station. He's just Joe — and he's still tied to her apron strings at eight." Maggie smiled fondly at the memory. She gave her brothers a hard time — that was her job, after all — but she loved them fiercely, and they knew it.

"That's how I was with my mama as well." There was a sadness in Leo's eyes as he mentioned his mother, and Maggie wanted to take him in her arms and comfort him. She had a feeling he would let her, too. "I have one older brother, and two older sisters — but they know I am Mama's favorite." He gave her a wicked smile, and she reached over to smack him with the shirt she was folding.

"You're incorrigible."

"I do not know what that means, but thank you." They continued in companionable silence for a few moments, both lost in thought. Finally, Leo asked, "Would you like to go to the pictures with me on Saturday night? I can get a pass, and I hear there is a movie with Cary Grant."

Maggie's eyes widened. Could she? Could she go into the Strand or the Star Theater on Leo's arm? Would the entire city talk, and report back to her mother? Being seen together in the camp was one thing; there were so many people and everyone was so busy that no one thought twice about a couple holding hands. But downtown on a Saturday night? And she had promised Betty she'd go to the USO on Friday—

"Guillermo and Sadie have a system," Leo explained, sensing her concern. "She goes to the box office and buys a ticket. Then he goes to the box office and buys a ticket. They sit together for the whole movie, and no one is the wiser."

"And Guillermo doesn't mind?"

"He would prefer to take her out on his arm and let the world know that a woman like her fell for a hairy little ogre like him,

91

but he knows that would be too hard on her. Her family would not understand. When the war is over, there will be time then to tell the whole world."

Maggie had the feeling that Leo wasn't talking just about Guillermo anymore.

"So," he said, moving the basket into which Maggie had placed the last folded item of clothing under the counter and holding out his hand for her to take, "will you go to see the pictures with me, *signorina*? I promise to be a gentleman."

"I'd love to," she replied, falling against him as he leaned down to seal their date with a kiss.

"Maggie?" he murmured against her lips, and she opened her eyes and looked at him with a quiet,

"Hmmm?"

"We'll always have laundry."

She kissed him again, laughing. "Here's looking at you, kid."

Chapter 17

Maggie — 1944

The USO dance was similar to the Catholic Youth dances Maggie was used to, except for three notable differences: There was a bar instead of a lemonade table, a haze of cigarette smoke filled the air, and there were no nuns moving around the dance floor and reminding couples to make room for the Holy Ghost. Other than that, Maggie could hardly tell the difference.

She dodged the wandering hands of several uniformed men as she made her way across the room, on the heels of Betty and Billy.

"I see a table," Billy called over his shoulder, his voice at risk of being drowned out by the cacophony of sounds around them. Finally, they sat down at a table on the outskirts of the dance floor, close enough to the band that Maggie could feel the horn section reverberating in her head.

"Can I get you ladies a drink?" Billy yelled to be heard over the noise.

"Champagne," Betty replied. "I like the bubbles."

"Just a Shirley Temple for me, thanks," Maggie said as loudly as she could. Billy nodded and disappeared in the direction of the bar, and Maggie hoped he heard her correctly.

"Just a Shirley Temple? Live a little, Mags," Betty advised. She looked gorgeous tonight. Betty's white-blonde hair had been teased and sprayed into a complicated updo, and her lips and nails were lacquered a fire-engine red that Maggie knew was designed to sing a siren song for Billy. Her eyes were lined in black, creating a smoky effect, and not for the first time that night did Maggie feel like a third wheel on their date.

"I'm having a Shirley Temple to make sure I don't end up living too much," she explained, scanning the ballroom for anyone else she might know. There were a few familiar faces from church, school, and around town, but unfortunately no one that Maggie knew well enough to go sit with and give Betty and Billy some quiet time.

"What are you looking for, a way to escape?" Betty yelled as the band launched into another fast and loud number.

"No — I just don't want to rain on your parade. You and Billy probably want to be alone."

"Mags, there must be close to five hundred people in this club, and you're worried that *you're* getting in our way?" She raised an eyebrow, and Maggie shrugged in response. If she was being honest with herself, she wished Leo was here. She wished Leo could put on a uniform and twirl her around the dance floor in front of all these people, instead of just in the back room of Camp Laundry #4. She wished he could sit at this table, sipping a highball and swapping stories with Billy, and then walk her home and kiss her under the stars on her front steps.

But Leo wasn't here, and every time Maggie caught a glimpse of Billy out of the corner of her eye, looking so much like his twin brother that even their own family got them confused sometimes, she felt sick at her betrayal. She might have had plans to end things with Charlie as soon as he was stateside again, but as far as everyone around her knew, Maggie was still a devoted girlfriend. Devoted girlfriends didn't look forward to dates with other men, and they certainly didn't let other men kiss them in a way that made them forget to breathe. But as fond as Maggie was of Charlie, and as much as she prayed for his safe return every night before she went to sleep, it wasn't Charlie's face that she saw when she closed her eyes. It was Leo's.

* * *

In the interest of giving Betty and Billy some privacy, however short-lived, Maggie used some of her hard earned, independent American woman money to take a taxi home from the USO and arrived a full two hours earlier than her curfew dictated. She didn't expect to hear from Betty until at least noon the next day, given how late she had been out and her parents' tendency to let her sleep in, so her heart jumped into her throat in surprise when Betty burst through the front door on Saturday morning as she was dusting the living room.

"You're up early," Maggie said when her heartbeat returned to a normal rhythm, wiping down the coffee table with a spray of furniture polish and a rag.

"Oh, I haven't gone to sleep yet." Betty breezed into the room, leaving the door wide open in her wake. *What on earth...* Betty held out her left hand, waving it through the air so quickly that Maggie had to grab the flying appendage and hold it steady in order to be able to see the glittering diamond solitaire on her finger.

It took Maggie a few seconds to register the news, but as soon as it hit her that *her best friend was engaged*, Maggie squealed and grabbed Betty in her arms, the two girls twirling around the living room in a state of pure joy.

"Jaysus, Mary, and Joseph, girls. What in blazes has gotten into you?" Maggie's mam came halfway down from upstairs, where she had been changing the bed linens like she did every Saturday. Betty flashed her ring at Annie, who gasped, both hands to her mouth.

"Blessed Mary and Bride, let me see that beautiful thing." Annie flew down the remainder of the stairs, moving like a woman half her age, and took Betty's left hand in both of her cracked, work-hardened ones. "Oh, it's brilliant, Elisabeth. Just brilliant," she cooed, her brogue thick with emotion.

She's shown more pride for that blasted ring that she has ever shown for anything I've done in my whole life, Maggie thought in frustration as Annie moved her hands from Betty's finger to her face, cupping her cheeks like she was a baby who'd just taken her first steps rather than a grown woman who'd just announced her engagement. "Aw, yer mam must be so proud. Bless ye, Elisabeth. And God bless that Billy Morris of yours too." *My God, were those tears in Mam's eyes? What in the name of...?*

"Excuse my mother, Betty. Her accent goes right back

to County Leitrim when she gets excited." Maggie grabbed her friend's hand and started for the stairs, brushing by her mother and dragging Betty along behind her. When they were finally behind the closed door of Maggie's room, she scrambled onto her bed like she had when they were children. "So, what happened?"

"We left the dance not long after you did," Betty smiled, basking in the attention. "Billy took me for a walk around the Green, and then he got down on one knee, right there in front of the fountain, and asked me to marry him."

Wow. Maggie sat back on her heels, grabbing a pink dotted swiss throw pillow from her bed and holding it to her middle. Betty was engaged.

"We just walked for ages, talking about the future, and the war, and then..." She trailed off, her cheeks stained tomato red and a nervous giggle escaping her lips.

Oh, my goodness. "And then *what*?"

"Well." Betty fiddled with a piece of thread that had pulled loose from the coverlet, and Maggie had the distinct impression that Betty was avoiding her eyes. "Billy had a room at the Taunton Inn."

"Elisabeth Louise Curran!" Maggie whisper-yelled. "You went..." she grasped for the words, "*all the way*?"

To be fair, Maggie didn't have more than a vague idea of what "all the way" even entailed. She knew it was something that boys were after, it evolved from kissing, it involved nudity, and it was a mortal sin if you weren't married.

Betty nodded, her eyes searching Maggie's face for a reaction. "Are you angry with me, Mags?"

"Angry?" Maggie was surprised by the question. "Why on earth would I be angry?"

97

"Because Charlie's still overseas, and I've got a ring now, and we always said we'd do all this together."

A pebble of dread dropped into Maggie's stomach at the mention of Charlie, but she pushed it aside as something that could be dealt with later. She smiled at Betty, truly happy for her friend.

"Betty, I'm delighted for you. The ring is beautiful." She paused, unsure if she should say it or not, and then finally blurted out, "I can't believe you saw his *thing*."

Betty turned an even deeper shade of red than she had previously, giving her the look of a platinum-blonde tomato. "He's only here until Monday, and then the next time I see him, we'll be getting married. So, we just skirted the rules a bit. I couldn't let him go back to the front and not..." She trailed off, unable to finish, but Maggie knew what she meant.

"I can understand that, although you know your mother wouldn't." Betty's eyes widened in fear, and Maggie couldn't help laughing. "Well, I'm sure not going to tell her! But are you... that is, were you..." Goodness, this was an awkward conversation.

"Bets, how do you know you're not going to have a baby?" That was the other thing Maggie knew about going all the way, the thing her mother had drilled into her since she had first gotten her period at thirteen: girls who go all the way have babies, and then they go to hell.

"Oh, don't worry about that," Betty breezed with a wave of her hand. "Billy knew all about it." Maggie raised her eyebrows and tilted her head, and Betty continued. "See, you get pregnant, because when a man... finishes... and he does it inside, that makes a baby. But Billy did it outside."

Maggie wanted to ask how she knew Billy was finished, and

inside and outside of where, but that seemed like a bit too much information for one morning.

"Do you want to come tell Nadine with me? And will you be one of my maids of honor? Of course, Charlie will be the best man." The giddy excitement was back on Betty's face, but at the mention of Charlie's name, Maggie's excitement dimmed. By the time Betty and Billy's wedding rolled around, Charlie was sure to despise her for breaking his heart. She didn't want to marry him, but could she stand being the object of his hatred? What would Betty think? Would she be compelled to take sides? Surely she'd side with her husband, who would naturally side with his brother. How many people would she hurt by breaking things off with a man that she truly did love, just not in the same way he loved her?

"Yoo hoo, Maggie? Did I lose you for a moment there? Are you coming with me to Nadine's?"

Maggie snapped out of her thoughts to find Betty staring at her, a bemused expression on her cherubic face.

"Just give me ten minutes to put my face on and do something with my hair," Maggie heard herself say through the fog of her worries, "and off we'll go."

Doing her best to focus on Betty's good news, Maggie teased and rolled her hair, finishing it off with hairspray. She would be the best friend she could possibly be to Betty, Billy, and even Charlie for as long as they would allow her to be. She would compartmentalize that part of her life, and not let it interfere with the part of her that shimmered with anticipation each time she thought about her upcoming date with Leo tonight.

Chapter 18

Niamh — 2016

"You know, it's a funny thing about DNA tests," Christine said one night as they were cleaning up from dinner. "They only seem to work if you take them out of the box and actually *do* them."

Niamh glared at her over the top of the pizza stone she was washing. It had been three weeks since Christine had presented her wife with the DNA test, and Niamh was getting annoyed with Christine's constant comments about it. She wanted to take it, and she had said over and over again that she would do it when the time was right. The more Christine mentioned it, however, the less ready Niamh felt, and the more Niamh wanted to tell her where she could shove that little box.

"Chris, I'll get to it. Drop it." But, of course, she didn't.

"What's stopping you?" Christine asked, hand on her hip, head cocked to the side in her trademarked *I'm not letting you worm your way out of this one* pose.

"I'm doing the dishes." Niamh gestured to the sink full of suds. "I'll get to it later."

"Except that you won't. I know you. You'll find another reason not to do it, and then we'll be having this same conversation a month from now." Christine took the stone out of Niamh's hand and dried it before putting it in the drying rack with the other plates. She took Niamh's damp hand in hers, and pulled her away from the counter to face her. "Talk to me, Goose. What are you afraid of?"

Niamh sighed. One thing she loved about Christine was that she had an uncanny ability to read minds. One thing she couldn't stand about Christine was that she had an uncanny ability to read minds. "I'm not scared, per se, I'm — shit, Chris, I don't know what I am. I'm frozen."

"OK. So... are we talking Arendelle in July level frozen, like in deep, deep, deep, deep snow? Should I tell you to let it go?"

"Nerd," Niamh grumbled, but she felt the side of her mouth tugging up in slightest approximation of a smile. She looked down between them, studying the contrast between her own scuffed Converse sneakers and Christine's pointy-toed black boots. If one of them was usually the nerd, it was Niamh.

Christine lifted Niamh's chin with her index finger, forcing her to look up. "Seriously, love. What is it that you're afraid of?"

"I don't know," Niamh whined, realizing belatedly that she sounded like a child. "What if it comes back with nothing, Christine?"

The other woman wrinkled her nose in confusion. "That's not even possible. Do you know what percentage of the population has taken these tests?"

"OK, Madam MBA, but don't throw stats at me. What if I'm just... completely alone?" Niamh's eyes filled up, and she dropped one of Christine's hands to wipe at her face with the back of her own. Christine's face softened, and she took Niamh's face in both of her hands, dropping the tiniest kiss onto her wife's lips and sending shivers all the way down to her toes.

"You, Niamh Reilly, will never be alone again as long as I draw breath."

Niamh knew Christine meant the words as comfort, but they only made her cry harder as she thought about all that she had been through since that day, decades ago, when a social worker came into the hospital to tell her that her mom had died and that she was really, truly, completely alone. She took a shuddering breath, willing her tears to stop, and went up on her tiptoes to wrap her arms around Christine's warm neck and bury her face in her shoulder. Christine smelled like home, and fabric softener, and Niamh wondered again what in the world she had done to deserve her. Niamh pressed her lips to Christine's, eager to lose herself in her wife for a while, but Christine stepped back, disentangling herself from Niamh's arms. Niamh shivered at the sudden cold.

"Don't look so dejected, love. I like your train of thought, but I'm not letting you distract me with sex." She looked over at the windowsill, where the test sat, still in its box, patiently waiting. "You're doing this now." Christine opened the plastic seal with one elegant red fingernail, and opened the top of the box. She knew it was crazy, but part of Niamh expected to see a green light glowing from within, and to hear a mysterious voice hiss, "Niamh Reilly, I am your DNA." Instead, the box contained instructions, a vial into which she was supposed to spit more saliva than she thought possible, and a mailing envelope with a prepaid label.

"OK, fine," Niamh agreed, a vague tingling sensation in her hands. She was really going to do this. She was going to mail off a little vial of her genetic material and ask the fancy scientists to see if it was anything like all of the other little vials of genetic material they had in their creepy (in her mind, at least) headquarters.

"You've got this, honey," Christine encouraged. "All you have to do is spit."

Niamh glanced at her with a smile, her sense of humor returning. "Well, that's something I never thought I'd hear you say."

Chapter 19

Maggie — 1944

Sadie was the perfect cover.

She had borrowed her father's massive black 1939 Lincoln continental, and picked Maggie up for the movie at six-thirty pm on the dot. Mr. and Mrs. O'Callaghan waved the girls off on their way to go see *Arsenic and Old Lace* at the Strand Theater.

"This is swell," Sadie said as she drove around the Green and started looking for a parking spot on Main Street, "having a real person to meet up with when I go out with Guillermo, I mean. I always just tell my parents that I'm going out with my friend Agnes, and they've started asking why they've never met her." She deftly swung the car into a spot vacated by a convertible and said with a twinkle in her eye, "Agnes doesn't exist, but you do."

"I could answer to Agnes," Maggie mused, emboldened, as she stepped one t-strap heeled foot out of the car and onto the sidewalk. It was a nice night, and everywhere she looked, there were couples or groups of teenagers enjoying the Saturday night and the crisp fall weather. As this was her first *real* date with Leo, she'd taken care to look her best. New stockings, high heels, and a cherry-red dress she'd gotten at Pober's with her earnings from the camp. She'd even spent an hour in the bathroom after she got home from Betty's house, making sure that her victory rolls were perfect, and that her makeup was flawless.

She looked amazing, and she knew it. She made a conscious effort to push down any feelings of guilt, straightened her skirt, and followed her friend towards the box office in front of the theater.

"OK, so we buy our tickets, and the fellas will meet us inside with the popcorn." Sadie sounded remarkably like a general, laying out the marching orders for her troops.

"Right on, Sarge," Maggie replied with a fake salute.

Sadie's smile was resigned. "Sorry, but my dad has made it crystal clear that if I were ever to go out with one of those '*eye-talians*,' he'd ship me off to a convent school faster than I could say *arrivederci*."

"My father would likely be the same way, but from what I hear, Spain isn't exactly an Allied nation, so that might be tough to arrange." The girls got in line for tickets. Maggie could smell popcorn, and her skin tingled with excitement.

"Tell that to my dad," Sadie said with a wry smile. "Two for *Arsenic and Old Lace*, please."

Once the girls had their tickets, they proceeded into the darkened theater. Sadie stopped at the second row from the back and took what Maggie assumed was her usual seat. Maggie moved forward a few rows, and sat down one seat in from the aisle. Hopefully Leo would be able to find her in the dark.

Just as she was beginning to worry that he had gotten lost, or even worse, decided not to come, Leo arrived bearing popcorn and Coca-Cola, and folded his lanky frame into the seat beside her.

Maggie's heart did a little backflip as he turned to give her a lingering kiss before twisting the top off one of the Coke bottles and handing it to her. In that moment, they were just two young people, out on a Saturday-night date, just like countless others all over the world. A war raged in Europe, across Africa and Asia, and in the waters of the Pacific, but here in Taunton, there was just Leo and Maggie, holding hands over a bowl of popcorn and enjoying a comedy about two octogenarian serial killers.

The picture was a scream, and Maggie could feel Leo shaking with laughter each time Teddy Roosevelt Brewster yelled, "CHARGE." They finished their movie snacks, and Leo stretched his arm around Maggie's shoulders, allowing her to rest her head on his arm.

I should feel guilty about this, Maggie thought at several points. *Owen and Charlie are God only knows where right now, risking their lives in God only knows what conditions. It isn't fair.* And it wasn't fair, but staying home and not seeing Leo wouldn't bring her brother or her friend home any sooner. So again, Maggie pushed down the nagging voice that told her she was doing something wrong and snuggled into Leo's side, breathing in the spicy, smoky scent of him.

Leo was a gentleman. Every so often, he'd look down at her with those molten green eyes, and then lean in for a kiss. As much as Maggie loved the feel of his lips on hers, the electric heat of his hand on her neck, her shoulders, her arms, he never pushed it any further. Unlike some of the other couples in the darkened theater, who were clearly there to experience more than the comedic talents of Cary Grant, Leo and Maggie actually watched the picture. She was content to simply be there, enjoying a good film and snuggling into the side of the man who made her feel alive in a world constantly filled with the specter of death.

Chapter 20

Maggie — 1944

"I told my father I'll be taking the bus home with Sadie from now on. As long as I'm with her, he's fine with it."

"But you will not be with her," Leo said, turning away from the wringer he was taking apart to watch Maggie load wool pants and jackets into the dry-cleaning machine. "Sadie leaves for the day at three o'clock."

"No, I won't be," she grinned at him over her shoulder. "But that gives me more time to be with you."

Leo gave a small chuckle and shook his head. "Is that safe, *Margherita*? I need to know that you get home safely."

"I'll get home just fine." She crossed the room and stood on her tiptoes in front of Leo, planting a kiss on his Adam's apple, which was as high as she could reach. Leo dropped the socket wrench he was holding and wrapped his right arm around her waist, pulling her against him and lowering his face to hers for a kiss.

Time slowed to a crawl, and all there was in the world was Leo, and how the lean muscles of his back felt through the thin cotton of his shirt. It was all sensation, sensations Maggie hadn't even imagined before, and in that moment it was easy to see why Betty had been willing to go all the way with Billy the second there was a ring on her finger, even though it wasn't the right ring. The *ding ding ding* of the service bell in the front room alerted Maggie and Leo to the presence of a customer, and they instantly broke apart, breathing hard.

"I am so sorry," Leo panted, squeezing his eyes shut and adjusting the waistband of his trousers.

"It's OK." Maggie fixed her shirt, which had become twisted, and patted her hair into some semblance of neatness. The jittery feeling rushing through her veins reminded her of the time she had accidentally zapped herself when plugging in a lamp at home. Her heart raced, and her skin felt hyper-sensitive and alive. Her lips felt swollen. "Do I look OK? Do I look normal?"

Leo nodded, looking like he was still trying to slow his breathing, and Maggie ducked into the front room just as the shrill ringing of the bell pierced the air a second time.

After collecting a bag of soiled linens from a private due to ship out in two days' time, Maggie gave him a receipt and returned to the back room. Leo had resumed working on the wringer, and was doing so with a vigor and intensity he hadn't before.

"Leo?" she asked, coming up behind him and placing her hand on his back. "Are you alright?"

After a long moment of silence that left Maggie grasping for what to say or do, Leo responded without turning around: "I let that get out of control. I am sorry." His voice was ragged, and emotion rolled off him in waves.

"You let it get out of control? I was here too, you know. I kissed you."

Leo turned, and Maggie was floored by the haunted, hungry look in his eyes.

"I need you to know something, *Margherita*. This is not a game to me." He cleared his throat, searching for the right words in English. "You are so beautiful, *molto bella*, so good — I wish I could take you home to meet my mama. Do this the right way."

The sight of this big man, who had been through so much on both sides of the war, telling her he wanted to bring her home to his mother made tears spring to Maggie's eyes. She wasn't used to hearing people talk about their feelings. In an Irish Catholic home, there were two emotions — angry, and not angry — and that was it. Emotions like love, fear, and longing were not talked about, or even admitted.

Maggie knew her parents loved her — they fed her, clothed her, kept a roof over her head, and raised her to be the kind of girl they could be proud of — but they never openly talked about it. Leo, with his feelings on his uniformed sleeves, was so different from everyone and everything else that Maggie knew... and she wanted nothing more than to wrap her arms around him and promise to never let him go.

"Tell me about your mama," she said, settling herself on the floor by the wringer he was working on. "And your family. You know all about mine, but I know almost nothing of yours."

Leo's answering smile was wistful, and she could see the longing for home in his eyes. "My mama is what you would call a tough cookie. She would tell me I am the answer to her prayers in one breath, and then tan my bottom in the next."

"I bet you were a naughty child," Maggie grinned, picturing Leo smaller, softer, his cheeks rounder and his legs knobbier.

"The naughtiest." Leo's eyes twinkled at the memory. "We have a farm outside of *Milano* where we grow wheat and—" he searched for the English word, "Soya beans? Once, when I was maybe six years old, I wanted to sleep outside in the fields with my dog, Cagna. My mama and papa said no, but I thought I was a man. Why should I listen to them?"

"Oh no," Maggie chuckled. "You sound like my brothers, and that is *not* a compliment."

"Perhaps your brothers will like me then," Leo said hopefully. "Of course, I snuck out of the *cascina de corte* late at night, when my family was asleep. I took Cagna and a few supplies and we went out into the fields to prove my bravery. It was cold, so I lit a fire. Do you know what happens to a fire in a field of dry crops, *bella*?"

"You set the field on fire?" Maggie's eyes grew wide as she worried for the six-year-old version of the man in front of her. "What happened?"

"Cagna happened. She ran back to the *cascina* and woke my parents. My father and brothers put out the fire, and I took such a thrashing that I could not sit down for two weeks."

"Your dad whipped you?"

"No, my mama!" Leo threw back his head in laughter. "I wish it had been my father. He would have gone much easier on my poor bum."

She could see it now, the longing he felt for the family on the other side of the world that loved him, even after his childhood foolishness almost cost them their livelihood. As much freedom as Leo and the hundreds of other Italian co-belligerents were allowed here, they were still prisoners. He could work as a mechanic, he could take her to the movies, but he could not go home.

"I wish I could meet your mama," Maggie whispered, taking Leo's hand in hers and squeezing.

"I've written to her all about you," he said, squeezing back. "I hope I can take you home to her one day."

Maggie blushed, flustered at the implication of what Leo taking her to Italy meant. "I hope so too," she stammered. "Is that your intention, to go back to Italy after the war?"

"I cannot see a future without family in it," he replied. "And I am a cripple now. I'll have to see what the world has for me after the war."

"It has me," she offered, standing to kiss him again, not caring in the least if he lost control. Leo was right about one thing, she thought as she lost herself in him once again. This was not a game — for either of them.

Chapter 21

Maggie — 1944

"Put on your twinkle toes and your happy rags, *signorinas*. We are going dancing tonight," Guillermo cried as he burst into the laundry, looking so proud of himself that Maggie felt a swell of sisterly affection for the swarthy little man.

"You mean dancing shoes and glad rags, Guillermo," Sadie said with an exasperated sigh, not even bothering to look up from the receipt she was filling out.

"Twinkle toes, dancing shoes, whatever. I want to take my girl dancing." Guillermo's thick accent made the words sound like "take-a my girl-a dahncing," but some of the light dimmed in his brown eyes when he saw Sadie's reaction. "What is the matter, *amore mio*? Are you sad?"

"No, I just don't feel like going dancing," she said testily, jamming the receipt down onto the nail they used to hold them. "I don't feel well, and I just want to sit at home with a cup of tea and you, and we can't even do that." Sadie's eyes filled with tears, and Maggie felt a rush of empathy for her friend. She also felt the pangs of not being able to bring Leo home to meet her family and sit with them around the radio listening to Jack Benny. She wanted him to meet her brothers — Frankie would have a million questions about Italy, and what Leo had seen in North Africa. Beansie would size him up with those wise blue eyes of his, and Joe would worship him as a real-life hero, one of his army figures come to life.

Some of the Italian POWs were dating local girls out in the open. Most of them were from Italian American families, who lived over in East Taunton and whose fathers worked in the brickyard. Girls that Maggie had attended St. Mary's High with, and girls that Sadie had attended Taunton High with, were often seen strolling arm and arm with their Italian paramours up Main Street and Broadway on Friday and Saturday nights. The Irish American families, the Polish American families, the Portuguese American families and others were not so accepting, however. Maggie wondered how many other girls besides her and Sadie had to sneak around, stealing moments with their soldiers wherever and whenever they could.

"Maybe you should just stay home, Sades," Maggie suggested. "There will be other nights to go dancing."

"No, home is the last place I want to be tonight."

"But you just said—"

"NO!" Her exhalation was emphatic, and it left no room for doubt. Sadie did not want to stay home while Guillermo went out with Maggie and Leo, and she had no intention of doing so.

"If you want to go, *bella*, we go," Guillermo said, coming

around the counter to place an arm around his girlfriend's waist. "But if you don't feel right, we will make sure you get home, OK?"

"OK," she sniffed into Guillermo's shoulder, and Maggie's heart went out to her friend. She caught Guillermo's eyes over Sadie's head, but he simply shrugged. Sadie said they were going dancing, and they were going dancing.

* * *

"The parking lot?" Maggie gave Leo a bemused look an hour later. "I thought we were going dancing?"

"We are," Leo smirked and waved his arm around him, indicating the empty back lot of the Roseland Ballroom, Taunton's finest dance hall. Sinatra himself had played the Roseland in '42, and while he wasn't in town tonight, the music wafting out from the open back door sounded like whoever was playing was in full swing.

"We cannot dance inside; there are sure to be people who know you or know your parents or Sadie's parents. One of the guys from the mail room at the camp works here on Friday nights as security. He said the music gets plenty loud enough out here, and besides," he gestured to the wide expanse of blacktop, "we have the whole dance floor to ourselves."

Maggie laughed at Leo and Guillermo's plan, and she had to give them credit for creativity. The girls wanted to go dancing, and come hell or judgmental parents, their boys were going to take them dancing.

The band began a new song — a slow, seductive jazz number Maggie hadn't heard before. Leo held out a hand, and she

115

stepped into his embrace. Behind them, in the shadow of the streetlamp, she saw Guillermo and Sadie do the same.

Being out with Leo was thrilling. She knew it had something to do with the element of danger, and the idea that she was breaking the rules her parents made clear to her, but it was more than that. It was dancing under the stars on an autumn night, melting into her partner, and what could possibly be better than that?

As Maggie swayed to the music, her head on Leo's shoulder and his warm breath on her neck, she thought back to the USO dance she'd attended with Betty and Billy. It ticked every box for a fun night out — music, dancing, free-flowing drinks, and handsome American soldiers all looking to show a girl a good time. And yet she had been so lonely.

Tonight was proof that although Leo had nothing, not even his freedom, he was giving her every bit of himself. She owed him the same.

Chapter 22

Niamh — 2016

Niamh was having lunch in the faculty room at school when she got the email from the DNA company, alerting her that her results were ready, and that all she had to do to see her biological matches was log into their app with a specific code, and it would all be spelled out for her.

She put down her phone and her chicken salad sandwich with an eerie calm, went into the faculty bathroom, and proceeded to vomit up the contents of her stomach into the toilet. When she came back out, gray and sweating, Marcos immediately jumped to his feet.

"Niamh, what the hell? Are you OK? Do you want me to call Christine? Do you need someone to cover your classes?" Niamh shook her head, sitting back down at her seat and putting the remainder of her lunch back into her insulated lunch bag.

"No, I'll be OK. Just give me a sec." She stared out the window at the parking lot, willing herself to take slow, even breaths, and not to act like a woman who felt very much like she had just gone off the deep end. When she thought she had gained enough control of herself, and she could no longer hear her pulse thrumming in her ears, she brought up the email on her phone and handed it to Marcos.

"So, you did it," he said, emitting a long, low whistle through his teeth.

"This is big, Niamh. You OK? Should you download the app?"

"NO!" Niamh shouted, drawing the attention of several other teachers who were quietly eating their lunch like this was a perfectly normal Tuesday. "No," she repeated in a whisper, just a completely sane teacher eating her lunch. "I'm not ready to see it yet."

"Why not?" Marcos took a bite of his sandwich and waited for her to answer, his demeanor no different than if he had asked her what she was planning to have for dinner. He raised one eyebrow. "Well?"

"Because then I'll know stuff about my family," Niamh grumbled. She knew she sounded stupid. Wasn't finding out about her family kind of the whole point? She tried to explain, to make Marcos see where she was coming from. "It's like — these people, the ones whose names are in this email, or at least the ones that I'll find on the app with the code that's in this email — they already exist." Marcos nodded, not ready to call for the men in the white coats yet, so she continued. "They have lives, and baggage. Maybe they already know all about me and have just chosen to have nothing to do with me. Maybe they knew when my mom died, and they made the choice to let me go into the system."

Marcos put a comforting hand over Niamh's. "And maybe they have no idea."

She shrugged. "The point is that I don't know. I know it sounds crazy, but if I have a baby, then I'll be getting the genetic connection as well as a clean slate. This way, I don't know what I'm going to get."

"You seem pretty confident that you're not going to give birth to an asshole, girl." Marcos wrinkled his nose in a blatant attempt to make Niamh laugh. It worked.

"Dude, you can't call a baby an asshole."

"I absolutely can!" He held up his palms in a *don't shoot* gesture. "You've never met my nephew, Xander. The kid is a level five asshole."

Niamh laughed, and the tension in her shoulders eased at least slightly. "Thanks, Marcos. I'm not sure what for, but thanks."

"Promise me you'll look, kid? Maybe not today, but soon?" He extended his fourth finger across the table, asking for a pinky promise. Never one to refuse the power of the pinky promise, Niamh hooked her own finger through his and shook on it. She'd look. Just definitely not today.

* * *

Niamh stumbled down the interminable hallway, pounding on door after door, the skin on her knuckles blistered and bleeding. She couldn't hear her own screams over the roar in her ears, but even though she couldn't make it out, she knew she was screaming the name of her child. She couldn't find them, no matter how hard she looked, and panic rose in her chest, choking the breath from her lungs. Just behind her, Niamh caught a glimpse of her wife, kicking a door in a desperate attempt to get inside. Instinctively, she knew that she too was desperate to find their child. A dark cloud hovered closer and closer, threatening to swallow the panicked mothers. Niamh reached for Christine and opened her mouth to scream—

"Niamh — Niamh, you're asleep. Niamh baby, it's a bad dream. Wake up."

Niamh opened her eyes, jerked from the nightmare by what felt like her entire body weight landing heavily on the mattress. Panic still seized her limbs, and she gulped in oxygen in an attempt to regulate her pounding heart.

"My God, Niamh, where were you?" Christine leaned over her, brown eyes wide with concern.

Niamh squeezed her eyes shut, forcing her breath in and out with regularity, still shaking with fear. "We were somewhere... I don't know... and I was looking for our kids, and I couldn't find them, and I didn't know if they were OK, and then there was you, and there was this darkness—" She shivered and allowed Christine to gather her up in her arms. She wanted to stay there forever, held by someone who she knew would never intentionally hurt her, but she knew she couldn't. It wouldn't fix anything. "I need to look at the results and see if there are any matches," she said into Christine's shoulder.

"What, now?" Christine pulled back to look at her. "Niamh, it's the middle of the night."

"Well, apparently that's when I get my bursts of motivation." Niamh climbed out of bed and stumbled out of the room, Christine not far behind as she made her way down the stairs and into the kitchen where she had left her laptop. Sure, she could have done this on her phone, but this felt like it was something official enough to warrant an actual computer.

"Here." Christine came up behind Niamh and laid her bathrobe over her shoulders. "I don't want you dealing with hypothermia on top of everything else."

As soon as the laptop warmed up, Niamh went straight to her email and clicked on the message from Forefathers.com. "The name bugs me," she commented, pointing at the dark blue Forefathers logo as it flashed onto the screen. "What about foremothers, huh? They're the ones who did all the work, anyway."

Christine yawned. "I want to be supportive, baby, but can you save the feminist commentary for daylight hours?"

"Fine, fine."

Niamh scrolled through the email until she found the code she was looking for, and within maybe three minutes she had the account set up. Gathering strength from the comforting pressure of Christine's hands on her shoulders, she clicked the "results" button. The kitchen was quiet, and the glow from the stove light gave the whole tableau a feeling of sanctity.

Niamh held her breath as the home page loaded, as if she was about to come face to face with actual long-lost family members instead of just their names and genetic connections. She drummed her fingers on the granite top of the kitchen island, waiting.

The first page to load appeared to be a breakdown of her genetic makeup. Nothing terrifying there, right? Apparently she was 25% Irish, 25% Italian, and a hodgepodge of other European nationalities, none totaling more than 10% of her total profile.

Hmm.

"Twenty-five percent Italian, huh? That must be where you get your roguish charm," Christine teased, her breath tickling Niamh's ear and leaving a line of goosebumps in its wake.

"And the Irish must be why I'm so fun at parties."

"Really? I was going to say it's why you're such a stubborn pain in the—ow!" Christine yelped as Niamh jabbed her in the belly with an elbow.

"I'm scrappy," Niamh said with a smile that dripped from her face like melting snow when she saw the tab at the top of the page: Genetic Matches. Oh shit shit shit. Here we go. What if her actual father was on here? The one who knocked up her mom and then turned out to be married?

Before she could talk herself out of it, Niamh pointed the cursor over the tab and double clicked, holding her breath as the page loaded.

Ho. Ly. Shit. There was—

"You've got siblings," Christine breathed.

Sibling, to be exact. One sibling — a half-brother. A half-brother in Texas named Dwight Thompson. Without looking any further, Niamh closed the laptop and tugged on Christine's arm. "OK, so now we know. Let's go back to bed."

"Hold up, girl." Christine stood firm, refusing to move from her spot in the kitchen. She gestured to the laptop with her free hand. "You need to email him."

Niamh squirmed under her gaze, rubbing the back of her neck with her hand. She'd reached the end of her bravery as soon as the name of her bio-brother had appeared on the screen. "Can I do it in the morning?"

"Why?"

"I don't know," she stammered. "I need to think about this for a while."

"Niamh, baby." Christine crossed her arms and fixed her wife with a knowing look. "You've done nothing but think about this for months. Try again."

Niamh looked up at her wife, a lifetime of loss and disappointment by family members reflected in her eyes. "C'mon, Chris, he's from Texas. His fucking name is Dwight."

"So?"

"So how do you think he's going to feel about hearing from his long-lost half-sister who is probably a result of his dad cheating on his mom? Oh, and by the way, she's a gay liberal from New England." Niamh's voice broke on the last part, tears welling in her eyes.

"I think that you have every right to be nervous." Christine paused, considering. "But you don't know this guy. Doesn't he deserve the chance to prove you wrong?"

"Chris, my father never wanted anything to do with me. My mom died. And even though none of the insemination attempts worked, I feel like I've lost children too. Or at least my chance at children. Contacting this guy feels like I'm daring him to reject me as well, and I don't know if I can take that."

"Baby..." Christine's eyes softened, and the pity Niamh saw in their depths made her want to scream in frustration. She *hated* to be pitied.

"Fine. What do you want me to say?" Niamh wrenched open the laptop and navigated back to the Forefathers matches page, clicking on the name of her newly discovered brother. A message box opened on the screen, its empty white nothingness reminding her that she had absolutely no idea how to begin. Niamh's fingers hovered over the keyboard, shaking despite the bravado she was desperate to portray. What was she supposed to write? *Hi, so apparently your dad and my mom bumped uglies about thirty years ago, and it turns out that we're related. Want to get a coffee and chat about the weather?* Ew. No. Niamh was nearing panic when Christine's steady hands covered her pale and trembling fingers, infusing her with warmth and calm.

"Do you want me to write it?" she asked in Niamh's ear.

"Yes, please." Niamh sighed in relief, laying her head down on the keyboard. Christine would take care of it; she'd take care of everything, like she always did.

Christine sat down at the island next to Niamh and slid the laptop out from under her. Niamh kept her head down on the counter, the cool granite soothing against her fraught nerves, and listened to the sound of her wife's fingers tapping on the keyboard, potentially changing both of their lives.

"Do you want to read it?" Christine asked moments later. When Niamh opened her eyes, she saw Christine's finger hovering over the "send" button, the question in her eyes.

"Read it to me, please," Niamh sighed, her fingers searching for the comfort of Christine's in the space between them. Christine's hand found Niamh's first, and Niamh grasped her wife's strong fingers in her own as if she could suck the comfort and strength from the other woman like some sort of weird emotional vampire.

"Dear Dwight," Christine began, and Niamh closed her eyes and let the voice wash over her. "I hope this message finds you well. According to the geneticists at Forefathers.com, it appears that you and I are genetic half siblings. I was born in 1980 in Burlington, Vermont. My mother's name was Julie Reilly. I never knew my father, through whom we are related. I'd love to speak with you and find out more about both you and our father. I look forward to hearing from you soon. Sincerely,

Niamh Reilly." Once Christine stopped reading, Niamh opened her eyes to find her wife staring at her, concern, not pity, clouding her honey-brown eyes. She squeezed Niamh's hand before dropping it to brush her palm across her cheek. "Is that OK, baby?"

"It's perfect," Niamh managed to say around the lump that formed in her throat. What the hell? Why was she being so stupid about this? It was an email to some guy she'd never met with whom she just happened to share genetic material. She had done what she could; the ball was in his court now. "Hit send." Niamh slid off her chair as Christine sent the email and closed the laptop, coming around to stand in front of her.

"Thank you," Niamh whispered, and Christine reached out and pulled her closer, resting her forehead on Niamh's.

"No thanks needed. Can I go back to bed now?"

Niamh smiled and dropped a quick kiss on her lips. "Yeah. I think I can sleep now."

"No more nightmares?"

"No more nightmares," she replied, tugging her wife off the stool and leading her back upstairs to their bedroom.

Hours later, though, as Niamh lay wide awake watching Christine sleep, she couldn't shake the feeling that contacting Dwight Thompson would lead to nothing but more disappointment.

Chapter 23

Maggie — 1944

When she awoke on Sunday morning, the first thing Maggie noticed was that she couldn't open her left eye. The lid was crusted over along her lash line, and held down with a layer of goo.

After getting out of bed and applying a warm compress to her eye, Maggie was finally able to open it, but that's when she knew something definitely wasn't right. A rosy-pink rash covered her skin from head to toe, and her head pounded with a low-grade headache that made her stomach turn.

A trip downstairs revealed Frankie and Joe in much the same condition as Maggie, and their mother stood off to the side, shaking the thermometer to reset the mercury.

"One hundred and one, Joseph. Back to bed with ye." She waved him off with her hand. "Now it's your turn,

Francis. Under your tongue, now." Frankie complied, looking absolutely miserable as Mam watched the clock to determine when a minute was up.

"One hundred and... looks like one hundred and two. Up to bed, Francis."

"My throat hurts, Mam," he whined, sounding more like a four-year-old than a fourteen-year-old.

"I'll be up with an aspirin and some juice, pet. Get to bed."

"Yes, ma'am," Frankie grumbled, lumbering over to the stairs with all the grace of an intoxicated elephant.

"Not you too, Margaret Veronica," her mother sighed. "Well, I suppose if Dr. Killion is coming out to the house, we may as well make the most of his time. Under the tongue."

Maggie allowed her mother to place the thermometer in her mouth, and she sat heavily in her father's armchair, awaiting the results. The skin on her face was tight, and it itched where the rash had spread over her cheeks and chin. There was no way she'd be able to go into work today, and her heart sank at the thought of Leo showing up at the laundry with a fresh cup of coffee, and her not being there.

"Just over one hundred and one degrees," her mother declared after she pulled the thermometer from between Maggie's lips. "Back to bed, and I don't want any argument."

"But Mam, I need to phone the camp and let them know I won't be in—"

"I'll do it for you. Now go. Bed. Now."

Maggie thought, and not for the first time, that her mother had missed her true calling as a drill sergeant in The Marines. It was too bad she refused to take a position on the war, because Hitler would be terrified of her.

* * *

German Measles.

Maggie, Frankie, and Joe all had it, and Mam was keeping a hawk eye on Paul just in case he developed symptoms. Another way Annie O'Callaghan had missed her calling — she'd have made an excellent warden in the field hospital. Within an hour of Dr. Killion's diagnosis, Mam had Maggie set up in her own room with juice, crackers, aspirin, and a fresh copy of *The Lives of the Saints* — Maggie was glad to have a copy of *Strange Fruit* that she'd borrowed from Betty tucked safely under her pillow. Frankie and Joe were tucked into their beds with hot water bottles at their feet, juice and aspirin by their heads, and copies of *Ivanhoe*, *The Man in the Iron Mask*, and at least six comic books on their bureaus. Paul, on the other hand, had been packed off to school alone and told that he'd be sleeping on the couch that night to avoid contagion.

German Measles can spread for up to seven days after the rash appears, Dr. Killion had advised. *They should be kept home from school and work, and away from friends, for at least that long.*

Maggie was bereft at the thought of not seeing Leo for over a week. Worst of all, she had no way to get word to him and let him know why she wasn't coming to work. Of course, he would worry, but what if he thought that she wanted to break things off, and not see him anymore?

By noon, Maggie had worked herself into such a state that if she didn't already have a headache from the virus, she'd certainly have given herself one from stress. She tried to sleep, but couldn't because of the itching, and so she tossed and turned until finally an idea came to her — she'd write Leo a letter, and ask Sadie to deliver it for her. Perfect.

Maggie slid out of bed and sat down at the desk she'd used to complete her homework since she was five. She pulled out a piece of the nice stationary she'd gotten for her last birthday, and began to write.

November 4, 1944

Dear Leo,

I hope I didn't worry you by not being at the camp this morning. I have the German Measles, as do two of my brothers, and Mam has us all tucked up in bed. There's no need to worry; Dr. Killion says that German Measles is far more mild that the actual Measles, and that I'll be feeling much better in a few days. I can't go to work until at least next Monday though, as I am still contagious until then. Not seeing you is worse than the illness itself.

When I was in school, we read a play by William Shakespeare called Romeo and Juliet. *Shakespeare was English, so I don't know if you'd have learned about him, but the play takes place in Italy. There was a line that always stuck out to me, and I think of it every night when I leave for home and you go back to your barracks. "Love goes towards love like schoolboys from the books, but love from love, towards school with heavy looks." That's how I feel when I think about seeing you, my* caporale, *like a schoolgirl who cannot wait for the bell to ring on a Friday afternoon and release her into the bright sunshine. You are my sunshine. Please know that I am thinking of you every moment of every day until we see one another again. I am,*

Yours,

Maggie

Now all she had to do was wait until Sadie was home from work, phone her, and ask her to deliver the letter to the guard station at the entrance to the camp.

Easy peasy.

With that load off her mind, Maggie took an aspirin and was finally able to sleep.

* * *

No one was answering the telephone at Sadie's house.

Maggie called four times, checked the number, and then called twice again. No answer.

She slammed down the receiver and growled in frustration. How was she going to get the letter to Leo if she couldn't get in touch with Sadie before tomorrow morning?

"I wanted to leave these for Maggie." Nadine's voice floated down the hallway from the front door. "There are some copies of *Seventeen* magazine and another novel if she gets bored."

"Thank you, Nadine; that was very kind of you to think of her." Mam was about to close the door when Maggie ran in from the kitchen, her bathrobe flying out behind her.

"Nadine, wait!" Nadine turned around and looked back at her friend, standing in the doorway in her pajamas and a bathrobe. "I need to talk to you."

"Margaret Veronica O'Callaghan, you are going to catch your death out here!" Mam fussed, trying to herd her daughter back inside.

"Mother, it is at least fifty-five degrees outside and I'm wearing two layers of flannel. Please just let me talk to my friend for a minute."

Mam emitted an annoyed sigh, but finally nodded. "Fine. Five minutes, and go put your slippers on first." She turned back into the house, muttering, "Nineteen years old and the foolish girl thinks she can just walk around sick in her bare feet."

Maggie grabbed her slippers off the stairs and stepped outside onto the porch, closing the door behind her.

"Mags, you look terrible."

"Really? I was going to try this look for Betty's wedding,"

Nadine stuck out her tongue in response, and Maggie responded in kind, dissolving into laughter. "I need you to do me a huge favor, doll, and you can't ask any questions." Nadine's eyes lit up; she loved a good secret, and here Maggie was handing her one on a silver platter.

"Of course; what do you need?"

Maggie reached into the pocket of her bathrobe and withdrew the letter. It was encased in an ivory envelope, sprayed with Maggie's best *Evening in Paris* perfume, and had the words *Leonardo Castiglione, Italian Service Unit, 12674, Camp Myles Standish* scrawled across the front. She held the letter out to Nadine with both hands, eyes pleading. "Can you please see that this gets to the front gate at the camp? Maybe you can borrow your dad's car?"

Nadine stared at the envelope in Maggie's hand, making no move to take it from her. The secret hung in the air between them, and for the first time in her life, Maggie wasn't sure if her friend would catch her and keep her safe, or if she'd let her fall.

"You can't be serious," Nadine whispered. She stared from Maggie, to the letter, and then back to Maggie, her face a mask of surprise and disbelief. "Betty told me that you weren't going to get involved with him."

"No, Betty told *me* I wasn't going to get involved with him. But sometimes," she took a shuddering breath, praying that she hadn't just made the biggest mistake of her life in trusting

Nadine with this, "sometimes you fall in love with someone and it can't be helped."

"You love him?"

Maggie nodded. "He's a good man. He's kind, and he's funny, and—"

"—a prisoner of war." Nadine shook her head. "I don't understand this, Maggie. Help me understand this."

"Would you love your Jimmy if he was Italian?" Maggie asked, referencing Nadine's on again, off again boyfriend. "Or German? Or Japanese?"

"But he isn't—" Nadine began.

"—but what if he was? Would he still be Jimmy Murphy, the boy who gave you his pin, or would where he was born and what language he speaks make you change your mind about who he is?"

"Fine." Nadine held out her hand for the letter after a long minute. "I'll deliver it. I don't agree with what you're doing, but I'll deliver it. Just promise me that you won't do anything stupid, OK?"

Maggie nodded, relief flooding through her limbs and making her dizzy. "Thank you, thank you, thank you, really. You're a doll and I owe you one."

"Yes, you do." Nadine grimaced, and looked back to the driveway, where her father's Chevy sat waiting. "You owe me."

Chapter 24

Maggie — 1944

Maggie didn't return to work until the following Tuesday, when every last member of her family had been fever free for three days. She couldn't sleep the night before; she was so excited to see Leo, and the guilt from leaving Sadie with all the work in the laundry was eating her up inside.

The first thing she noticed when she arrived at the laundry was that the door was locked and all the lights were off. Maggie jogged over to the custodian's office to get the key, and the harried private who had shown her around on her first day looked delirious with relief to see her come in the door.

"Miss O'Callaghan — thank goodness you're back. We've been overrun. I trust you're feeling better?"

"Ship shape, Private," she replied. "But I need the key to the laundry. Why isn't Sadie Marshall here to open up? She not sick, is she?"

"Hell if I know," he responded with a grimace. "I haven't seen or heard from her since a week ago last Friday. At first, I thought she was down with whatever you had — German Measles, was it? — but you at least had the decency to phone us and let us know what was happening. Marshall just up and disappeared. We had to shut down #4 and divert all the linens to #3 and #5."

That was strange, Maggie thought, as she took the key and walked the short distance back to the laundry. Leaves crunched under her feet and the scent of wood smoke tinged the air as Maggie unlocked the door and stepped inside. Nothing had been touched in the eleven days since she had last been here. The same clothes were hanging on the rack by the door, waiting to be picked up, and the shirts by the ironing board were still waiting for Maggie to smooth out their creases.

Where was Sadie?

Maggie didn't have long to consider it, because within moments of her coming through the door, she was bombarded with soldiers dropping off bags of clothes, towels, and sheets.

"Can you have this done by tomorrow?" "How soon can I pick it up?"

"Please, doll, I need this jacket back as soon as I can get it."

Her mind spun as she took in more and more, mechanically writing out receipts, sorting, and getting started with the actual washing. By the time the line died down and she could really get down to business, it was well after ten o'clock in the morning, and Maggie felt as if she had run a marathon. She had just loaded her eighth washing machine with soiled clothes when she heard the door open.

What now? she thought with a sigh. Maggie grabbed onto the nearest machine and used it as leverage to stretch out the kinks in her back before stepping out front, but before she could go anywhere, the door to the back room opened and Leo strode through, a worried expression on his face.

"Maggie." His face broke into a wide smile, relief etched on his handsome features.

Before she could register what she was doing, Maggie flew across the room and threw herself at Leo, burying her face in his neck. He smelled like home, and she couldn't stop the tears that welled up in her eyes and spilled down her cheeks, dampening his collar.

"Did you get my letter?" she asked, her voice muffled by his shirt as he hugged her to him.

"I did," he replied, drawing her back to drink in her face. "But if you think that would stop me from worrying about you, *Margherita*, then you don't know me very well at all." He bent his lips to hers, and Maggie's knees buckled as she kissed him back with a hunger that both terrified and thrilled her. It was different than before, somehow, as if they had both decided that a week apart was too much, and they had resolved to make sure it never happened again.

Leo tasted of coffee, and of the toast and jam he must have had for breakfast. The combination was so *normal*, so completely and perfectly *right*, that Maggie couldn't get enough of him. They fell to the floor in a tangle of limbs, and she found herself sitting atop a very... delicate... situation.

"Oh." Maggie stopped, searching Leo's face to see if she had hurt him. The look in his eyes was strained, but not from pain.

"*Margherita*, I—" He rolled out from underneath her, his breathing labored.

"Did I do something wrong?" she asked, concern racing through her. She couldn't be sure, but she thought Leo had responded with a... *snort?* "Are you laughing at me?"

"Not at all, *bella*. *Mio Dio*, I missed you so much." He kissed her again, and Maggie again felt the sensation of coming home. His hand cupped the back of her neck, his fingers spread into her hair, and his tongue — whatever it was that he was doing with his tongue made Maggie shiver from the top of her head to the tips of her toes. Leo broke the kiss first, holding her forehead to his. "You are doing everything exactly right, *bella*. Some parts of me just get a bit too excited when you do."

"A bit too... oh." The meaning of his words suddenly dawned on Maggie, and she blushed crimson. *So that was how it happened.* "I didn't mean — I don't want you to think — I'm not—"

"Shhh," Leo interrupted her, his index finger gently caressing her lips. "I know you did not mean, I do not think, and you are not. I would never expect you to..." He trailed off, unsure of an English word to express himself.

"Go all the way?" Maggie supplied helpfully.

"Yes." Leo cleared his throat, uncomfortable. He leaned back against a tumble dryer, pulling Maggie in front of him and wrapping his arms around her waist with a sigh of contentment.

"I missed this," she sighed, laying her head back against his chest. "You can't imagine how much."

"I think I have a good idea," he chuckled into her hair. "You are well now?"

"I am," she replied. "It wasn't fun, but it wasn't serious." She looked around the room at the massive amount of work to be done. "And no one has heard from Sadie?"

"Guillermo was hoping that you might know something." Leo stood up, adjusted his trousers, and offered Maggie a hand up.

"I haven't heard a thing." Maggie shook her head. "I phoned her dozens of times, but no one ever picked up. I'm worried."

Leo nodded in agreement and did his own survey of the cluttered laundry room. "I am finished with my repair work for the day. I am not Sadie, but can I help you sort all of this?"

* * *

The amount of work to be done was staggering, but with Leo by her side, Maggie was able to get through a good deal by lunch time. They worked mostly in companionable silence, until finally breaking to share Maggie's pot roast sandwich and cookies in the back room while listening to *A Light in the Darkness.*

"How did you listen to the show while I was sick?" Maggie asked, taking a bite of her sandwich. "Were you able to use the radio in the mess hall?"

Leo shook his head. "I could not listen at all. Even if I could have, it didn't seem right listening without you."

Maggie flushed, guilt blooming on her cheeks. She had curled up on the sofa in the living room each afternoon of her illness, sipping her tea and leaning in towards the radio, following along with the drama. It had made her feel a mite better to think that perhaps Leo was also listening to the program at the same time she was, although it didn't do much to alleviate how much she missed him.

"You *did* listen without me, didn't you?" Leo cried, teasing. "Margherita." He shook his head. "Now I know where your

137

loyalties lie."

"I was sick," she replied, guilt still curling in her belly despite Leo's teasing.

"I was bored, and I missed you."

"And you wanted to find out who Captain Norton was having an affair with."

"Well," she smirked at him through lowered lashes, "that too."

"So, you know?" Leo sat up straight, green eyes wide, sending Maggie into peals of laughter.

"You look like a kid on Christmas Eve," she said through her giggles. "I love how excited you get about this stuff."

"I'm not a child at all." Leo glared at her in mock sternness. "And this is a very serious subject, *signorina*. I may have to torture the answer out of you."

Maggie placed what was left of her sandwich into its waxed paper wrapping on the floor next to her, leaning towards Leo with a glint in her eye. "Do your worst, Corporal. I'll never crack."

Within seconds, Leo had scooped Maggie onto his lap with his one arm, and began tickling her right over her rib cage, eliciting hysterical laughter and pleas of surrender.

"Tell me, *signorina*, or I'll have to resort to even crueler methods of torture." Leo's voice was full of laughter as he tried his best to remain stern.

"Alright, alright! Mercy, please," Maggie begged through tears and gasps. "It was Constance Jennings! The Captain is having an affair with Constance Jennings."

"No," Leo gasped, instantly ceasing his tickle assault. "But isn't she—?"

"Dead?" Maggie cut in. "I thought so too, but no. She's

been hiding in the basement of the hospital, and that's where the Captain has been meeting her."

"Well, I'll be..." Leo whistled. "That is not what I thought you were going to tell me." He gazed down at Maggie, who was resting her head on his knee. "And a hospital basement does not feel romantic, does it?"

"There was a time I would have said that the back room of a military laundry facility wasn't particularly romantic either," she said with a wink. "But I think it depends on the person that you're with, because this is pretty nice."

Leo's eyes softened, and he leaned down to kiss her as she sat up on her elbows to meet him halfway. Maggie was so caught up in the feeling of Leo's lips on hers, the planes of his muscles under her hands, that she didn't hear the bell ringing on the front desk, and she didn't hear the door to the back room swing open. The first thing she did hear to alert her to the fact that they were no longer alone was Owen's furious voice, yelling, "Who the fuck are you and what the fuck are you doing to my sister!?"

Chapter 25

Niamh — 2016

"Annalise, can you read today's sight word for the class?" Niamh held out her pointer to the little girl, who scrambled to her feet and rushed to the front of the room. All of the kindergartners loved getting to hold the pointer, a long white stick with a red plastic hand on the end, and little Annalise beamed with pride as she took it from Niamh and turned to the board.

"A — N — D. And," the little nugget read triumphantly, eyes shining from the attention.

"Excellent, honey." Niamh clapped her hands together before turning to the rest of the five-year-olds who were seated on the rug in front of her, criss-cross apple sauce. "Now all of our friends can say it after Annalise. Ready? A — N — D spells AND."

The children dutifully repeated the word of the day with

varying degrees of enthusiasm, and Niamh had to reach deep into her reserve of kindergarten teacher cheerfulness to congratulate them on their hard work. "Great job, friends! A — N — D spells AND!" She glanced at the clock and wanted to cry with relief when she saw that it was finally time for lunch and recess, and finally time for her to have a few minutes to check her phone. It had been three weeks since Christine had sent the message to Dwight Thompson, and Niamh had been checking her phone for a response with a frequency bordering on obsession. Still, there had been nothing.

"OK, friends, please line up by the door for lunch. Who's my line leader today?" A skinny little boy with a permanent cowlick raised his hand and ran to the door to take his place. "Alex G., wonderful."

"Are we ready to go?" Ms. Jones, the aide who floated between the two kindergarten classrooms, appeared in the doorway.

"Yaaaaaasss," replied the chorus of tiny, high-pitched voices, and Niamh had to smile at their innocent enthusiasm for something as simple as a walk to the cafeteria. Oh, to be five again.

As soon as the students paraded out of the room, Niamh leaped for her phone, clicking on the familiar Forefathers icon and clicking through the log-in and facial recognition screens. *C'mon, Dwight. C'mon.*

You have no new messages.

"Son of a bitch," Niamh exclaimed in a distinctly un-kindergarten teacher-esque tone. What was up with this guy?

"Excuse me, Ms. Reilly?"

Niamh jumped at the interruption, nearly tossing her phone

141

into the air, and spun around to face the door, guilt written all over her face. Luckily, the intruder was only Marcos, who was doubled over with laughter at the results of his little prank.

"Marcos Mejia, I swear to God I'm going to kill you! You scared the hell out of me!"

He wiped the tears from his eyes as he leaned against the door frame, still chuckling. "You ready for lunch, potty mouth?"

Lacking a better response, Niamh stuck her tongue out at him and sashayed out the door of the classroom.

"I'm sorry, Niamhy. It's just too easy sometimes." Marcos jogged to catch up with her. "Any word from your literal brother from another mother?"

"Nope."

* * *

"Just a thought," Marcos said as he opened the door to the faculty room and held it for Niamh to pass through. "Have you tried Googling him?" Niamh went to the fridge to retrieve her lunch bag and sat down at their usual table, unboxing her salad, cookie, and ginger ale before answering.

"No...?"

"Haven't thought about it or haven't done it?" Marcos raised an eyebrow and fixed Niamh with a look that made her feel like one of her students.

"Of course I've thought about it," she replied around a bite of romaine. "It's 2016 — I'm well versed in the art of Google stalking. I just haven't done it."

"Why not?" Marcos propped his chin up on his fists and

stared at her with his infuriating brown eyes, daring her to come up with a good excuse for not making more of an effort to contact her brother.

"Because," Niamh finally replied, exasperated. "I don't know. I'm scared, I guess? Seriously, though," she said as Marcos reached into his pocket for his phone, "I'm getting enough of this at home from Christine. I don't need it from you too."

"We nag because we care," he replied absentmindedly, scrolling through his iPhone. "You're one lucky bitch to have us and you know it."

Niamh grumbled something unintelligible into her salad and popped the tab on her soda can for effect. She'd give him another week, maybe two, and then she'd do a Google search to see if she could find out more about this stranger in Texas.

"Speaking of lucky bitches," Marcos spun his phone around to face Niamh with a triumphant grin, "I'm the best. I found him."

"Oh, for the love of—" Against her better instincts, Niamh reached across the table, taking the phone from Marcos and studying the screen. It was a website for an accounting firm in Laredo, TX, and there on the main page was a man in a blue suit with a red tie and an enormous cowboy hat, seated behind a desk with a nameplate that read, "Dwight Thompson, CPA."

"He looks..." Marco began, before trailing off.

"Like he's voting for Trump," Niamh finished with a dismissive sigh, returning the phone. "How do I share DNA with that?"

"C'mon, Niamh. Give the man a chance — you don't know him from a hole in the wall. He might be lovely."

"And he might be an asshole," she replied curtly before

turning to pitch her trash into the trash bin. "Score!"

"We'll know once we email him, won't we?" Marcos was typing something on his phone, and Niamh felt a buzz in her pocket. She removed her phone and read the text, which contained Dwight's email address.

"I'm not emailing him, Marcos."

"How's this — either you email him, or I email him pretending to be you and demand that he gives me one of his kidneys."

Niamh stared at him, attempting to discern whether or not he was telling the truth. "You wouldn't."

Marcos's lips curled into a wicked smile. "Wouldn't I?"

"Fine." Niamh opened her Gmail app and copy and pasted Dwight's email address into a new message. "But I'm warning you that if he turns out to be a serial killer who stuffs my body into a suitcase and uses me to perfect his taxidermy techniques, I'm going to haunt the shit out of you."

"Noted." Marcos grinned at her over the top of her phone screen. "So, what are we saying to this guy?"

"Nothing special," she sighed. "I'm just copying and pasting the message I sent from the Forefathers site. I suppose it's possible that he just didn't check the app and didn't see it." She clicked send, tucked her phone into her back pocket, and turned back to Marcos. "Now can we please talk about something else?"

Chapter 26

Maggie — 1944

Maggie leapt to her feet, straightening her blouse and trying like hell to wrap her brain around what was happening. Owen O'Callaghan, her big brother, who was supposed to be on an aircraft carrier in the Pacific Ocean, stood framed in the doorway, his face a mix of shock and rage.

"Owen, I—"

"I wasn't talking to you, Margaret," he spat, voice thunderous. "Who the fuck is he?"

Behind her, Maggie could feel Leo getting to his feet and coming to stand behind her, strength and calm radiating from his body to hers. He reached around Maggie, offering Owen his right hand.

"*Caporale* Leo Castiglione, Private O'Callaghan. I am so pleased to meet you."

Owen stared down at the proffered hand, his pale lips curling into a sneer. "I find you all over my sister, and you want me to shake your hand? How about I rearrange your face, you fascist bastard?"

"Owen, no—" Maggie began, placing a hand squarely on her brother's chest in an attempt to hold him back. "Leo wasn't — I — he's—"

"What your sister is trying to say is that I am sorry, Private. I should not have taken liberties—"

"And you think I'll believe that this is the first time?" Owen's hands were balled into fists at his sides, grenades about to go off.

"Will both of you just shut up!" Maggie yelled, looking back and forth between the two men. "Owen, you have no right to barge in here and start yelling like you're my warden, and Leo, don't ever presume to decide what I'm trying to say again. I'm a grown woman. I can speak for myself and I can decide who I want to spend my time with and how I want to spend it. Is. That. Clear?"

Leo stepped back, showing enough sense to let Maggie handle her brother on her own. Owen, on the other hand, doubled down.

"I don't know what you think you're doing, Margaret, but—"

"Maybe you don't, but it's also none of your goddamned business. And how dare you come in here like a tornado and ruin my seeing you again! I've been worried about you every day for a year and a half, and I'm so happy to see that you're alive and well because now I can kill you myself." Maggie's voice was a low growl, but Owen wasn't picking up on the serrated edges to her tone.

"I assume that Mam and Da don't know you're seeing an

Italian?" Owen's threat was clear.

"They do not," Maggie hissed though clenched teeth, "and if you breathe a word of this to them, I'll make sure to tell Mam about the time you stole the consecrated hosts from the tabernacle at church and sold them to your friends for a nickel a piece."

"You bought one too, Maggie."

"Because you sold me a line of horseshit about how they'd been gifted to you by Jesus Christ himself. I was a child, Owen, and I've kept that secret for fifteen years. If the threat of telling Mam on you isn't enough to keep your mouth shut about Leo, then how about I tell her what you and Roberta Sullivan were up to in the choir loft the Easter before last?"

Owen's face paled, and it was a moment before he could respond. "You wouldn't dare."

"Try me." Maggie stood on tiptoe, staring down her brother and daring him to take the bait. From behind her, she heard Leo clear his throat, although she couldn't be sure if it was in warning or in appreciation.

"Fine, you win." Owen admitted defeat through gritted teeth. "Christ, Maggie, what if it had been Charlie coming through that door instead of me? You'd break his goddamn heart. I'll be keeping an eye on you, *Corporal*." Owen spat Leo's title with disgust before turning on his heel and marching out of the laundry, leaving Maggie to consider what this new development meant for her, for Leo, and for their ability to continue seeing one another.

* * *

"Who is Charlie?"

Maggie held a hand in front of her face, watching it tremble as it if it weren't a part of her own body at all, but something entirely separate. She drew a ragged breath in through her mouth, and followed it up with a shuddering sigh, starting at the door through which her beloved big brother had just departed in a rush of fury.

"*Margherita?*"

She registered the pressure of Leo's hand, stronger and steadier than her own, on her shoulder. She turned, slow and deliberate, to face both him and what had just occurred.

"I—" Maggie opened her mouth to speak but was at a total loss for what to say. What did a girl say to her boyfriend, who by the way once fought on the opposing side of the war, when her brother, who might have once shot at him or been shot by him, walked in on them fooling around in the back room of the military laundry? She didn't realize she was crying until she felt Leo's warm hand cupping her cheek and wiping away her tears with the side of his thumb.

"Shhhhh," he soothed, in a voice so gentle that it broke Maggie's heart open, releasing a choked sob before she allowed herself to bury her head into his chest and wet his shirt with her tears. They stood for several minutes, Maggie crying and Leo holding her against him, until finally she took a deep, cleansing breath and whispered, "I'm so sorry."

Leo pulled back, holding Maggie by the elbows and gazing down into her reddened eyes. "What do you have to be sorry for?"

"For my brother — for crying all over you — for all of it." She sniffed, and Leo offered her a clean handkerchief from his pants pocket. She took it, blew her nose, and stuffed the handkerchief into her own pocket to launder later. "For not telling you about Charlie."

"Will you tell me about him?"

The tremor of uncertainty in Leo's tone was enough to bring on a fresh bout of tears, but Maggie stood rigid and dug her nails into her palms until they were numb to the pain, not speaking until she was sure she could do so without breaking.

"Charlie is the boy — the man, really, I suppose — that everyone expects me to be with. My parents, my brothers, Betty and Billy, and of course Charlie himself." She trailed off with a bitter laugh. "Everyone except me."

"You do not love him?"

Maggie shook her head, reaching up to cup her palm over the twitch in Leo's jaw. He was hurting and trying not to show it, breaking a bit of Maggie's heart.

"I love him like I love my brothers. But I don't love him like he deserves to be loved." I don't love him like I love you, she thought, but let the words remain unspoken. Leo placed a gentle kiss on the edge of Maggie's finger, and she continued, "I can't put that in a letter while he's in the middle of the ocean. I promised myself I'd tell him as soon as he comes home, but then I didn't expect *you*, and then... God, Leo, I'm so sorry."

"Let us get one thing straight." Leo relaxed, wrapping his arms around Maggie's lower back and pulling her into him. "You have nothing to be sorry for."

"But I should have told you. And my brother is—"

"Your brother is a brother." Leo cut her off, and Maggie huffed in response. "If I walked in on my sister with a man — I don't care who he was, friend or enemy — I would kill the *bastardo* first before I asked any questions. Your Owen showed great restraint."

Maggie glowered up at him. "You men are all the same — why can't you trust us to make our own decisions?"

"Owen trusts you. It's me he doesn't know. He has no reason to trust me." "How about trusting you because clearly I do? Shouldn't the fact that I vouch for you be enough?"

"If Owen is anything like me, then no one is ever good enough for his sister." Leo's eyes softened, and Maggie knew he was thinking about his own sisters, on the other side of the world.

"Isn't one of your sisters married? And you haven't killed your brother-in-law, have you?" Maggie argued, determined to gain the upper hand in this argument.

"And how do you know that, *Margherita*? I told you that I have a sister, yes, and that she has children, but I never said her husband was still living." His green eyes danced, and for a moment, Maggie wasn't sure if he was serious or not. She stepped back, eyeing him through crinkled lids before offering him a half-smile.

"Your sisters must think you're a brute."

"That and many, many other things, most of which I will not repeat," Leo said with a laugh, the tension finally broken. "But *Margherita*, don't let this ruin your joy at seeing your brother. You don't know how long he will be home. There will be plenty of time later to convince him that I have the best of intentions towards his sister."

Maggie's cheeks warmed at Leo's casual mention of the future, and at his apparent intention to be in her life long after the war's conclusion. If it *ever* came to a conclusion.

"Now," he said with an air of authority. "We must finish your work and get you home to your family." Maggie nodded, wiping the remnants of her tears from her cheeks and grabbing a stack of hangers on which to hang the newly ironed uniforms. They'd finish up the day's work and she would go home to a proper reunion with her brother. As Leo walked her to the guard station at the end of the day, however, Maggie couldn't avoid the feeling of guilt curling in her belly. Guilt for making Owen feel betrayed, however unwarranted, but mostly guilt for the opportunity to go home and see her family. It was an opportunity Leo didn't get, and based on the tightness with which he squeezed her hand when they parted for the night, it was one he desperately wanted.

Chapter 27

Maggie — 1944

Owen was on leave for four precious days that November, meaning that the family got to enjoy Thanksgiving with their favored son and brother. Mam and Dad were over the moon, and the younger boys followed Owen everywhere he went like puppies, waiting for him to drop a morsel about life aboard ship. Maggie, however, did everything she could to avoid being in Owen's presence. She spent an inordinate amount of time in her bedroom, over at Betty's or Nadine's houses, and she even went to work early under the pretense of helping Sadie with the workload.

What she didn't mention, however, was that she still hadn't heard a word from Sadie since before her bout of German Measles. No one answered the telephone at the Marshalls' house — it was as if she had completely disappeared. Maggie might be overwhelmed at the laundry, but no one was more affected by Sadie's sudden disappearance than Guillermo.

"Has he lost weight?" Maggie whispered to Leo the afternoon after Owen had returned home, as she transferred armloads of uniforms from the washing machine to the dryer. Guillermo had come by the laundry on his lunch hour with Leo, but his usual ebullient smile was nowhere to be seen. He sat in the corner of the front room, staring out the window with an occasional sigh. Leo responded with a solemn nod.

"He's so worried about her. He hasn't been eating or sleeping well. It would be one thing if she simply broke his heart — he could hate her and move on — but to just vanish? It's concerning."

"That's an understatement," Maggie agreed, casting an anxious glance through the door at their friend. "Are they letting you celebrate Thanksgiving at all tomorrow?"

Leo's face broke into a wide grin. "We learned about your Thanksgiving in the civics class. Pilgrims and Indians celebrating brotherhood with turkey and mashed potatoes — ironic in a time of war, no?"

"Ironic, but delicious. And my family is ready to celebrate now that Owen's home."

Leo's smile faltered for just the barest of seconds, but Maggie caught it and was immediately awash in guilt. How could she talk about celebrating the holiday with her family when he hadn't seen his own in years?

"Well then," Leo said with a bright smile, "I will be excited to hear about all your Thanksgiving traditions when I see you on Friday. The Altieris have invited us to their home for dinner tomorrow. And now, I need to get Guillermo back to the shop before his backside grows into your window seat."

Maggie nodded, but just before Leo could disappear through

153

the door and gather his friend, she reached out a hand and touched his side.

"I wish you could come home with me," she blurted out, heat immediately flooding her features at the admission. Leo's face softened, and for a moment he looked almost pained before he rearranged his features into their customary teasing expression.

"Is that so your brother could serve me to the family on a silver plate? Perhaps with an apple in my mouth?" Leo waggled his eyebrows, and Maggie couldn't decide between laughter or tears.

"No, it's because Thanksgiving is about recognizing the good things in your life and being grateful for them." Maggie's neck began to itch, and she rubbed at the back of it, looking anywhere but at Leo.

"*Margherita*, are you saying that you're thankful for me?" Leo tipped her chin with one finger, forcing her to look at him. Her cheeks burned, but Maggie bit back her own embarrassment.

"Yes," she said with a tremor in her voice. "That is what I'm trying to say."

"And I am grateful for you too." He placed a gentle kiss on the tip of her nose, and stepped back, leaving her wanting more. "We will have more Thanksgivings, *Margherita*."

As Maggie watched the men leave, Guillermo moving beside Leo like a man asleep, she couldn't help but think how strange it was that the very thing she was most grateful for this Thanksgiving was only in her life because of the war and all the atrocities that went with it.

Chapter 28

Maggie — 1944

Hours after Thanksgiving dinner, when her parents and brothers were sound asleep, Maggie tiptoed down the stairs and into the kitchen, determined to somehow smuggle out a Thanksgiving feast for Leo. She removed each platter of leftovers from the refrigerator one by one, careful to make as little noise as possible as she transferred enough for two portions into packets of waxed paper. Two portions of turkey, two portions of potato, and so on until she had a neat pile of leftovers ready to be packed into a picnic basket for a hungry soldier.

She transferred the packages into a basket, covered them over with some old towels and sheets that her mother had been meaning to donate for months, and placed the basket in the garage to chill for the night. In the morning, she'd put the basket in the backseat of her father's car with a story about donations for needy soldiers, and no one would be any the wiser.

By the time Maggie slid under the covers, it was after one o'clock in the morning, but she fell asleep with a smile on her face in anticipation of Leo's first ever American Thanksgiving dinner.

* * *

Maggie had never worked so quickly in her life.

Getting all of the work at the cleaners done on her own without Sadie was difficult any day, but the Friday after Thanksgiving was especially difficult.

She had two days of work to do in one, and she wanted to be absolutely certain she got it done by five o'clock, so she could close and lock the door as soon as Leo arrived.

One hundred and twenty-five uniforms had to be washed, dried, pressed, and hung. Three hundred individual pairs of men's underwear, socks, and t-shirts had to be washed, dried, and folded. The sheets and towels could wait until Monday. Maggie worked through lunch, only stopping to use the powder room once the entire day, and she was just slipping the last uniform onto a hanger and into its cloth garment bag when Leo came whistling through the door.

Still whistling — was that "Que Sera Sera?" — Leo wrapped Maggie in an embrace and whisked her into a waltz around the room before leaning down to place a lingering kiss on her lips.

"*Buona Serata, caro mio,*" he whispered, and Maggie couldn't control her excitement any longer.

"Come into the back," she said with a smile, bouncing up

and down on the balls of her feet. "I have a surprise for you." She took him by the hand and led him into the back room, where she had laid out a Thanksgiving feast that would make Myles Standish himself jealous.

A white, standard-issue linen bed sheet was spread out on the floor and set with flickering candles, a handmade centerpiece of leaves, pinecones, and acorns, and a feast for two. Leftover turkey, stuffing, potatoes, green beans, and cranberry sauce were arranged on two ceramic plates that Maggie had smuggled from home.

"Surprise," Maggie exclaimed, crossing her fingers and praying that Leo would see and appreciate all the trouble she had gone to to make this dinner a reality.

The expression on Leo's face was blank as he took in the surprise Maggie had laid out for him. Finally, he turned to her, green eyes glistening, and asked in a hoarse voice that was barely above a whisper, "What's all this?"

"This is Thanksgiving," she replied with a nervous smile. "You said they taught about Thanksgiving in those American civics classes you take?"

"They do, but I never imagined..." he trailed off, walking further into the room and then turning back to reach for Maggie. "The Altieris served fish last night — eel, octopus, prawns. But this — this looks like something out of an American movie. Leave it to the Yanks to celebrate a holiday based on food." Both Leo and Guillermo had mentioned that what surprised them most about their tenure in the States was the food. Cornflakes, eggs, bacon, coffee, and juice for every breakfast. Sandwiches, salads, and side dishes for lunch. Meat and potato and a vegetable every night for dinner. Even under rationing, the Italian POWs were given more food than they

157

had ever seen before, and they were beyond grateful. Everyone knows that the way to a man's heart is through his stomach, and Uncle Sam had taken that adage to heart.

"Sit down," Maggie encouraged him, doing so herself and arranging her skirt so that it was tucked neatly underneath her. She unfolded her cloth napkin — borrowed from the laundry, of course — and placed it neatly across her lap before opening one of the two bottles of Coca-Cola she had swiped from her father's store and handing it to Leo.

"A toast," he suggested, holding his bottle aloft and throwing his shadow into relief against the ceramic laundry machines in the flickering candlelight. "To my Maggie, mi *Margherita*, for making me feel at home for the first time in three long years." Maggie blushed but held up her bottle to join in the toast. "*Salude.*"

"*Slainte.*"

* * *

"That was the best meal I have ever eaten." Leo leaned back against a tumble dryer, a hand on his belly. "And that includes my Mama's *osso bucco*."

"I'm sorry I couldn't find a way to heat it up," Maggie apologized, fussing with the corner of the tablecloth. She had racked her brain for any conceivable way she could heat up the food before she served it, but nothing came to mind.

She briefly considered putting it in the tumble dryer, but quickly decided against that for obvious reasons.

"You made me feel like a part of something for the first time in three long years, and you're going to apologize because the food wasn't hot enough?" Leo joked before turning serious again, his eyes giving off enough heat to light an inferno, never mind warm up some turkey. "This was— Maggie—" he sighed. "First I was a soldier, then a prisoner, and now a co-belligerent. This is the first time I have felt like home since I left my parents' house. You have given me family."

Maggie was speechless. A myriad of emotions ran through her, but she didn't have the words to express how this funny, generous, intelligent, kind man had touched her soul and changed her life forever. Leo leaned forward across the makeshift dining table, kissing Maggie once, twice, three times, before gazing down at her, a question in his eyes.

"Do you know that I love you, Maggie?" Her breath caught in her throat, and every fiber of her being was electrified, as if somehow even her fingers and toes had heard Leo's words and reacted to their meaning. She opened her mouth to say it back, but the words wouldn't come.

Finally, after what seemed like an eternity, she managed, "No one's ever said that to me before."

"I've never said it to a woman before either," Leo admitted, reassuring her. He moved the sheet/tablecloth out of the way, giving him enough room to slide over next to her. "I've had feelings, yes. Crushes, you call them. But never this."

"No," Maggie said, needing Leo to understand her meaning. "No one has ever said those words to me. *No one*."

Leo's brow furrowed in confusion. "Not your mother or your father? Your brothers? Not," he cleared his throat, clearly uncomfortable, "your Charlie?"

Maggie shook her head.

"First of all, he's not *my* Charlie. It's just not something we ever said." She offered Leo a weak smile, and he visibly relaxed.

"I told you, you have nothing to worry about there. And I know my parents love me. We just—" she paused, looking for exactly the right words to convey her Irish Catholic family and how they moved around one another. "I know they love me because they provide for me. They make sure I have everything I need, and they push me to be my best. They pray for me, and they look out for me. We just — we don't talk about it." Leo stared at her, aghast at this revelation. "I suppose your parents told you all the time?"

He nodded. Maggie shrugged.

"I love you," Leo said, his tone suddenly insistent, needing to be under- stood. "I love you, and I promise to tell you that every day for the rest of my life."

The words crashed into Maggie like a wave at the seashore, threatening to drag her under with their weight. For the rest of his life, she thought through the roaring sound in her ears. Does he know what he's saying?

"Hey, now. You look like you're about to panic." Leo smiled down at her, cupping her face in his hand. "We're in no rush; there's a war on, remember? And then there's the issue of your family hating me." Maggie grimaced, but Leo held her gaze. "I do not know how it will work, *Margherita*, but it will. That I know."

"How do you always manage to make me believe that everything is going to be okay?" Maggie asked, and Leo leaned in for another kiss. At the feeling of his lips on hers, Maggie used her body to tell him what her words could not. She pulled him down to her until they were both on the floor, and kissed him until they were both sweaty, out of breath, and hungry for more.

"Leo?"

He paused his attentions on her neck and looked up at her, questioning. "I love you too."

Chapter 29

Niamh — 2016

By the time Christine came home from the office most nights, Niamh had dinner started and was sitting at the kitchen island either grading papers or working on tomorrow's lesson. That night, however, Niamh didn't bother with practicalities, choosing instead to sit on the wraparound couch in the living room, cocoon herself in an enormous blanket, and stare blankly at an episode of *Buffy the Vampire Slayer* on TV. She heard Christine's car in the driveway and briefly considered getting up to greet her wife, but the siren song of her nest on the couch was simply too strong to resist.

"Oh no, you're watching *Buffy*." Christine tossed her keys onto the granite countertop with a clack before turning on the light in the darkened hallway and stepping into Niamh's line of sight. "What's the matter?"

"How do you know something is the matter?" Niamh replied

without taking her eyes off the screen. "I might just really like this episode."

"Baby, this is season five. No one watches season five of Buffy unless they've got some demons of their own to exorcise." Christine sat down on the couch, moving Niamh's blanket-wrapped feet onto her lap. "Plus, you didn't make me dinner, woman."

Niamh sighed, a deep exhalation of ennui. "You've got a law degree, Chris. I think you can manage takeout." She grabbed her phone off the coffee table and unlocked it before turning the screen to face Christine. The email was curt and succinct enough to fit entirely onto the tiny cell phone screen: *I have blocked your email. Do not contact me again. Dwight Thompson.* Christine took the phone from Niamh's outstretched hand and stared at it long enough to read the email at least ten times over before sighing and placing it gently back on the coffee table.

"Do you want to talk about it?"

"Other than to say I told you so, not really." Niamh sniffed, willing back the tears that rose stinging into her eyes, but it was no use. The traitorous tears spilled down her cheeks, blurring her vision before finally convincing her to let go and cry.

"Come here," she heard Christine croon softly before she felt her snuggle down behind her on the couch. Niamh tucked herself back against her wife, the little spoon, and allowed herself a sardonic laugh through her tears.

"The crazy thing is that I never wanted to do this in the first place," she said into Christine's shoulder. "I knew it would go wrong, and now it's like being abandoned by my father all over again. I'm their dirty little secret." She hiccuped and tried to focus on the feeling of Christine's fingers combing gently through her hair.

"I think we can agree that your father is an asshat, and that his son is probably no different," Christine murmured. "But they can't be the only family you have out there."

"So, I'm 50% asshat?" Niamh asked.

"Yes, but you're 100% my asshat."

Niamh pulled back to grimace at her wife. "That has to be the worst line I have ever heard — and I once had a guy introduce himself to me in a club with 'Hey, I'm Arthur. You know, like the king.'"

"But did it make you laugh?" Christine raised one perfectly arched and plucked brow.

"No, it made me a bit nauseated. Can we get Thai? I have feelings I need to eat."

"Absolutely." Christine sat up, pulling Niamh with her. "Pad Thai?"

"You know me so well," Niamh smiled and began hunting under the couch for her sneakers.

"Exactly, because you're my—" Christine shrieked, breaking off mid- sentence as Niamh rose up, one hot pink running shoe held aloft in an attack position.

"Don't you dare," she cried, climbing onto Christine's lap and waving the shoe around in a threatening manner. Christine grabbed her wrist and pulled it down, causing Niamh to drop her weapon and bringing their faces within an inch of each other. Niamh stopped, distracted by Christine's full lips, and before she knew what she was doing, she had pushed her wife down on the couch.

Chapter 30

Maggie — 1944

Something had changed since Thanksgiving. If pressed, neither Maggie nor Leo could put into words what exactly was different, but it was tangible enough that they both knew it was there and felt its presence settling over their every moment together. One thing they could not ignore, however, was Guillermo.

"He just mopes around; it's as if the light has gone out of his eyes," Leo reported one evening about a week after Thanksgiving as they strolled through the camp together. "You still haven't heard anything about Sadie?" Maggie shook her head.

"It's like she disappeared into thin air. I've gone by her house three or four times now, and no one answers the door. I just hope she's OK." Maggie tucked her hands inside her pockets to keep them warm, and within seconds, Leo had removed his own mittens and placed them on her hands. "I look ridiculous," she laughed.

"Ridiculous does not get a head cold." Leo nodded his head firmly, sure of the truth of the statement.

"Is that a direct translation from your mother?" Maggie asked with a laugh.

"My nonna — my grandmother," he smiled. "But she is not wrong." He shook his head, still perplexed by the mystery of what could possibly have happened to Sadie. "Guillermo has himself convinced it's something he did. He thinks she's mad at him and that's why she never came back to the camp."

Maggie shook her head. "That can't be true. If it was, surely she'd have told me. She'd have answered the telephone. Something!" They walked in silence for a few moments, their shoes leaving barely perceptible prints on the frosted blacktop. Finally, Maggie asked, "What would you like for Christmas?"

"Christmas?" Leo laughed, as if he had forgotten about the holiday entirely. "You don't have to get me anything for Christmas, *Margherita*."

"I know I don't have to," she protested. "I want to." She pulled on his arm, a child eager to deliver the perfect present on Christmas morning. "Come on, Leo. If you could have anything in the world for Christmas, what would it be?"

Leo was silent for a few minutes, lost in thought, and when he finally stopped and turned to look at Maggie, his smile was sad and his eyes were far away. "If I could have my heart's desire for Christmas, I'd be with my family in *Milano*, drinking good wine, eating my mama's and my nonna's cooking, and I'd wake up with you in my bed on Christmas morning." After that heartfelt declaration, Leo simply turned, looped Maggie's arm through his once again, and continued walking.

I should say something, she thought. I should respond and tell him that nothing would make me happier than going to Italy, meeting his family, and... sharing his bed. I should say something.

When the words finally came, however, Maggie found herself saying, "I was imagining something like a watch or some new socks."

Idiot, she berated herself. The man just told you he wants to marry you and take you back to Italy with him, and you offer him socks? What's wrong with you?

"Socks are nice too," Leo said with a laugh. "Everyone needs socks. But promise me, Maggie?" He stopped and turned her towards him, and it was then that she noticed it was starting to snow. Fluffy, fuzzy white flakes fell from the sky and clung to her eyelashes, causing Leo to grin with unbridled joy. "Promise me that one day, when this war is over, you will come to Italy with me as my wife."

How is it that he always knows exactly what to say? Maggie wondered. The words that she found so awkward and unco-operative fell from his lips like snow from the clouds, perfect and well timed.

"Promise me." All of his hope was in his eyes, and Maggie knew that she had the power to cherish or crush this man, however she chose. He gave so much of himself, and all he asked for in return was her promise of a life that she'd give anything to live with him. She stood on tiptoe, and he met her halfway, sealing this deal with a kiss.

"I promise."

Chapter 31

Maggie — 1944

"I can't wait for you to see this movie." Maggie leaned over in her seat, snuggling into Leo's side as they waited for *Casablanca* to begin.

Leo raised an eyebrow and tossed a piece of popcorn into his mouth. "I have seen this already, Mags. We have talked about it."

Maggie felt a warmth spread through her veins when he called her by the familiar nickname her friends used. She still preferred it when he called her *Margherita*, or *ma bella*, but somehow the causal use of "Mags" marked Leo as part of her everyday world in a way that the others didn't.

"I know, but you told me that you barely understood English the last time."

"True," he laughed. "I am sure the picture will be more

enjoyable now that I speak the language." They kissed, the taste of salt from the popcorn mingling on their tongues. There was an urgency to their kisses now, a promise of more, and Maggie wondered if Leo felt the same way she did when they broke apart — like a piece was suddenly missing.

The picture began with a map of Africa, the title city of Casablanca on the north-western corner of the continent. Maggie was struck with the realization this was where Leo had landed with the Italian Army. It was where he had been shot, it was where he had been captured, and it was where he eventually lost his arm after nearly losing his life. Maggie was momentarily overcome with emotion; this wasn't just a beautiful film with a tragic love story. This was somewhere that Leo had almost died. Where would she be right now if he had? Could she miss someone she had never known? She reached out to take Leo's hand, which had been resting on his lap, and squeezed it in her own, reassuring herself with his solid warmth beside her.

Leo squeezed back, as if he knew exactly what was going through her mind. He confirmed it by leaning down and whispering, his warm breath tickling her ear. "Everything that happened to me in Africa led me here, to you." He dropped a kiss on her neck, just behind her earlobe, that left a trail of shivers down her spine.

* * *

By the time the picture came to a close, and Rick told Ilsa that "the problems of three little people don't amount to a hill of beans in this crazy world," Maggie was openly weeping, tears sliding down her cheeks faster than she could wipe them away. How could she have ever thought this was a beautiful story? When Rick uttered the final line to Captain Renault, "Louis, I think this is the beginning of a beautiful friendship," and the music swelled, Maggie emitted a gulping sob, catching Leo's attention.

"*Margherita. Bellisima*, what is wrong?" He turned her to him, cupping the side of her face with his hand and searching her eyes as if to find the reason for her tears. Maggie shook her head. How could she put into words her fear that no matter how much they loved each other, no matter how many promises they made, their families or countries or this blasted war would tear them apart like it had done to Rick and Ilsa?

Maggie moved back out of Leo's embrace in anticipation of the lights coming up in the theater. They couldn't be seen.

"The movie's over," she sniffed, dabbing at the skin under her eyes with the handkerchief he held out to her. How many of these hankies had she washed, dried, ironed, and folded in the past few months? Hundreds? Thousands? How many more would she launder before the end of the war, and before Leo went home to Italy?

"I am not sending you home like this. Come on." He stood and offered Maggie his arm, which she took after only a moment of hesitation.

"We might be seen," she hissed, but Leo shook his head, determined.

"There are forty thousand people in this city, and forty thousand more in the camp. I will take my chances to make sure you are OK."

Maggie knew she should object, knew that she should allow Leo to walk her within sight of her house and then turn back towards downtown to catch the bus. But she didn't want to leave his warmth any more than he wanted to leave hers, and so she followed as Leo walked her out of the theater, hailed a taxi cab, and asked to be brought to the hole in the fence at Camp Myles Standish.

The driver didn't even hesitate at the directions — the hole in the fence had become a recognized entrance and exit from the camp over the past few months, where American soldiers and Italian co-belligerents sneaked in or out of the camp to avoid the hassle of the main gate and their superior officers.

"Where are we going?" Maggie whispered in the darkened cab, and Leo placed his hand on her knee in reassurance.

"The laundry. Do you have your key?"

She did — it was in her handbag along with her lipstick, a compact, and the dollar bill she kept for emergencies. She nodded, the thought of her compact making her grateful for the darkness of the night. She'd been crying on and off for the entire movie, and she must have raccoon eyes from her mascara.

Leo paid the driver when they reached their destination, and any other night Maggie would have felt the thrill of adventure as he led her through the hole in the fence, through the woods, and onto the main road of the camp.

Tonight, however, their trek added to her sense of desperation.

Once they reached Myles Standish Laundry #4 and let themselves inside, Maggie was shaking from the cold. Leo led her into the back room, turning on the lights and closing the door to the front so that no one passing by would have any idea that there were people inside.

"Maggie, come, sit down," Leo instructed her, and she

complied robotically. He grabbed two woolen blankets from where she had left them folded next to the dry-cleaning machines the day before and wrapped Maggie in one of them before retrieving a bottle of Coca-Cola and a tin of potato chips from their secret stash behind the wringers. He then sat beside Maggie and pulled her onto his lap, wrapping them both in the second blanket with a bit of help from her.

Within seconds of being safely settled on the ground, wrapped in the warmth of the blankets and their shared heat, Maggie began to cry afresh. Leo seemed to know enough not to stop her; instead he simply made lazy circles on her back with the tips of his fingers and soothing, hushing sounds in his throat, letting her cry as much as she needed to before she could open up and tell him what the matter was.

Instead of talking, however, Maggie reached up and brought Leo's face down to hers, pressing her lips to his with an urgency she hadn't felt before. She needed him, needed to know that he was there and so was she, and that for the moment there was nothing that could get in the way of these feelings that so many would condemn them for.

"Leo," she whispered, turning to reach her hand between the top two buttons on his shirt and popping them open to reveal the white cotton vest underneath, and the warm olive skin that was physical proof of Leo's presence in this moment.

Leo reacted like kindling touched by flame, and with more strength in his remaining arm than most men had in two, he hoisted her up into a seated position in front of him, sucking air between his teeth at the sensation of her chilly hands on his skin.

Maggie continued to explore his torso with her fingers, until finally Leo removed the shirt altogether, pulling it over his head and tossing it to the floor next to him. She wanted to kiss him everywhere, and she tried, pressing her lips to the hollows of his collar bone, his shoulder, and the small patch of dark hair in the center of his chest. It was becoming more and more clear that he was as desperate for her as she was for him, and she could feel the proof of that on her leg, straining against the fabric of his trousers with an urgency that couldn't be comfortable.

Allowing her curiosity to get the better of her, she moved her hand down until it rested lightly over Leo's hardness, and he groaned against her lips in response.

"Maggie," he breathed, the look on his face a perfect mix between pleasure and plain. "Maggie, wait."

She continued to kiss down his shoulder, marveling at the hills and valleys of him, until she arrived at the ruin of his arm, a mass of twisted flesh and scar tissue. She felt him hold his breath, waiting to see what she would do next. Maggie looked up at Leo, holding his emerald gaze with her own, and deliberately placed a soft kiss on the skin covering his wound.

"I wish I had been there," she said, her tone almost reverent as she thought of all that he had been through. "I wish I could have been there with you to hold your hand."

"Well," Leo cleared his throat, struggling for humor, "that would have been awkward when they took my arm off, if you were still holding onto it. Maggie, wait, stop—"

She pulled back and looked into Leo's eyes, which burned with a green fire that threatened to consume them both. "Hmm?"

"I do not want you to think that I — that is, when I brought you back here tonight, I had no intention—" She silenced him for the moment with a kiss, and that was when he realized that she was crying again. "*Margherita*, what is it? What is it, *bellisima*?"

The tenderness in his voice and on his face only made Maggie cry harder, and he wrapped both of them tighter in the blanket until she could put her thoughts together enough to tell him. "What if we end up like Rick and Ilsa?"

Leo wrinkled his brow, bemused. "What if I put you on a plane with a resistance fighter in order to save the world?"

"Leo, I'm serious," Maggie sniffled, and his face softened, concerned. "Didn't you hear what he said? *The problems of three* — or in our case, two — *little people don't add up to a hill of beans in this crazy world.* There's the war, and my parents, and Charlie, and your parents — what are the odds that we'll be able to live happily ever after together, in the middle of all this?"

Leo, choked with emotion, gathered Maggie even more tightly to his chest and held on while he formulated a response. "Maggie, I said that I wanted you to come home with me when this is all over. I want you to be my wife. How and what that will look like, I don't know, but that is one thing I am completely sure of. Hey," he leaned back, tilting her chin up with one finger, "*Casablanca* is a movie. This is real life. Rick was selfless; he let Ilsa go for the good of the world. I am a selfish man, Maggie. I wouldn't get you go for anything."

Maggie kissed him again, desperate to believe as he did that they would get their happy ending.

Chapter 32

Maggie — 1944

"You are sure?" Leo asked, dropping light kisses on each of Maggie's cheeks before meeting her lips, salt meeting sweet.

She nodded. "I'm sure."

"There's no one else, Maggie. There will never be anyone else for me." "There's never been anyone else for me," she smiled shyly.

"Stay here," Leo placed a kiss on her nose before standing up, and Maggie felt suddenly cold without him there next to her. He grabbed a stack of blankets from the corner, and was struggling to create a makeshift pallet on the floor. Maggie rose to her knees and grabbed one side of the blankets to help.

Mother of God, he was beautiful. Tanned olive skin, eyes the color of Christmas trees, and that beautiful black hair that refused to stay in place no matter how much pomade he put in it. She could see the definition in his chest and stomach through the thin cotton of his vest, and not for the first time, she felt the urge to run her fingers over his bare skin.

Her intentions must have shown on her face, because after locating the candles that had once adorned their Thanksgiving table and lighting them, Leo shut off the overhead light and beckoned her to him with a smile that made her heart jump in her chest.

"Maggie." His voice was a growl as he pulled her to him and put his mouth over hers. They lay back on the blankets, and Maggie was intoxicated by the weight of Leo's body on top of her. She could feel him, every muscle, every breath, as he nudged her legs apart with his knee, and she could feel his hardness pressing against her belly.

"May I?" he asked, fingering the buttons at the neckline of her dress. She nodded, not trusting herself to speak, and Leo began to slowly undo the buttons, unwrapping her like a present he had always wanted but never imagined he could have.

"*Mio Dio, Margherita*," he inhaled as she sat up to slip the dress over her shoulders and down her legs, leaving her in nothing but her nylon slip and her stockings. "*Sei la donna più bella.*" She had no idea what the words meant, but given the hunger in his eyes, she assumed they were complimentary. Emboldened, she reached over and untucked the bottom of his vest from his trousers, lifting it over his head, and finally allowing her eyes to travel over the ridges and planes of his body.

"*Ti amo tesoro*," Leo groaned, reaching out to cup her breasts and then finally unclasping her bra.

Within moments, they were both completely naked, and Maggie delighted in the heat and the strength of him, all hers. She ran her hands up his chest and over his shoulders, stopping a second time to place a kiss on the spot where his arm had been removed.

"You are sure that does not bother you?" Leo asked, and Maggie shook her head.

"Some of us wear our scars on the inside, and some of us on the outside. This is part of what makes you you, and it is part of what brought you to me," she declared, and sealed it with a kiss before moving her hand lower and wrapping it around the length and heat of him, tentatively at first, and then with more confidence as his eyes closed and he sucked in air through clenched teeth. She liked this feeling, that she could bring Leo such pleasure, and that she wielded so much power over him with it.

"Wait," he gasped, pulling her hand from his cock and breathing heavily, nostrils flaring.

"Did I do something wrong?" she said, scooting back, face hot with embarrassment.

"Not at all," Leo managed, eyes still closed. "I just don't want this to be over before it begins." Maggie, unsure of his meaning, sat up and reached for a sheet with which to awkwardly cover herself. "No." Leo covered her hand with his, pushing back the sheet and pulling her close to him. "Maggie, do you — do you know how this all works?"

Maggie shook her head, cheeks aflame She didn't trust herself to speak. "Hey," Leo said, gently turning her to face him. "This is me. You don't need to be shy. What *do* you know?"

"I — I know that I want to touch you," she began, hesitant at first but then gaining in confidence under Leo's patient gaze. "I know that I want you to touch me. And I know that the nuns say it is a sin."

"Does this feel like a sin?" he asked, grazing his lips against the side of her neck while also running his hand along the curve where her waist met her thigh.

"No—" she breathed.

"Because I don't want you to do anything that you'll feel the need to confess tomorrow." His fingers slid along until they slipped between her legs, and Maggie gasped at the sensation.

"What are you...?"

"Do you want me to stop?"

"No," she nearly yelped, and Leo laughed as he kissed her, so that Maggie could feel his shoulders shaking under her hands. What was this feeling? She had never even come close to experiencing anything like this before, as if every fiber of her being was focused on Leo's fingers and the delicious reaction they were eliciting from a part of her body that she'd always been told was dirty and shameful.

She reached out, eager to touch him as he was touching her, but Leo just moved out of her reach, and she was too focused on her own pleasure to object. "*Shhh, Amore.* Let me do this for you," he whispered, his mouth to her breast.

"Leo, I feel — I can't—"

"Let go, *Amore.* I've got you." *I've got you.* His words brought her dimly back to the first words he'd ever said to her, and Maggie did as he instructed, letting go and riding a wave of such intense feeling that she was surprised to find herself still in the back room of the laundry when she eventually opened her eyes.

"What was that?" she asked hazily, reaching out a hand to cup Leo's face and bring him back down to her.

"That was the beginning, *bella.*" He kissed her, softly at

first, then more deeply, as if this were the first time and the last time and every time in between. He held himself on top of her, bracing himself on his arm, and pushed himself into her.

Again, Maggie sucked in her breath, amazed that there seemed no end to these new sensations. It hurt, at first, but then gave way to something stronger, as she realized that she already knew what to do. Maggie wrapped her legs around Leo's waist, taking him in deeper and holding on as he drove them both beyond expectations to somewhere where there was no war, no disapproving parents, no government laws or prisoners. There was just Leo and Maggie, and whatever this was between them that neither of them had expected but both had welcomed.

Maggie gasped as Leo reared up, pulling out of her and collapsing onto the sheets. He lay beside her, twitching, eyes squeezed shut, and for a moment Maggie was convinced she had killed the poor man. "Leo?" she asked tentatively, and was surprised when he rolled to face her, arm up over his head and an expression of absolute bliss on his face. "Was that—" she asked, "was that what you did to me? Before, I mean."

Leo nodded and pulled her to him, placing her head on his chest. Maggie could feel his heart beating steadily against her chest, and she counted the beats as they slowly returned to a normal rhythm. Leo looked ready to fall asleep, completely relaxed and satiated, naked as the day he was born. Maggie, on the other hand, was full of questions and exclamations.

"My God," she breathed. "The nuns have no idea what they're talking about. That can't be a sin — it's too wonderful." The rumble of laughter from Leo's chest under her cheek proved that he was not, in fact, asleep, and Maggie pulled herself up on one shoulder to look down at him. "Don't you dare laugh at me, Leo Castiglione. Not after—" she gestured around them, "that."

"I am not laughing at you, *caro mio*. I promise. But I am honored to be here, with you, and to have—" he gestured to their entwined bodies.

"Yes?" she asked, baiting him. "Does the man who prides himself on knowing everything not know the correct terminology?"

"I know plenty of words." Leo's eyes widened at the thought. "But all of the words I know in English for... that... are words I learned from other soldiers, and I assume they're not fit for a *signorina*."

"Are you blushing?" she asked, running a finger down his warm cheek and reveling in the chance to tease him.

"I am a man; men do not blush," he replied, all bravado. But then his eyes softened and Maggie melted into the crook of his arm and he pushed a delicate kiss to her temple. "I wish we could stay here all night. Your parents will worry."

"My parents will sleep," Maggie said. "They think I'm at Nadine's house; nothing could possibly happen there that would concern them."

"How long do we have?" Leo's voice was thick and his eyes were closed, his long lashes painting dark shadows on his cheeks.

"Long enough, love," Maggie whispered.

* * *

By the time Maggie snuck into the house and closed the front door behind her with caution usually reserved for handling a bomb, the ebony of the night sky was giving way to the navy blues that signified the approach of dawn.

The silence of the house was punctuated only by Da's occasional snores, and Maggie removed her pumps to tiptoe up the front stairs as slowly and unobtrusively as she possibly could. Testing every step for creaks, she managed to make it to the top in under five minutes, before scurrying into her own bedroom, closing the door, and jumping under her coverlet fully clothed.

She had had *sex* with Leo. The nuns called it *intercourse*, her friends called it *marital relations* or *rounding the bases*, and her mother didn't admit to its existence at all. But she, Margaret O'Callaghan, had gone all the way with Leo Castiglione.

And she didn't feel one bit guilty.

She felt sore, to be sure. Her inner thighs ached, and there was a soreness *down there* that most certainly must be normal. But the rest of her felt like she was walking on clouds — not so much from what she and Leo had done, but from the way he had treated her and looked at her. It was like she had never known she was starved for touch until she felt Leo's; never knew she was beautiful until she felt so under his gaze.

After she undressed under the covers and tossed her clothes to the side of her bed, Maggie turned on her side and gave herself a moment to savor the events of the past hours. She was sure she had never been so happy.

Chapter 33

Niamh — 2016

"I don't want you to be mad."

Niamh looked up from her book to see Christine standing in the doorway of their bedroom, her laptop closed and clutched against her chest. Christine was chewing her bottom lip and hopping slightly from foot to foot.

"Why does that make me nervous?" Niamh scrambled to sit up on the bed, hastily dog-earing her page despite the dirty look she knew Christine would shoot her as a result. "What's up?"

"OK, the whole Forefathers thing," Christine began, padding into the room and taking a seat on the far edge of the bed. "I know you said you were done with it, and I didn't want to see you hurt, so I agreed." She placed the laptop on the blue flowered comforter, opened it, and moved her fingers around the keyboard for a moment before looking up to meet Niamh's eyes. "But there was another match."

Niamh threw her head back and emitted a frustrated groan. "Chris*tine*," she said, emphasizing the last syllable. "I'm done. I don't want to think about it anymore."

"Exactly, which is why I emailed your cousin for you."

Niamh opened one eye and glared. "You did what now?"

Christine slid across the bed, pushing her open laptop in front of her until it bumped against Niamh's side like a child demanding attention. "You had another match. A first cousin named Isabella." Niamh didn't speak, so Christine continued. "I emailed her to see if she could help, and she said she'd be happy to."

Niamh closed her eyes again, leaning her head back against the headboard and considering. A cousin who was interested in helping Niamh discover her heritage? The door behind which she had crammed all her remaining hope burst open a crack, allowing warmth to rush out and stifle her fears where they stood. This Isabella person wanted to help, maybe even to meet her?

"Let me see," Niamh groaned, hauling the laptop onto her lap so she could see the message for herself.

"I emailed her about two weeks ago, and we've been talking back and forth. She hasn't heard of you, but she's checking with her parents and grandparents to see if any of them know anything." Christine wrung her hands as Niamh skimmed the email chain.

"So, she knows I'm a liberal, pro-choice, pro-gun control lesbian?"

Christine grinned. "Well, since I introduced myself as your wife, the African American environmental rights attorney from Boston, I think there's a chance she put it all together."

"What the hell do I say to her?" Niamh asked, staring at the screen.

"I'd start with 'hello.'"

"Smart ass," Niamh replied with a smirk before turning back to the computer.

"Why don't you ask about her parents? Where she comes from? According to this..." Christine leaned across Niamh's lap to click on an open tab. The Forefathers website flashed onto the screen, and Christine navigated deftly to Niamh's genetic matches, and clicked something. The name *Isabella Ricci* appeared, followed in smaller text by the words, *likely first cousin*. "Right. See here? One of her parents is a sibling of one of your parents. See what she can tell you about her family."

"Okaaaay." Niamh drew out the word, taking her time to think before clicking back into her email and beginning to type.

Dear Isabella,

Hi. Apparently we're cousins, which you already knew since my wife contacted you before mentioning any of it to me. Can you tell me anything about your family? I was raised by a single mother, Julie Reilly, outside of Burlington, VT. My mother was born in Boston, Massachusetts in August of 1945, but she passed away when I was a teenager, and I don't know anything about her family. I'm not looking to disrupt anyone's life or pull skeletons from anyone's closet; I simply want to know where and who I come from, and I'd appreciate anything you can do to assist me with that.

Yours hopefully,
Niamh Reilly

"That look good?" Niamh asked, chewing on her bottom lip. Christine had been reading over her shoulder as she typed.

Christine pulled herself to lie on the bed next to Niamh. "I think it's perfect."

Niamh rested her head on her wife's shoulder and allowed Christine to fiddle with the ends of her short hair. "And now," she said with a sigh that was half contented and half foreboding, "we wait."

Chapter 34

Maggie — 1944

Yuletide celebrations on Randall Street always began with Midnight Mass on Christmas Eve at St. Mary's Church. The mood in the usually dour and imposing building was one of joy and anticipation, and even now, with the constant worries of the war, the people of Taunton were able to come together to celebrate, to ask for the safe return of each other's men, and to pray for the souls of the boys who would not be coming home.

As Maggie walked into the church at eleven-forty pm (because according to Mam, if you weren't early for church, you were too late), she marveled at how beautiful it looked. Evergreen wreaths with fat red bows adorned all of the pillars holding up the vaulted wood ceiling, and smaller bouquets of pine and cedar hung at the entrance to every pew. The altar was covered with poinsettia plants, interspersed with candles, and the air was filled with the scent of incense and something indescribable that Maggie could only think of as "Christmas." It all came together to give the church the air of an enchanted yuletide forest, softened in the flickering candlelight, and when it came time for Maggie to genuflect before following Frankie into the pew, she did so with an air of absolute reverence for the magic of the season.

"What's Da doing?" Frankie whispered, watching as their father circled around the back of the row and came into the pew on the other side, next to their mother. Normally, he sat on the aisle, but for some reason he chose not to that night, and Maggie was the one sitting at the end of the pew, enjoying the splendid view.

"I don't know, but I'm not going to complain," Maggie whispered back, and Frankie grinned. It was Christmas, they were out and about in the middle of the night, and now they were separated from the watchful eyes of their parents by at least three bodies.

Mam and Dad always enforced the expectation that their children were to remain seated in reverent silence until the Mass began, no matter how long that might take. The boys always found it difficult, but Maggie liked to use the opportunity to look around — and tonight she was looking for Leo. He and Guillermo had been invited to attend church with the Altieris, and Maggie fixed her eyes on their usual pew, determined to see Leo the moment he walked into the church.

She had certainly put in as much effort as she could for the Christmas festivities. She wore a new wool skirt in red, white, and black plaid that she had been eyeing in the Pober's window for months. When it finally went on sale, she snatched it up, along with a red blouse and white cardigan. Once she put on the whole outfit, including a precious new pair of stockings and some new "Siren Red" lipstick from Revlon, she felt like one of those girls from the USO posters, the ones soldiers went crazy for. Maggie felt beautiful, and she wanted Leo to see her like this.

By eleven fifty-six, the Altieris and Leo hadn't arrived yet, and the choir was practicing their rendition of "We Three Kings," which would presumably be sung during the Mass. Next to her, Francis and Paul sang under their breath the version that was sure to get them slapped by the nuns in school: "We three kings of Commonwealth Square, selling ladies' underwear. So fantastic, no elastic. Only a nickel a pair." She kicked Francis in the leg, but had to smile at the song she had sung many, many times in her own childhood.

Father Murray donned his robes and was getting into position at the back of the church for his procession down the aisle when Maggie felt a hand on her shoulder. Adrenaline raced through her veins, and Maggie spun around, half expecting to see Leo standing right there in the open, and wishing her a Merry Christmas. But instead of Leo's dark, handsome features, Maggie saw someone far more fair, someone she'd known since they were barely out of diapers, and someone she desperately did not want to see that Christmas Eve: Charlie Morris.

Poor Charlie must have taken Maggie's shocked expression for joy, because he leaned down in front of God and half the population of the city to place a kiss on her lips. Unfortunately for him, Maggie turned at the last second, and Charlie's lips ended up grazing her cheek.

"Really, Mags," Beansie hissed. "The man comes home from a goddamn war for the first time in two years, and you give him the brush off?" Somewhere over the rush in her ears, Maggie heard Frankie shush their younger brother; at the same time, she noticed Leo, walking in behind Guillermo and Mr. Altieri, and staring right at her. No no no no no. This couldn't be happening.

"That's OK," Charlie grinned with that easy manner of his. She had forgotten how easily everything rolled off Charlie, how cool he kept in almost every situation. "We are in church, and I think I've given our Maggie a bit of a shock." He continued to stand in the aisle, and Maggie dimly realized through the fog that he was waiting for her to slide over so he could sit next to her. One glance down the aisle at her mother and father's glowing smiles confirmed this; they had known. They had known Charlie was coming to Midnight Mass and had given her no warning whatsoever.

Emotions churned through Maggie's entire body as she met Leo's gaze across the church and slid over to allow Charlie to take a seat.

What was he even doing here? Her thoughts raced along, looking for something to hold onto. Did Betty know? And Leo — did he realize that the soldier sitting next her was Charlie, the man she claimed to have no romantic feelings for? What is he thinking right now? Oh, God, would he think she had lied? Maggie's head spun as she thought of all the ways this beautiful night had gone sideways, and she had to get out of there. She grabbed the front of the pew and tried to stand, but a wave of dizziness washed over her, and she half sat, half fell onto her brother, right before vomiting her Christmas Eve dinner all over Charlie Morris's lap.

* * *

Charlie came by the house at eight o'clock sharp on Christmas morning to see if Maggie was feeling better, and to ask if she might want to go on a walk with him. Before Maggie could formulate a response — no, she wasn't feeling any better, she hadn't slept a wink all night, and a walk with him was the last thing that would settle her nervous stomach — Mam was already pulling her coat out of the hall closet, and Dad was waving them off with a clap on the back for Charlie and a flask of Christmas whiskey in his pocket.

The air outside was biting cold, and it hit Maggie like a wall of tiny needles driving into her face and neck. She gasped, wanting to turn around and run back inside, but Charlie removed his own scarf and wrapped it snugly around her neck before pulling her hat down over her ears and tucking her arm securely through his.

"I can't let my girl freeze, now, can I?" Charlie chuckled.

"No, you can't," Maggie murmured, allowing herself to be led down the street and around the corner towards downtown. She wanted to say something — no, she *needed* to say something, but how in the world should she go about breaking a good man's heart? They walked without talking for what seemed like ages, the only sounds coming from the crunch of their boots on the frozen sidewalk. Maggie studied Charlie out of the corner of her eye, noting all the ways he had changed since she last saw him. Both Charlie and his twin had always been tall, but their time in the Service had filled them both out, turning lanky lines into hard muscle. His reddish hair was cropped close to his head, making Maggie nostalgic for the mop of curls he had sported in their childhood. How she had envied those curls! The freckles across his cheeks and nose had multiplied exponentially, as if he'd been granted a new one for each new place he'd seen or atrocity he had witnessed. He was different, but he was still good, sweet, dependable Charlie, and Maggie hated herself for not being able to love him.

"Mags, I've written to you every week since I've been gone," he finally said, his deep, melodic voice slicing through the frozen morning like a knife. "And over the past year, I've poured my heart out in those letters. I've told you everything I feel, everything I want for our future, but your letters have always been about the here and now. Scrap metal drives, victory gardens, dances in the church basement and at the USO — I need to make sure you know where I stand." Charlie stopped in front of the Bristol County Savings Bank, and tugged Maggie over to the bench in front of the doors. She sat automatically, as if she was a marionette and Charlie was pulling her strings. He dropped to one knee on the frigid concrete, and Maggie felt her gorge rise, her Christmas breakfast of eggs and bacon threatening to make a reappearance and ruin what she was sure Charlie imagined was a beautiful moment. She swallowed, squeezing her eyes shut and willing the contents of her stomach back to their rightful place. When she opened her eyes again, Charlie had taken a velvet ring box out of his pocket and was holding it front of her.

Holy Mary Mother of God, no. He was going to make her do it. He was going to make her refuse his proposal on Christmas morning and send him back to Europe with a shot through his heart. Maggie looked at the pale blue eyes that had been such a constant through every moment of her childhood. He was so kind, so steady, and he always wanted the best for her. She loved him; of course she did.

But she wasn't *in* love with him.

"Charlie, wait…" She paused as a shadow fell across his features, turning his blue eyes to gray in the morning haze. "Not now. You've just come home, and it's Christmas, and you have to go back when, Wednesday?" Charlie opened his mouth to object, but she pressed one gloved finger to his lips, silencing him. "Don't ask me, please. Don't ask me now." She knew that *now* carried an implicit promise that there would be a *later*, and it was a later she had no intention of reaching with this boy, but she just couldn't bring herself to hurt him like she knew she should by telling him that her heart belonged, and would always belong, to someone else. Charlie's shoulders sagged, but he got up from the ground to sit next to Maggie on the bench.

"I don't understand, Mags. I wanted to ask now because Billy and Betty… and I want you to know how I feel about you. Sometimes the thought of coming home to you, and a little house with a picket fence, and a dog, and our kids — that's all that keeps me going."

Maggie couldn't have felt worse if he had grabbed one of the icicles that hung from the roof of the bank and stabbed her through the heart with it. Charlie was putting his life on the line to stop Hitler and the Japanese from destroying life as she knew it, and she just couldn't find it within herself to love him enough to tell him so?

"You dream about it too, don't you, Maggie? The life we could have? That's why I want you to wear the ring; it's a promise that one day this war will be over, and I'll come home and we can give it a go." The hope of that life was visible in his eyes, and Maggie closed her eyes against a wave of dizziness and promises she'd have to break.

"You just focus on coming home safe after this is all over. The rest will sort itself out." Maggie reached over and snapped the ring box closed before squeezing Charlie's cold hands in hers. He was hurt, that much was clear, but she hadn't said no. She just hadn't said yes. Maggie swallowed down the guilt that threatened to overwhelm her. *He's going back to war*, she wanted to shout at the sky, justifying her actions. *At least when I break his heart for real, he'll only be going home and not into the middle of an ocean full of submarines and torpedoes.*

She thought about Leo, and the question in his eyes when he'd learned about Charlie. *Do you love him?* No, for Christ's sake, she didn't. If she did, then she wouldn't be so twisted inside. But if she loved Charlie, then she wouldn't have gotten involved with Leo, and how could she possibly regret what had become the most defining relationship of her life?

Maggie glanced at Charlie, sitting beside her in the cold, and imagined the boy he had been and the man he would become. Once the war was over, and life could return to normal, he really would be an amazing husband and father.

Just not for her.

Chapter 35

Maggie — 1944

Mr. and Mrs. O'Callaghan seemed to assume that Maggie and Charlie had a simple, lovely walk through town, and Maggie wasn't about to disabuse them of this notion. Slight disappointment registered on Mam's craggy face when Maggie walked through the door later on Christmas morning without Charlie and without a ring on her left hand, but she must have decided not to say anything about it. That was how the O'Callaghan family worked — if talking about something could be avoided, then it should be, at all costs.

Christmas dinner was served and eaten without incident, and prayers were said for Owen and for all the boys at the front. After dinner, Maggie helped Mam with the dishes, and then the entire family retired to the living room where they each curled up with a Christmas gift: Maggie had a beautiful clothbound version of *Pride and Prejudice*, Frankie a copy of *The Man in the Iron Mask*, Paul a collection of civil war battlefield maps, Joe a sports almanac, and Ambrose a book of crossword puzzles. Mam, as usual, eschewed any type of entertainment, and simply watched her family at theirs.

"Aren't you going to visit Charlie tonight?" Dad asked, glancing up at Maggie over the top of his reading glasses. "I thought we wouldn't be able to keep you two away from one another, right, Annie?"

Maggie moved her lips into something resembling a smile, and replied that she still wasn't feeling well. It wasn't a complete lie; her nervous stomach hadn't felt normal since last night, but it was still a nice excuse to avoid going out. "Actually, I think I'll go to bed," she said, closing her book and heading for the stairs. The sooner she went to sleep, the sooner this strange Christmas would be over.

"It's seven o'clock," Joe exclaimed, looking up at his sister from his spot on the floor. "You're being a drip, Maggie."

"Joseph Edward," their mother huffed. "You're getting a little too bold, young man. Apologize to your sister."

"Sorry, Maggie."

"That's OK, champ." She ruffled her littlest brother's hair on her way upstairs. "Some day, when you're as old as me, you'll see that going to bed early isn't always a bad thing."

"You're nineteen — not ninety," Paul called after her, but Maggie was already halfway to her bedroom, closing the door and looking for her nightgown.

* * *

Thwomp.

Maggie rolled over in bed, dimly aware that it was the middle of the night, but just as she let sleep pull her back into its cozy embrace, she heard it again.

Thwomp.

She sat up in bed and rubbed her eyes, struggling to find a foothold in consciousness. What in God's name was that noise? Maggie swung her legs over the side of her bed just in time to both hear *and* see the snowball hit her bedroom window.

Thwomp. What on earth?

Maggie ran to the window, feeling very much like the speaker in *The Night Before Christmas* as she tore open the curtains and threw up the sash. She peered out into the night, but saw nothing except her front yard and, in the distance, the lights from the center of the city. She was about to give up and close the window again when she heard Leo whisper-call from below.

"*Buon Natal, Margherita.*"

"Merry Christmas," she hissed back with a surprised grin that split her face in two. "What are you doing here?"

"Christmas is for family, no? You are my family. Come down!"

"Now?" Maggie's hand flew to her throat. She was wearing a nightgown and slippers, and her hair was in pin curls. He couldn't mean now.

"Yes, now. Put on some warm clothes and come see the stars with me." She could just barely make out Leo's figure under the shadow of the oak tree. He stepped out of the shadow and onto a moonlit patch of snow, and any reservations she had were dashed away by the sight of Leo Castiglione standing under her bedroom window on Christmas night.

"Give me five minutes." She shut the window, and debated changing into a skirt and sweater before thinking better of it. She finally decided to leave on her flannel nightgown, but added some wool socks and snow boots. She hastily brushed out her curls and donned her coat, hat, and mittens before tiptoeing down the stairs and out the front door, right into Leo's solid form.

"You're like a brick wall," she laughed, delighting in this eleventh-hour Christmas surprise and lifting her face for a kiss.

"A brick wall? Is that the kind of compliment that's popular with American girls?" Leo teased, leading Maggie around the back so they wouldn't be seen.

"You're my brick wall. My dashing Italian brick wall." Maggie wrinkled her nose. "I think I've lost the metaphor."

"I will accept dashing," he grinned. "I had Christmas dinner at the Italian Club with the Altieris. You have never seen so much food. And Tommy Altieri let me borrow his pickup truck."

"What?" Maggie's jaw dropped in disbelief. "Why?"

"Because it's Christmas, *bella*. And he wanted me to show my girl a good time." Leo reached out to chuck her under the chin, but Maggie pulled back.

"Tommy Altieri knows about us?"

"Tommy can be trusted," he assured her. "Really, Maggie. He's a good man, and he even said that he'd ask his uncle if he could get me a job at the brickyard after the war, once I come back to America."

Maggie's heart swelled at the best Christmas present Leo could possibly bring her.

"After the war, we'll get married, and then I can apply to

197

stay in America permanently. The food here is reason enough — wait until I tell you about the seven fishes." He laughed as Maggie smacked him in the side with all her might, and he fell giggling into the snow.

"Come on," she said, offering him a hand up. "Show me this truck."

* * *

No one in their right mind would ever have given Leo a driver's license. Prior to Christmas night, 1944, his only experience driving had been behind the wheel of a tractor back in Italy. The Ford's transmission wasn't particularly difficult to figure out in comparison, but due to the fact that Leo was missing his left arm, negotiating back and forth between the stick shift and the steering was enough to make a lesser man give up.

Thank goodness they didn't drive far, and by the time Leo stopped the truck at a turn-off over by the park, Maggie was sure all of her hair had gone completely white.

"This was a lovely surprise, but can I ask for just one more thing for Christmas?" she asked when Leo engaged the emergency brake and turned off the engine.

"Absolutely," he replied with a flourish. "What can I do for you?"

"You can let me drive home."

Leo threw back his head in a laugh, the glow from the street lights highlighting his long neck, Adam's apple, and squared jaw line. Without stopping to think, Maggie leaned over the gear shift and pressed her lips to the spot just under his jaw, whispering, "Merry Christmas."

"*Buon Natale*," Leo sighed, before sliding his arm behind

Maggie and lifting her effortlessly, albeit awkwardly, onto his lap. She wrapped her arms around his neck and buried her face in his shoulder, reveling in his scent and his *thereness*. *This*, she thought to herself, *this* is Christmas.

"*Margherita*, can I ask you a question? I do not want you to be upset."

Maggie felt his words more than heard them, a melodic rumbling against her cheek. She pulled back, searching his eyes in the semi-darkness of the truck's cab. "Of course."

"Last night, at Mass..." Leo cleared his throat and rubbed a hand across the back of his neck, causing Maggie to sit up. "Was that him? Charlie?"

"Leo." She placed a finger under his chin, lifting his face to meet hers like he so often did with her. "Are you jealous? I did get sick all over the poor man."

His green eyes flashed with something Maggie couldn't recognize, and he immediately looked away.

"I saw him come into the church, and your mother and father were so happy to see him. And you looked..."

"Surprised? Confused?" Maggie sighed, shaking her head. "I was both. And yes, my parents have... expectations for Charlie and me. Expectations," she said pointedly to Leo, "that I have told you I do not share."

"Have you told him?" Leo asked, voice low.

"He knows how I feel. We — we talked about it this morning." The half-truth caught in Maggie's throat, but she pushed through, reminding herself that it wouldn't do Leo any good to know she had delayed breaking things all the way off with Charlie. It didn't change how she felt about—

"Does he know about me?" Leo asked with his heart in his eyes.

199

"Leo—"

"No. Please do not remember that I asked." Leo closed his eyes and leaned back against the driver's seat headrest. "I know why. I know what your family thinks and how hard they would make it for you if they knew. And I am in no position to protect you from that right now."

Maggie laid her head against Leo's chest, cursing herself for not being able to tell him the whole truth, but comforted by the warm solidity of him and the sound of his heart, beating like a metronome mere inches from her ear. With all the freedoms Leo's status in the ISU afforded him, it was easy to forget that in the eyes of the United States Armed Forces, he was still a prisoner. He lived at the mercy of the government, and his privileges could be revoked as quickly as they were given. As much as they both hated it, they needed to be patient and wait out the war before they could be open about who they were to one another with her family.

* * *

Leo had certainly planned out a lovely Christmas surprise for Maggie. The bed of the truck was loaded down with blankets and pillows, and as soon as they were settled in the back, looking up at the stars with Maggie's head resting on Leo's chest, he pulled out a box and handed it to her.

"For me?" Maggie asked, delighted that Leo had thought to get her something for Christmas, however unnecessary.

"It is not much. You know that if I could, I'd take down all the stars for you and string them on a necklace, *bellisima*." There was that shy smile again, the one that was always just there, just under all of Leo's flirting and bluster, and it was the one that made Maggie want to crawl onto his lap and bury herself in his chest forever.

She untied the red and white cord that held the box closed, and opened it to reveal a stack of freshly baked Italian *pizzelle* cookies. She shivered with delight, inhaling the sweet smell of sugar and anisette. "Can I eat one?"

"That is what one does with sweets," Leo laughed. "*Signora* Altieri made them for me, but I had nothing to give to you, so my *pizzelles* are your *pizzelles*."

"We'll share." Maggie took the top cookie off the pile, marveling at its thin, delicate structure, like edible lace. She broke it in two, and handed half to Leo. "*Slainte*."

"We toast with cookies now?" Leo laughed, taking it from her. "*Salud*."

"Unless you've got any champagne hidden under those blankets," Maggie replied before taking a decadent bite and savoring the sweet, sharp flavor as it melted on her tongue. "Leo, these should be illegal. They're scrumptious."

"I do not know *scrumptious*," he repeated, "but I think I am probably right to say that you, *Margherita* O'Callaghan, are scrumptious as well." He pulled her on top of him, and Maggie didn't need any more invitation than that to kiss him. He tasted like *pizzelles* and smelled of Old Spice, and he was just so utterly Leo that Maggie wanted to thank the universe for giving him to her for Christmas.

The temperature was below freezing, but their nest of blankets in the bed of the truck was enough to keep them warm, and they provided plenty of heat on their own. Maggie pulled at the buttons of Leo's shirt, desperate to feel his skin against hers, and when he finally sank himself inside her, she let out a guttural noise at the sensation. The nuns might have taught her that this was a mortal sin, but Maggie knew better. She knew that being here with Leo, under the wide, clear expanse of winter sky on the most magical night of the year, was as close to the divine as she was ever going to come in this lifetime. And she was grateful.

When they finished, Leo turned his head discreetly so Maggie could clean herself up, and they lay back together under the crisp, cloudless sky.

"Do you ever feel guilty," she asked, thinking of her conversation that morning with Charlie and snuggling into Leo's warmth, "being this happy when so many people have been through so much?"

"Every day," Leo replied immediately. "I feel guilty that I cannot fight for the Allies, to help bring the war to a close faster. I feel guilty that my family is in Italy, probably without enough to eat, while I am here living like a king even while I am a prisoner. I feel guilty that so many other men do not get to hold their women tonight, or see their children being born, and that some of them will never come home." He paused, and Maggie thought that the conversation was over, until he said, "But does our happiness add to anyone else's pain? If I had never come here, and never met you, would the war be over any sooner?"

"No," she whispered, the exhalation making a visible cloud of vapor before her eyes, proof that they were here, they were alive, and they were together.

"There is so much ugliness in the world," Leo continued, staring up at the same sky his brothers and sisters in Italy could also see. "I think it is our duty to hold on to happiness wherever we can find it."

Maggie nodded, dropping a kiss on his shoulder and trying

to avoid the realization that they'd need to get home soon if she didn't want to get caught, and if she had any hope of being functional at work tomorrow. "I just can't get over the fact that this Christmas is probably the worst in history for so many people around the world, and yet it's the best one I have ever had." Leo turned to kiss her again, and Maggie responded in kind for all those in the world who didn't get to see the people they loved tonight, and might never again. "I need to get home," Maggie breathed, breaking away and trying to slow the racing of blood through her veins.

Leo nodded, kissing her again with agonizing slowness. "I know. I'll get you home."

And he did — an hour and a half later.

Chapter 36

Maggie — 1945

At first, the nausea was intermittent, but by the third week of January, Maggie's days were punctuated with bouts of vomiting, and smelling food of any kind made her run for the powder room, the trash bin, or whatever else she could find to catch the meager contents of her stomach. She thought of it as little more than a nuisance that occasionally kept her from work, but when January turned into February, and her period had still not made its monthly visit, a terrifying realization began to dawn.

When was the last time she bled? Maggie went over and over it in her mind, and she couldn't be sure, but she thought it was before Thanksgiving. She'd never kept a calendar of her menstrual cycle like her mother had suggested; there had never been a need. She had been more or less regular since the day she had first noticed blood in her underwear at age twelve and run into the backyard screaming for her mother, sure that she must be dying.

Now, however, Maggie would have done anything to see the telltale stain in her underwear. She couldn't be pregnant. She just couldn't be. Betty had said that if the man didn't finish off inside, then it wasn't possible to get pregnant, and Leo had been fastidious about pulling out every time they were together. So, she could not be pregnant and that's all there was to it.

Denial was Maggie's main way of coping with the situation. After living in an Irish Catholic home for twenty years, she was an expert at ignoring feelings that she didn't want to feel. She kept it all locked inside, deep down inside of her, where her worries weren't the only thing growing.

Maggie managed to keep it together until the middle of February, when one Saturday afternoon at Betty's house, she realized that she could no longer button her favorite navy skirt. She crumpled to the floor, wave after wave of denied emotions washing over her: Fear of what Leo would say, what her parents would say, what this would mean for her future. And now she couldn't even fasten the button on her favorite skirt; it was too much.

"Maggie, darling, come on now. Tell me what's wrong?" Betty hurried to sit down next to her friend, lifting Maggie's head into her lap and soothing her like Maggie had always wished her mother would. The thought of her mother and her inevitable fury brought on another bout of tears, and Betty had to wait several more minutes until Maggie's sobs had slowed down enough for her to reveal what was wrong.

"You're *pregnant*?" Betty exclaimed in a whisper, lest her parents hear what they were talking about. "Maggie, that's wonderful!"

"Wonderful?" Maggie lifted her swollen and tear-stained face from her friend's lap to look her in the face, incredulous. "Please, please explain to me how this is wonderful."

"You're having a baby, Mags!" Betty stated the obvious with a smile — was that actually a *smile* on her face?

"Thank you, Elisabeth." Maggie's tone was clipped, annoyed. "I am aware of what it means to be pregnant."

"Does Charlie know? Oh, I know it's impossible, but I would give anything to see the look on his face — you know he's always wanted to be a father."

"Charlie..." Maggie trailed off. Of course, Betty would think it was Charlie's baby. Charlie had been home for Christmas, and he'd probably told his brother he was planning to propose. Betty had always talked about how much fun it would be to have houses next door to one another and raise their children side by side. "It's not Charlie's," Maggie blurted before she lost her nerve.

"Not — I don't understand." Betty scrambled to her feet, gobsmacked. She began to pace, stopping after a full minute to ask, "If it's not Charlie's... gosh, Maggie. Whose is it?"

Maggie just sat on the floor, gazing up at Betty with a forlorn expression on her tear-stained face, until light dawned in her friend's eyes. "No. No, no, no. Margaret O'Callaghan, someone from work? One of those Italian boys you were going on about? No ma'am, you are *not* pregnant with the child of a — a — war criminal." She hissed the last words, and Maggie was on her feet in a second, the desperation in her eyes replaced by fury.

"He's not a war criminal. Officially he's not even a prisoner of war. He's a co-belligerent, and he's a good man, Betty!"

"If he was a good man, would he have gotten you up the pole?"

"How is it ANY different than you and Billy? You told me yourself that you'd gone all the way?"

"Billy is an *American*, and he's going to marry me."

"Are you saying that Leo has no intention of marrying *me*?" The girls were nose to nose, vitriol racing through Maggie's body. Betty was her best friend; she was supposed to be supportive. She was supposed to be the one person in this whole city that Maggie could confide anything in. Betty's words hurt, but the betrayal behind them cut deeper, leaving a wound that Maggie was certain would never heal.

"I don't see a ring on your finger, Margaret. If he was such a good man, he'd have made arrangements by now. Unless—" Betty eyes widened, staring at Maggie's trembling chin. "You haven't told him, have you?" Maggie shook her head.

"I haven't told anyone."

Betty placed her hands on her hips, all business. "It looks to me like you have two choices here. You can tell him and hope that he does the right thing, or you can tell his superior officer and they will force him to do the right thing. Either way, you're married to a traitor."

The tears spilled down Maggie's cheeks were no longer born of fear or desperation, but rage. "How can you be so cold?" she asked this stranger who had been her best friend since they were both in diapers.

"You ruined everything, Maggie. Everything! All the plans we made — it's all gone now. And *you're* angry with *me*?"

Betty was never going to understand. She couldn't.

Maggie had heard enough. Wiping away tears with the back of her hand, she brushed past Betty and ran down the stairs and out of the house. It was three-thirty. If she rushed, she could make the next bus to the camp, and from there she could tell Leo exactly what had been going on. Maggie prayed fervently as she jogged toward the bus stop, hoping against hope that Leo would have some idea what to do — because one way or another, everything was about to change.

* * *

"Miss, with all due respect, I can't just radio down to the ISU guys and tell 'em that there's a pretty girl here to see one of 'em," the man at the guard station told Maggie for the third time in a row.

"Please, Private—" she read the name on his uniform, "—Moskovitz." She smiled sweetly, doing everything short of batting her eyelashes at the man to convince him to get Leo for her. "It's very, very important." Maggie could get into the camp herself with her work badge, but that wasn't the problem. The problem was that a civilian young woman couldn't just walk down into the barracks unaccompanied. That was asking for trouble, and Maggie really didn't need any more trouble in her life at the moment.

"Lady, I said no. If he was up here at the gate to meet you, fine. But I'm not radioing down there." Maggie was just about to go around to the hole in the fence and take her chances on her own when she heard a familiar, heavily accented voice inside the guard station.

"I think that the machine is fixed, Private. Can you please sign the work order for me?"

"Guillermo!" Maggie called, nearly collapsing with relief. Guillermo did a double take at the frizzy-haired, blotchy-faced woman standing at the gate before finally responding.

"Maggie?"

"See?" Maggie said to the private, throwing up her hands in exasperation. "He can take me."

"Do you know this woman?" He looked from Maggie to Guillermo with an expression usually reserved for bad smells or rabid raccoons.

"I do, yes. She is my friend." Guillermo shoved the work order into the private's hand for signature, then crossed to Maggie, frown lines creasing his face. "Maggie, something is wrong?"

"I need to see Leo," she said succinctly. "Can you take me to him?"

Guillermo nodded. "Of course. The work order?" The private held out the signed paper, and Guillermo slid it into his toolbox. "Let's go."

The ISU barracks were on the opposite side of the camp, and therefore a fifteen-minute walk for Maggie and Guillermo. They walked together in silence until they passed the stone grotto to the Virgin Mary that was built by the first Italian POWs to be brought to Taunton in 1942. Guillermo stopped in front of the statue, made the sign of the cross, bringing the metal crucifix he wore around his neck to his lips for a quick kiss before continuing on next to Maggie.

"I still pray for her every night," Maggie said softly, letting Guillermo know that if he needed or wanted to talk about Sadie, she was there to listen.

"I pray for her all day, every day," he replied, looking straight ahead at the road in front of them. "And still I do not know what happened."

"I know she loves you," Maggie said. "I don't know where

she is, and I don't know what happened, but I know that much."

Guillermo took a cigarette out of his pocket, lit it, and took a long drag before replying. "Do you see, though, how knowing that makes it even harder for me? If I thought she did not love me, it would break my soul, but I would know she was alright. This way, I know something bad must have happened, and I cannot be there to help her."

Maggie felt an ache in her chest for what Guillermo was going through, and for Sadie, wherever she was. She might be in an impossible situation, but at least she had Leo, and he had her.

* * *

Guillermo left Maggie on a bench outside the mess hall while he ran inside to fetch Leo. In what felt like less than a minute, Leo burst out the door and into the snow, turning his head left and right in an effort to find her.

"I'm here," Maggie called, and Leo jogged toward her, concern and worry written across his handsome features.

"Maggie, what is the matter? Something is the matter, yes?" His questions made clouds in the bitter air, and he put his arm on her shoulder, pulling her to him before she could even respond. It took everything in her not to let all her fears and feelings loose into the comfort of his chest. But she couldn't — she needed to talk to him, and she was freezing.

"Is there somewhere we can go? Somewhere private?"

Leo pondered for a moment, eyebrows scrunched in thought, before suggesting that there probably wouldn't be anyone in the rec hall at the moment. The gymnasium wouldn't be particularly comfortable, but it was warm and dry, and it was empty.

Maggie managed, through herculean effort, to hold herself in check as Leo guided her across the snow-covered grass to the door of the gymnasium, his arm around her shoulders a strong and comforting presence. Leo would fix this; he had to.

Once they were out of the cold, Leo grabbed two wooden folding chairs from the stack by the basketball hoop, and opened them each with a flick of his wrist. The click of the chair's hinges and the following bang as they hit the wooden floor echoed off the walls, and Maggie was flooded with memories of childhood physical education class with Sister Winifred Marie. Things were so much easier back then...

"*Margherita. Bella.* Tell me what is wrong." Leo led her to a chair and helped her to sit, as if she was suddenly incapable of doing so herself. "Maggie?" His green eyes shone with compassion and concern, and her heart clenched painfully in her chest. "You're scaring me."

"I'm pregnant." The words left her mouth of their own accord, so easy to say, but impossible to take back. Maggie held her breath as she waited for Leo's reaction, whatever it might be.

Leo's expression was blank, as if the information Maggie had just given him was floating in front of him but hadn't quite yet made it into his brain. Maggie heard a rushing sound, and she grabbed onto the seat of the chair to steady herself as a wave of dizziness made the room tilt sideways.

Almost before she knew what was happening, Leo swept her up into his embrace, kissing her with a tenderness that brought tears back to her eyes. Hadn't she cried enough for

211

one day?

"A baby? We are having a baby?" Leo's eyes shone with unshed tears, and the pure joy on his face was enough to make her laugh, even now when she feared that her life was over.

"You're" — she almost didn't dare to believe it — "you're happy?"

"Happy? I am — what is the English word? Ah! — I am over the moon, Maggie! We are going to have a baby." Leo's hand, which had been caressing her face, moved slowly down to her middle, where he laid it with absolute reverence over her belly.

All of the fear and tension she had been holding left her body in that instant, and she sagged against him in relief. Thank God. Thank God for Leo, who could have strength enough for both of them.

For all three of them.

"I was so worried," she whispered into his chest. "I didn't know what you'd say. I *know* what my parents will say—"

"You didn't know what I'd say?" Leo leaned back, lifting her chin and gazing down at her, his teasing smile somehow older now, more knowing. "I have told you that I am in love with you, my Maggie. I will find a priest tonight and we will be married as soon as it can be arranged."

"Can we?" she swallowed, the very real limitations of their situation foremost in her mind. "Are you allowed, I mean?"

Leo's cheeks puffed out as he let out an audible breath, running his hand through his hair as he worked it out. "I don't know. I don't know that anyone has requested to get married. But this is hardly a normal situation. Even if I can find a priest to marry us until after the war, and then we can make it legal. We don't have the time to waste." A grin lit up his features, and Maggie couldn't help but respond with a tiny smile of her own. "We have a baby on the way."

After she repeatedly reassured him that she was fine, and that she did need to go home eventually before her parents sent the police looking for her, Maggie and Leo walked to the bus stop, making plans the whole way.

"This is not how I had planned to marry you, *bella*, but now that it is happening, I would not have it any other way."

"Let's see if you still say that when I'm the size of a tank," Maggie scoffed, tucking herself into his side for warmth. "What do you think of the name Owen, after my older brother?"

"I think it would be an honor to name my son after him." *My son.* The words lay between them, so new that they shimmered in the cold, delicate and almost visible. "And for a girl, I have always loved the name Guliana. That is my nonna's name," he said with a smile that was tinged with longing.

"It's beautiful," Maggie assured him. "And your nonna will love it when she finds out."

They reached the bus stop by the main gate of the camp, and Leo opened his coat to hold Maggie in his warmth until it arrived. "Go home and get some sleep," he whispered into her hair as the headlights of a bus appeared in the distance. "I will find us a priest tonight, and I will send you word tomorrow. It's going to be better than OK, *Margherita*. It's going to be wonderful." He pressed his lips to hers as the bus pulled up to the curb, and she returned the kiss with all the relief and tentative excitement in her heart.

"I love you." He dropped a final kiss on the top of her head. "Take care of *il patatino* for me."

"I love you too, and I will." Maggie squeezed Leo's hand, walked through the gate, and stepped onto the bus. As it pulled onto the street and back towards the center of the city, Maggie could still see Leo standing steadfast, growing smaller and smaller under the lights from the camp.

Chapter 37

Niamh — 2016

She was out of tissues.

The students had given Niamh one of those spring head colds that made her nose drip continuously like a leaky faucet, while simultaneously stuffing her sinuses to the point where she could neither actually blow her nose nor breathe through it. And now she was out of friggin' tissues.

Niamh hauled herself off the couch, leaving *The Price is Right* long enough to pad into the bathroom and retrieve a roll of toilet paper. She promptly rolled up two squares and stuffed them into her nostrils. It wasn't pretty—or comfortable — but it did the trick, and Niamh snapped a selfie in the bathroom mirror to send to Christine.

As she moved back into the living room, toilet paper and trash bin in tow, the phone rang. Assuming that it was Christine calling to check on her, Niamh didn't even bother to look at the screen before answering. "Hello?"

"Hello, I am looking for Niamh Reilly — is this she?" The voice on the other end of the phone was hesitant, yet deep and melodic, with an accent that Niamh couldn't immediately place.

"Yes, this is she. Who's calling, please?" If this was another telemarketer, she was going to scream. Niamh cradled the phone between her shoulder and her ear and settled herself back on the couch. She heard a sharp intake of breath on the line, and after a few seconds of silence, the voice, considerably shakier than it had been a moment before, said, "Niamh, my name is Leo Castiglione, and I think—" he paused, and she immediately grabbed the remote to pause the TV, as if sensing the importance of what he was about to say, "—I think I am your grandfather."

Niamh dropped the remote to the ground, almost dropping the phone as well as she scrambled to her feet and yanked the wads of toilet paper from her nose. She opened her mouth once, twice, three times before any words were able to escape her racing mind and she simply said, "Hi, Leo." The warm chuckle that came through the phone sailed across Niamh's frayed nerves like a tropical breeze, and she felt her shoulders relax as she sat back down on the edge of the couch, wanting to know everything at once. "How do you — what—?" She wasn't able to slow her mind down enough to pluck the right questions from the morass of thoughts racing around and getting tangled up in one another.

"My granddaughter — my other granddaughter, that is, my Bella —" he cleared his throat, a rasping sound like torn paper. "She came to see me this morning and told me about the messages you have been exchanging." Isabella had taken a full month to respond to Niamh's initial email, but once she had emailed back, she had been very helpful. She spoke to both of her parents, but they knew nothing of any use, so she had promised to visit her grandparents and check in with them.

"Yes, she's been lovely." Niamh stated the obvious.

There was that chuckle again, like warm milk to a tired soul. "Bella is a good girl, yes, but she did not know, and neither did her father. I never told them, though I have carried *your* mother in my heart for sixty-five years."

Niamh's breath caught in her throat, and she could feel the tears begin to well, stinging, into her eyes as she asked, "My mother? Can you confirm her birth date for me?"

"Of course." Leo's reply was immediate. "It is a day I have celebrated in my own way every year since. Bella tells me that your mother went by Julie. Her mother and I wanted to name her Guliana. She was born in the late summer, 1945, correct?"

Niamh's jaw dropped. Everything around her seemed to go out of focus, everything except the voice on the other end of the line — the voice of her grandfather — and what he had just told her. "I think—" she paused, fighting to regain control over her swirling emotions, "I think I need to meet you, Mr. Castiglione."

"Please call me Nonno," he said, and Niamh could have sworn she actually heard the smile in his voice. "That is what Isabella calls me. It means grandfather in Italian."

"So, then, your accent, it's Italian?"

"It is, but I have lived in Brooklyn for almost seventy years now."

Niamh smiled as a picture of the man on the phone began to form in her mind. Did he look like her? "I think I need to meet you—" she paused, trying on the word for size, "Nonno."

"Nothing would make this old man happier, *mi nipotina*. Bella tells me you are not far away, just outside of Boston."

"Can I come tomorrow?" Now that Niamh had found this man, this grandfather, she didn't want to waste another second not knowing hm in person. She was already calculating sub plans in her head and trying to determine if it was quicker to take the train to Grand Central Station, or if she should book a flight from Logan to LaGuardia.

"Of course you may come tomorrow. Just let me know your arrangements and if you need Bella to pick you up anywhere. I understand if you wish to book a hotel, but you are welcome to stay with me, with my son, or with my granddaughter and her husband." The emotion in his voice was clear through the phone line. "You are family, Niamh."

Again, it took Niamh a moment to gather herself enough to formulate a response. Other than Christine, Niamh hadn't had a family to call her own since she was too young to really appreciate what that meant. She'd had friends, and foster families — some of whom treated her as one of their own— but she hadn't had real family of her own since her mother died. Leo's words wrapped themselves around her heart and she wanted nothing more than to melt into his welcome, but first she had to know if this elderly man would accept everything about her. Niamh took a deep breath and put it all on the line. "May I bring my wife to meet you as well?"

"Of course," Leo cried. "My Bella told me that your wife is the one who made this happen, and therefore I must meet her and thank her from the bottom of my heart for bringing us together. Please bring her along, Niamh."

Niamh nodded, as if Leo was right in front of her, before sniffling into the phone, "Thank you, Nonno."

"Family is family, *my nipotina.* I look forward to seeing you tomorrow, and I feel as if I know you already."

After saying their goodbyes and promising to be in touch with travel arrangements, Niamh hung up and proceeded to stare at her phone for an additional few minutes with a dopey grin on her face. She had to call Christine.

Chapter 38

Maggie — 1945

When Maggie finally turned the corner onto Randall Street, the first thing she noticed was the car in the driveway. It wasn't one she recognized, and the first thought that occurred to her turned her blood to ice in her veins and gripped her throat in its icy fingers. Owen. Had something happened to Owen?

Maggie ran the last few steps to the front door, throwing it open in her haste to get inside. Inside, she hit a wall of curated calm as thick and impenetrable as stone. Mam, Dad, and Father Murray all sat in absolute silence on the very edge of their chairs in the living room. The only thing that set them apart was the look on their faces: Mam looked furious, Dad looked defeated, and Father Murray looked like he was about to deliver devastating news.

"What is it?" Maggie asked, frantic. "Tell me quickly — is it Owen?" The only sound in the room was the whisper of a clink as Father's teacup settled into its saucer.

"We've had a visit this afternoon, Margaret—" Mam was calling her Margaret; this could not be good. Was it the army? A letter? What? "From Elisabeth Curran."

Betty.

They knew.

Shock, betrayal, fear, and devastation all vied for purchase in Maggie's mind, and she grabbed onto the banister to steady herself. How could Betty have betrayed her like that? Would her mother ever be able to forgive her? And what was the priest doing here? Surely he was the last person Mam would want to know about her daughter's loose morals.

Maggie's face burned and she had the unsettling feeling that she was no longer *in* her body, but rather floating above it, looking down at her own worst fear.

"Margaret, your parents called me here tonight to discuss your situation, and what can be done about it." Father Murray had the expression of a man inordinately pleased with himself, as if he had every right to come into Maggie's house and discuss the most personal of topics, and she should thank him for the honor.

"There is nothing to discuss, Father," Maggie replied in a strangled voice. She threw back her shoulders, held her head high, and proceeded towards the staircase.

"Margaret. Veronica." Da's voice, filled with agony, acted like an arm, reaching out to grab Maggie and stop her mid-step. "You will come in here and you will listen to us."

Maggie turned, as if caught in an invisible web of her father's disappointment, walked over to the sofa, and sat.

"Margaret, your parents telephoned me because they have recently learned that you are with child. Is that correct?"

Father Murray asked before lifting his teacup oh-so-delicately to his lips and taking a sip.

She might feel terrible upsetting her father, but the Catholic priest was *not* her father, and Maggie felt no obligation to speak to him. "Da, what did Elisabeth tell you?"

"You may direct your responses to me, Margaret," Father Murray instructed. "Your parents have engaged my help to deal with this difficult matter."

Maggie, who had never spoken a disrespectful word to a member of the clergy in her life, bristled. This was *her* life, and *her* baby, and who the hell was this man to come into her house and act like he knew her? She dug her fingernails into the palms of her hands deep enough to cause pain, and that pain was a momentary relief from the anguish and the fury of the moment. "Excuse me, Father, but I fail to see how this is any of your business."

"Margaret!" her mother roared, rising to her feet — but one hand motion from the priest had her seated again, staring daggers at her daughter from across the room.

"That is where you are wrong," the priest continued. "Any threat to my congregation is absolutely my business, in that it is God's business. Now, Margaret," he continued, crossing one knee over the other in a gesture of casual familiarity which made her teeth clench, "do you know who the father of the child is?"

"What kind of a question is that?" Maggie exclaimed, rising to her feet. "Of course I know who the father of my baby is."

"There's no need to be angry, Margaret. It was simply a question." Simply a question that impugned her character, Maggie fumed.

"The father is overseas, Father. He's at the front, and I

222

don't know that we can get him home to get a ring on her finger before it's too late," Mam clipped, biting off the words like stale crackers.

"Charlie is *not* the father, Mam. Da." Maggie looked between her two parents. Dad looked ready to have an embolism, and Mam's face was blank with shock. Before they could ask, she took a deep breath and let it all come pouring out. "The father is Corporal Leonardo Castiglione of the Italian Service Unit at Camp Myles Standish, and we are getting married."

The little room was absolutely silent in response to Maggie's declaration, save for the *tick tock* of the grandmother clock by the fireplace. Father Murray gaped at her, mouth open, looking rather like a landed fish. Da closed his eyes and pinched the bridge of his nose, and Mam looked at her with such utter revulsion that Maggie could feel herself shriveling under the gaze.

"We are getting married," Maggie repeated. "That's where I was just now, with Leo at the camp. He's finding us a priest. It's going to be alright, Mam."

One thing Maggie had learned from experience with her mother was that long periods of silence often ended with violent explosions of temper, and this one was no different.

"My. Daughter. Is. Not. Marrying. A. God. Damned. Prisoner. Of. War." Mam started to rise from her chair, but got stuck somewhere between standing and sitting, as if her body simply couldn't decide which position to take and her brain was far too preoccupied with her overwhelming disappointment in her daughter to be of any help. "And that is final."

"Mam, Leo and I were going to get married anyway. This just speeds things up a bit." Maggie tried without success to

223

console her mother. "I met him at work, at the camp. He's a wonderful man; I think you'll like him. He's Catholic," she added with a glance at Father Murray, who hadn't moved from his spot by the fire.

"You heard your mother," Dad managed to say without opening his eyes. "You are not marrying some fascist who thought he could use you as his plaything."

"He didn't *use* me, Daddy. He loves me. We're going to get married."

"Margaret, listen to yourself. If I had a nickel for every young girl who thought that the father of her baby loved her and wanted to marry her, I'd be able to put a new roof on the rectory," Father Murray sighed, rising to his feet. "Margaret, it comes down to this. You're coming with me, and I'll be taking you to St. Gerard's Home for Unwed Mothers in Boston. They will look after you until the baby is born, and then they will find a good Catholic family with a mother and a father to raise it."

It was then that Maggie noticed the battered suitcase at the foot of the stairs. Sweet Jesus, that was for her.

"You can't make me go." Maggie turned to look at her father. "Da, you can't let them take me. This is your grandchild!" He didn't respond, but simply fell into silent sobs as his wife crossed the room and handed the suitcase to Maggie.

"You are nineteen, Margaret. You're right — we cannot force you." Father Murray placed a hand on her elbow, and Maggie's skin began to crawl. "But I can tell you that the young man who did this to you will be arrested. He has broken the law by assaulting an American civilian, and he will be prosecuted to the fullest extent of the law."

"Assault me? He most certainly did not assault me," she

spat, ripping her arm out of the priest's grasp. "We're going to get married."

"The child you carry proves otherwise, my child," the priest argued. "He will not be allowed to marry you — he is a prisoner. You will be alone. You have no husband, and your mother and father will not allow you to live under their roof while you carry an Italian soldier's bastard. Am I right, Mrs. O'Callaghan?" Maggie caught her mother's nod out of the corner of her eye, and she felt like a rat, trapped in a cage and unable to escape as her demise came nearer and nearer. "Come with me to St. Gerard's, and we can work this out when you are in a better state of mind." Sensing Maggie's hesitation, the priest added, "You have no other option."

And that was why Maggie allowed the parish priest to lead her to the backseat of an unfamiliar car on a frigid night in February, and her parents didn't do a thing to stop it.

Chapter 39

Maggie — 1945

It took a little over an hour to get to the Edwardian-style mansion, which stood set back on a quiet street in Dorchester, and Maggie spent the entire ride wringing her hands and trying to find a way out of her situation. She hadn't come up with anything. When they arrived, Father Murray took her suitcase out of the trunk of the car and greeted the nun who opened the door, before turning around and getting back into his car without a word of farewell.

"Hello, Sister," Maggie greeted the ancient figure at the door, more out of a lifetime of training than any desire to be polite. She assumed that the creature was a nun, based on her outfit, but the face beneath the severe black habit was nothing but a mass of wrinkles and liver spots, interspersed with more than a few chin hairs.

"Follow me," the woman croaked, turning and gliding

through the front hall of the building with nary a footfall to suggest that there were actual legs hiding underneath her habit. Maggie turned to look back the way she had come, but there wasn't even a trace of Father Murray's taillights visible in the darkness. She had no choice but to lift her suitcase off the steps and follow this strange little nun into the house.

St. Gerard's Home for Unwed Mothers looked like it belonged to someone's rich maiden aunt, and it smelled like boiled cabbage and bleach. After the decorative furnishings and the smell, the next thing Maggie noticed was the absence of any actual unwed mothers. The only living creature she could see was the nun she was following, which gave her an eerie feeling that she was the only one here, and that St. Gerard's had been built specifically for the purpose of shaming and jailing her. The house lay still and silent, daring her to reach out and disturb a silk fern or one of the figures of the Virgin Mary that were everywhere.

Ironic, Maggie thought, considering.

"Wait here," her guide commanded, indicating a single wooden chair against the cream damask wallpaper before disappearing behind a closed door. Maggie did as she was told, disgusted at her own compliance but too scared to rebel. She waited maybe ten minutes, fidgeting on the chair to ease the strain in her shoulders, and trying to make a game out of *not* yawning. What time was it? Ten? Eleven? It was late, she knew that, and she felt as if she'd been awake for days. Could she just leave, she wondered? Make a run for the door and hail a taxi from the street? But where would it bring her except back home to parents who had sent her away like a bundle of old newspapers?

"Sister Jane Regina will see you now," the craggy little

nun said, reappearing as if from nowhere and giving Maggie enough of a fright to set her heart racing and her hands shaking — or perhaps that was hunger. She hadn't eaten since lunch, and that had just been a ham sandwich.

Maggie stood and squared her shoulders before stepping through the door to what must have been some sort of an office. Behind a massive mahogany desk and underneath an ornate and gruesome-looking crucifix stood another impossibly tiny nun in a full black habit.

"Sit."

Maggie sat. Twelve years of Catholic schooling had taught Maggie that when a nun gave a command, it was best to obey. The nun, presumably Sister Jane Regina, sat behind the desk and shuffled through the papers in front of her.

"It says here that you are nineteen years old and from St. Mary's parish in Taunton, is that correct?"

Maggie nodded.

"How far along are you?"

"I'm not sure," Maggie replied honestly. "Three months, I think."

Sister pursed her lips and gave a curt nod before writing something down in Maggie's file, putting the papers in a neat stack, and placing the cap back onto her pen with a definitive *click*.

"Right, then." She stood, and Maggie instinctively rose to hear feet as well. "I will show you to your room. It is past bedtime, and you will not disturb the other residents. Mass will be held in the chapel at seven am sharp, followed by breakfast, and then I will meet with you again to go over your assigned duties while you are here." She walked around the desk and directed a pointed look at Maggie's midsection, adding, "We'll need to get you in to see the doctor at some point to confirm your dates."

Maggie nodded, understanding that no verbal response was required of her, nor would one be appreciated. As she turned to follow Sister out of the room, the older woman paused, and without turning around or making eye contact, said, "While you are here, your name will be Ethel. You will answer to Ethel, and you will not reveal your true name to anyone. Is that understood?"

"Yes, Sister," Maggie murmured, a hand to her heart. In one day, she had lost her future, her autonomy, her family, and now even her name.

* * *

"Well, well, well, looks like Santa Claus left us a little present, girls. We've got a fresh one."

Maggie opened her eyes to see a freckle-faced young woman with wispy strawberry-blonde hair standing over her and peering down into her face. She started, making the other girl laugh.

"Leave her alone, Mairead. The poor thing got in late last night." Freckles, whose moniker must have been Mairead, smiled at the admonishment but otherwise completely ignored it.

"What's your name?" she asked, landing on Maggie's bed with a *thwomp* and causing Maggie to sit up in a hurry. "Your real name, that is, as well as whatever it is the nuns told you to use."

Maggie shook her head to clear out the cobwebs with little to no success before replying, "Maggie — and Ethel. My real

229

name is Maggie, but I'm supposed to go by Ethel."

"Delighted to meet you, Maggie slash Ethel. I'm Mairead, but you can call me Mary anywhere the nuns can hear you. This little lady over here is Tricia; you can call her Pattie." Maggie followed Mairead's gaze to the bed in the corner of the room, which was occupied by a young girl with an enormous belly who couldn't have been more than twelve or thirteen.

"Hullo," the girl offered, and Maggie responded with a shy wave.

"And this over here is Grace. We don't know her real name, because she doesn't speak, but she makes herself understood just fine, don't you, Grace?" Grace, a tall, broad-shouldered, round-bellied woman in her thirties, stared at Maggie with wide, unblinking brown eyes before offering her a small smile. Maggie smiled back.

"So, what's your story?" Mairead asked Maggie.

"Give her a minute to get her bearings," Tricia advised, slipping out of her bed and stretching her back under her enormous belly. "We need to get to Mass anyway, or the Sisters will have our heads."

"We're already sinners and whores in their eyes," Mairead scoffed. "Tardiness can't make it too much worse. So, tell me." She turned back to Maggie. "Where are you from and what happened that got you sent here?"

Maggie raised one eyebrow, and Mairead burst into gales of hoarse laughter. "Right. That's how I got myself sent here too." She rubbed her bump lovingly. "My fella's in the Navy and I wanted to give him a little present before he shipped out. Looks like I'm the one who ended up with a surprise."

"I'm desperate for the restroom, and I don't want to be late for Mass," Tricia said, brushing past the bed with a towel and a toothbrush in her arms. "You'd do well to get dressed yourselves, or all of us will end up on dish duty."

Mairead made a gagging face. "The food is edible, but just barely." She bounced off Maggie's bed and over to her own, giving Maggie the chance to take in the room. It was sparsely furnished — wooden floors and white walls, four twin-sized beds with metal frames, and four small dressers, one next to each bed. The only adornments in the room were four simple wooden crucifixes, one hung over each bed. It wasn't fancy, but it was serviceable, and Maggie found herself wondering what Leo's accommodations in the camp looked like. She had never thought to ask him.

Maggie's heart clutched painfully in her chest at the thought of Leo, and what he would think when he went to the laundry to find her this morning only to discover that she was gone without a trace. He'd be so worried for her. And that's if her mother hadn't followed through on her threat to have him arrested...

"Mairead," she asked, "Are we allowed to send letters home?"

"Of course," the other girl replied. "We're not in prison." Mairead took her nightgown off over her head without an ounce of self-consciousness, revealing her rounded belly and swollen breasts. Maggie found herself staring — was that what she was going to look like in a few months' time?

"Don't mind me, doll," Mairead said as she reached behind her back to fasten her bra. "There's no need for modesty. We're all in the same boat, and the line for the ladies' room is a joke in the morning. Do you need help with that, Grace?" Grace was struggling to button up the back of her maternity smock — a hideous olive-green number with a ridiculous white bow in the front.

"Oh, let me help you," Maggie said, rushing over to help. Grace gave her another shy smile in response, and somehow Maggie knew she had found a kindred spirit. Mairead was right; Grace didn't speak, but she was able to get her message across.

Tricia, now dressed, let herself back into the room with the air of a tiny drill sergeant. "You'd better get some clothes on, Ethel, or you'll end up on the wrong side of the Sisters, and trust me when I tell you that is not where you want to be."

Mairead winked at Maggie, who hurried to open her suitcase and pull out a suitable dress that still fit her. She hastily ran a brush through her hair, put on her shoes and stockings, and within minutes she was out of the room and heading down the stairs to Mass with Mairead, Tricia, and Grace.

The despair she felt without Leo was crushing, but at least now she knew she could write him a letter, and she vowed to do so as soon as she could get her hands on a pen and some paper. The other girls were a comfort as well.

As Mairead said, at least they were all in the same boat.

Chapter 40

Maggie — 1945

By the end of her first week at St. Gerard's, Maggie's hands were blistered and bleeding. Ironically, she had been assigned to the laundry room as her "duty," but the laundry room at St. Gerard's was very different from the military laundry at Camp Myles Standish. There were only three washers, all of which had manual wringers, and part of Maggie's job was to plunge her hands into the hot water to retrieve linens and then manually crank the wringer to get the water out of them. There were no tumble dryers, so Maggie then had to bring the large baskets of still wet clothes, towels, and sheets outside in the icy March air to hang them on the line. The constant movement from hot to cold, from wet to dry, left her fingers so badly cracked that it was painful for her to hold a fork or a pen.

And yet every night Maggie would take the pen in her raw hands and write to Leo. The mail was only picked up once per week, and so she made sure that every Friday she had seven letters to put into an envelope to deliver seven days' worth of news to Leo. She was certain by then that her mother's threat to have him arrested was an empty one. However much her family might disagree with the morality of Maggie's relationship with Leo, she was a consenting adult. They'd broken no laws. Still, she knew Leo couldn't visit her — the military was permissive with the ISU men, but giving one a pass and transportation all the way to Boston to see his pregnant American girlfriend was so out of the realm of possibility that Maggie didn't even ask.

Instead her letters were filled with the ins and outs of her daily life at St. Gerard's. She wrote to Leo about Mairead, and about Tricia, who Maggie learned was there because she had been assaulted by her stepfather. Tricia said that she was looking forward to giving her baby to a good Catholic family and putting all this behind her, and then she hoped to one day become a nun herself, the kind that taught in schools. Maggie struggled to see how being forced to have a baby and give it up at such a young age could ever be put behind her, and she told Leo so, but she prayed that Tricia would have a good future.

Sometimes Maggie and Mairead would write to their sweethearts together. Mairead didn't know where her boyfriend Jeffrey was, just that he was on a ship somewhere in the South Pacific, but she indulged herself in vivid fantasies about the day that Jeffrey would come home and take her away from St. Gerard's. They'd have a little house somewhere on Cape Cod, she said, and they'd have their baby, and perhaps a dog. Maggie prayed for Mairead as well, hoping that the war would end soon, Jeffrey would come home, and her beautiful fairy-tale life would become a reality.

Grace, due in large part to her inability to speak, was a bit of a mystery. *She's older than any of the other girls here,* Maggie wrote one night after nighttime Rosary and before lights out. *She never alludes to a husband or a boyfriend; she has no photographs and no one comes to visit her.* Maggie wanted to believe that Grace had a safe and loving home she could go back to when this was all over, but she knew deep down that this probably wouldn't be the case.

Maggie poured every thought and hope for the future she had into those letters to Leo, and she ended each one with, "I'm longing for the day when the three of us will be together again. I love you, and I remain yours, faithfully, Maggie."

She mailed the letters without fail every Friday, and she met the mailman at the door as he delivered letters and packages from the outside world.

But there was never any reply from Corporal Leonardo Castiglione, ISU.

* * *

One afternoon at the end of May, Maggie and Mairead were folding towels in the laundry room when another girl told them that Tricia had been taken "through the tunnel" to have her baby.

The tunnel connected St. Gerard's to Boston Bethlehem Hospital, where the unwed mothers from the home were taken to deliver their babies. No one really knew what happened to the women who went "through the tunnel" — they just knew that the girls left the home pregnant, and that they rarely, if ever, returned.

"Poor kid," Mairead said, referring to Tricia. "Her home life really is the worst. Her dad ran out on the family, and her mother married this shit head who started in on Tricia when she was only eight."

Maggie's skin crawled with revulsion. Tricia may have had the eyes of a woman three times her age, but she was still a child, and Maggie's heart broke for her.

"I hope she can move on and build a life for herself," Maggie said. "Have you ever seen any of the girls, you know, after?"

Mairead paused, the towel she was folding hanging down in front of her. "Once or twice," she said, her eyes far away. "From what I hear, those are the sad cases, where the baby doesn't make it, or the girl goes a little crazy after."

"Crazy?"

"Well, not everyone is as lucky as you and me. Our babies' fathers are good men who just can't marry us right now because they're off saving the world." Mairead shrugged, and Maggie felt a stab of guilt through her belly. She had told the girls that Leo was a soldier, and when they of course believed him to be an American soldier fighting on the other side of the world, she just didn't correct them. After all, who would that help?

"There was one girl here until about a week before you came," Mairead continued. "We called her Sarah, but her real name was Sadie. She insisted till the end that her boyfriend was coming to claim her and the baby, but he never came. And do you know why?"

A horrifying realization washed over Maggie. It couldn't possibly be the same Sadie she knew...

"Because her baby's father was a *prisoner of war* — one of those Italians they captured and brought over here. Can you believe it?" When Maggie didn't say anything, Mairead continued. "She went a little crazy after that. They took the baby but brought her back here for a few days because she was in no fit state to go home. Screamed the roof down for two nights so that none of us got any sleep."

Jesus, Mary, and Joseph — it was Sadie; Guillermo's Sadie. Had Father Murray dropped her on the doorstep of St. Gerard's like a bundle of soiled linens, just like he had done to her? Maggie's vision went blurry and she had to grab hold of the wall to keep herself from falling down. Thank goodness Mairead was facing the other way and didn't notice. "This Sadie—" Maggie took a slow breath and willed her voice not to shake. "What happened to her?"

Again, Mairead shrugged. "Who knows? I feel terrible for what she had to go through. She was so sure that Italian boyfriend of hers was going to come riding in here like a white knight and save her. I'm just glad that I know Jeffrey is a good man, and that he'll come for me and the baby."

Maggie had to close her eyes and will the bile that rose in her throat back down to her stomach. Guillermo hadn't come because Guillermo had no idea what had happened to Sadie. Surely if he knew she was here and that she was having his baby, the entire United States Armed Forces couldn't have kept him from getting to her. A horrifying thought came into Maggie's head. "Did she write to him?"

"She sure did." Mairead put the now neatly folded towel on top of the stack and moved on to a set of sheets. "Just about every day, but he never responded. I guess he didn't love her after all."

He did, Maggie wanted to scream. *He loved her and he still does; he just didn't know!* The whole revelation left Maggie feeling like she had gone four rounds with Joe Lewis. The next realization, however, had her slumping against the wall and falling to the floor, just missing hitting her head on a metal washtub by mere inches.

"Maggie," Mairead cried, dropped her sheet and running over to help her friend. "Help!" she cried. "Ethel's fainted. Someone please help!"

But Maggie hadn't actually fainted — although a loss of consciousness would have been a welcome relief. She had simply realized the similarity between Sadie's situation and her own. Sadie had written to Guillermo every day, and he had never gotten her letters.

Leo had no idea where Maggie was.

Chapter 41

Niamh — 2016

Roughly eighteen hours after getting Leo's phone call, Niamh was getting out of a taxi cab in Brooklyn, her suitcase in her hand and her heart on her sleeve. She took in the stately brownstone before her, and double checked the address against the one in her phone for at least the fourth time before marching up the stairs to the front door and depositing a firm knock.

"Niamh!" The door swung open to reveal a young brunette woman of about thirty-five who immediately introduced herself as Isabella, the cousin who had provided the missing piece. She was warm and inviting, and she enveloped Niamh in a hug that spoke of a lifetime of connection, rather than just a few emails and some genetic markers. What struck Niamh the most, however, was the fact that Bella's eyes were exactly the same shade of emerald green as her own.

"I see the resemblance," Bella smiled when she noticed Niamh studying her face like a textbook. "And you've got Nonno's dark hair, or at least I think that's what his hair used to look like when he was younger."

Nonno, Niamh thought. Italian for grandfather. Her grandfather.

"Is he here?" she asked, trying desperately to sound like meeting her immediate family for the first time was an everyday occurrence.

"He's in the kitchen with the gravy." Bella waved behind her. "We try to keep him from wearing himself out, but he was up at the crack of dawn this morning. He insisted that he needed to make a pot of gravy for your arrival." Bella stepped back, inviting Niamh into the comfortably furnished front room and whispering conspiratorially, "He does make the most delicious gravy I've ever tasted — spoiled the jarred stuff for me forever."

"Is that her? Is she here?"

Before Niamh had the opportunity to ask about the gravy, jarred or otherwise, a voice boomed from further inside the house and within seconds, Niamh's nonno strode into the room with the vigor of a man half his age.

He was tall, well over six feet, and although he was quite slim, he stood with the confidence of a man who was used to filling the room with his presence. When his eyes lit on Niamh standing in the entrance way with her coat and her suitcase, a smile of pure joy broke over his lined face. He held out an arm, and before Niamh could move towards him, he had crossed the room to her, wrapping her up in a hug that smelled of Old Spice and the wool of his green sweater vest. This was it, Niamh thought as she closed her eyes and breathed him in. This was the feeling of recognition, of family, that she had been longing for. Hugging Leo felt like coming home, and when she finally stepped back to look up at him, she was surprised to see tears streaming from his bright green eyes as well.

"Niamh, *mi bambolina*, I never thought this day would come." He took a shuddering breath, and suddenly Bella was by his side, easing him back and into the brown leather recliner that dominated the room. "This one," he said, waving Bella off, "she wants to treat me like I'm an old man."

"Nonno, you're ninety-four years old," Bella reminded him with an eye roll that told Niamh this was an oft-practiced conversation.

"And I'm still a handsome devil," he said to Niamh with a wink, making her laugh and feel right at home in this place with people she had only just met.

Now that Leo was seated, Niamh edged over to the brown leather sofa, a match to his reclining chair, and settled herself on the edge of it to look around the room. It was small and homey, decorated in tones of cream and brown around a central fireplace that now housed a more practical pellet stove. Off the living room, Niamh could see a formal dining room which led to a kitchen in the back. From there, she could smell something delicious, which must have been the gravy Bella mentioned earlier.

"And where is your lovely wife?" Leo asked, leaning forward in his chair to study Niamh's features. It was then that she noticed he was missing his left arm. The sleeve of his plaid shirt was pinned neatly to the shoulder. He reached out with his right hand to squeeze her arm, and Niamh's heart swelled at the gesture.

"She's sorry, but she couldn't make it. She was due in court this morning and there was no way of getting it postponed. And," Niamh admitted with a shy smile, "I couldn't wait another few days for her to be able to come with me."

"I look forward to meeting her soon," Leo squeezed Niamh's fingers in his own, "but I am delighted you are here today."

"Can you tell me," Niamh edged forward in her seat, unable to wait a moment longer, "anything about you, about my grandmother? My mother wasn't close with her family, but I know she was adopted." Niamh reached into her purse, from which she retrieved a carefully folded document printed on crisp, yellowed paper. "This is her birth certificate. I found it with her things when she..." Niamh trailed off, unsure how to finish the sentence.

Leo took the paper, studying it for a moment before placing it gently on the table in front of him. "Bella tells me that your mother died when you were twelve? In a car accident?" Leo's voice was thick with emotion, and it hit Niamh suddenly that her mother was this man's daughter. She knew that, obviously, but she hadn't really processed the reality of it until now. Leo was trying to remain strong for her, but he was still asking her to tell him how his daughter died.

"You named her Guliana?" Niamh asked, shifting in her seat a bit so that they faced one another sharing what was, for both of them, life's greatest tragedy.

"Her mother and I, we decided to call her Guliana if she was a girl, after my nonna back in Italy."

Niamh watched as Leo drew in a deep breath through his nose, visibly grasping to keep hold of his emotions. "I am sorry, Niamh; I never had the chance to hold your mother. I never met her — and then she was gone."

"She was wonderful," Niamh told him. "Really, the most

amazing mother I could ever ask for. I never knew my father, but I didn't need to. My mother and I were a team. She was a librarian, and she'd bring me to work with her and let me sit under the desk and read to my heart's content." Niamh smiled at the memory of being small, curled up by her mother's high-heeled feet with a copy of *Little House on the Prairie*. "We never had much, but I really didn't notice that until much later."

"And the accident?" Leo asked.

"Drunk driver and icy roads. I don't remember much of it — just waking up after in the hospital, and then they told me—" Niamh didn't realize that the tears were spilling down her cheeks until she felt her grandfather's warm fingers brushing them away. It was his pain too. "Why didn't you ever hold my mother? You knew about her?"

Leo's eyes hardened, and Niamh could see the regret that had lived within him for seventy years.

"Her mother — your grandmother— her name was Maggie O'Callaghan, but I always called her my *Margherita* — she came to me and told me about the baby. She was scared, of course, but I had never felt such joy. I said right then that I was going to find us a priest, and that I would make her my wife. That's what I had always intended to do after the war, you see," he smiled at Niamh, his gaze far away, "but the baby sped things up a bit." He sighed and closed his eyes, still clinging to Niamh's hands. "Father Antonio Liotti agreed to marry us, under the circumstances, and the next day he stopped by her house to give her the news, but she was gone. No one had seen her or heard from her, and her family refused to open the door and explain what happened. I left the camp and tried myself, but her father threatened to have me arrested, and—" he broke off, overcome. Niamh rubbed her thumb over the spotted back of his hand before finally asking, "The camp?"

Leo took a starched white handkerchief from his pants pocket and blew his nose before replying. "Yes, Camp Myles Standish — the US Armed Forces embarkation camp. You see, Niamh, your grandmother was an American citizen, but I was a prisoner of war."

* * *

Niamh was desperate to know the rest of the story, but she could see that Leo was tiring. Bella bustled in from the kitchen, wooden spoon in hand, to announce that lunch was ready. Ignoring Leo's protestations that he was perfectly capable and not an invalid, Niamh let him use her arm for balance as he got up from the chair.

"This is lunch?" Niamh gasped upon seeing the spread that was laid out on the dining room table. "It looks more like Christmas dinner for twelve!"

"Clearly she's never seen an Italian feast, eh, Nonno?" Bella laughed. "Would you like some *vino*, Niamh?" Niamh nodded, and after helping Leo to his seat at the head of the table, she sat beside him and watched as Bella poured wine into all of their glasses.

"*Salud*," Leo declared, raising his glass into the air in a toast. "To Niamh, who has come home at last."

Niamh blushed happily, wondering if it were possible to feel more content than she already did, and twirled some pasta on her fork before bringing it to her lips. The explosion of taste was instant, as soon as the fork hit her tongue. She closed her eyes, savoring the intense flavors of tomato, basil, and garlic, and was almost sad when she finally swallowed the bite.

She opened her eyes, fork poised to take another, when she noticed Bella and Leo watching her with identical grins spread across their faces.

"What?" she asked, twirling another bite's worth of pasta on her fork.

"Do you like my gravy?" Leo asked, looking like nothing so much as a little boy asking Santa for his favorite toy.

Niamh looked around the table in confusion. "Gravy?"

"On your pasta," Bella hissed. "The sauce."

"Oh, the spaghetti sauce? It's delicious," Niamh declared, proving her point by shoving another forkful of the delicious concoction into her mouth. Leo, meanwhile, clasped his hand over his heart and closed his eyes in a dramatic show of emotion.

"You wound me, Niamh. Right here." He thumped his chest again for emphasis. "That is not *spaghetti sauce*. That, my American granddaughter, is homemade gravy. Do you see what not having me in her life has done to her, Bella?" He turned his dramatic expression on his other granddaughter, who rolled her eyes.

"Don't get him started, Niamh. I can't deal with him."

Niamh laughed, and Leo winked at her from his seat at the head of the table. For as long as she could remember, she had dreamed of finding her family, but even then, she'd scarcely dared to dream that said family would make her feel so at ease, or that it would include a chuckling, teasing nonno and the spicy sweet tang of homemade spaghetti sauce. Homemade *gravy*, she corrected herself.

"Can you tell me more about my grandmother?" she asked in between bites. "I'd love to hear about her — if you're up to it, that is. And you were a POW?"

"Not a day goes by when I don't think about my Maggie," Leo said, reaching across the table to pat Niamh's arm. The skin on his hand was papery-thin, but warm, and Niamh got the sense that Leo Castiglione wasn't a man who was amenable to fading gently into old age. He sat back in his chair, eyes far away as he looked into the past, his lips curled into a teasing smile. Her nonno must have been a looker in his day, Niamh thought. My grandmother Maggie was a lucky lady.

"I came to America in 1943, Niamh, on a Navy ship from North Africa with hundreds of other Italian boys on board." Leo leaned back in his chair, settling into the story. "We were told that we'd be held in camps in the States until the end of the war, but we had no idea what the conditions would be like. I was barely more than a boy, and I'd never have admitted it then, but I was so scared." He looked to Niamh, a sheepish grin breaking across his craggy features. "I missed my mama."

"Of course you did." Niamh's heart broke for this man she'd known for less than an afternoon. "Was that after your..." She trailed off, unsure of the polite way to ask her grandfather how he'd lost his arm.

"After," he said matter-of-factly, twirling some spaghetti onto his fork and lifting it to his mouth. "I lost the arm in North Africa. Damn near lost my life too, while I was at it." He washed down the bite with a swallow of milk. "Good thing I didn't, *bellisimas*, or neither of you would be here now." Niamh caught Bella's eye across the table, and the other woman shrugged as if to say, *this grandfather of ours is a trip, isn't he?* He certainly was, and Niamh warred with herself between wanting to ask the old man every single detail of his life, especially the ones having to do with her grandmother, and not wanting to tire him out. She chose the former.

"Was it my grandmother who saved you when you were wounded?" She took a sip of wine, savoring the explosion of flavors on her tongue.

"In a way," Leo replied. "The medics in Casablanca saved me from infection, but Maggie made me want to live again. She made me whole." His eyes were miles, or decades, away. "I was young, in a strange country, a prisoner of men I had been told were my enemy. Maggie was the first good thing that came into my life in a long time. Well," he shrugged, "Maggie and the food."

Niamh gave a startled laugh, choked on a sip of wine and coughed into her napkin. When she had regained her composure, she asked, "The food?"

"The food, Niamh! I had never seen food like I saw when I first came to America." Leo held his good arm out wide, indicating the sheer amount that he had seen. "For breakfast every day we had cornflakes, bacon, toast, milk, coffee, orange juice — I'd never seen so much food in my life. And we were the prisoners. What were the Americans eating?"

"You'll find that Nonno's mind is almost always on his stomach," Bella said with a wry smile for her new cousin. "Can I take your plate?" Niamh nodded, and Bella began to clear the table.

"*Gracie*, Bella." Leo gave the young woman an affectionate nod before continuing. "Often my stomach, yes, but always my heart first, girls. Always my heart. The food helped, but as soon as I laid eyes on my *Margherita*, I was a goner."

"Was she very beautiful?"

"She had skin the color of milk, and long dark hair — almost black. And her eyes... her eyes were blue fire, Niamh. You look a bit like her yourself — shorter, perhaps, but I can see her in you."

Niamh's cheeks flushed with pleasure at the idea that she bore a resemblance to this mysterious grandmother she'd never met. She rolled the stem of her wineglass between her fingers, trying to picture Leo in his early twenties, walking hand in hand with a woman who looked like her. "And you were in love with her?"

"Besotted." He turned to face Niamh directly, a sad smile on his face. "I wanted to marry her long before we knew about the baby. I wanted to build a life with her, but her family... and that goddamn priest..." Leo trailed off, a tick in his jaw alerting Niamh to the fact that seven decades of water under the bridge had done little to cool his fury over losing her grandmother.

"They wouldn't tell you anything? And she never came home?" Niamh asked, striving to make her voice as low and gentle as she could so as to not upset the old man more than necessary. Leo shook his head.

"Father Liotti was able to learn from one of his fellow priests that she was taken to a maternity home, but no one would tell me where. I wrote to her — so many letters — but I didn't know where to send them. Then the next summer we — that is, all the Italian boys from the camp — we were shipped back to Italy. I didn't want to go. I needed to stay and find my Maggie and our baby, but what is one man against the United States government?"

The desperation in Leo's voice pulled at Niamh's heart, and she scooted her chair closer to his so that she could rest her hands on his knees. She didn't have any words that would ease the burden he'd been carrying since 1945, but perhaps her presence could offer comfort.

"I went back to Italy," Leo continued. "Back to my family's

farm, and I tried to get used to an idea of a life without *Margherita*. I assumed that her family had forced her to give up the baby, but I didn't even know if both of them had survived the birth. My family was overjoyed to have me home, but I wasn't the same. I may as well have died in that blasted camp. It was my nonna Guiliana who finally gave me the talking to I needed."

"What did she say to you?" Niamh asked, keeping her voice low and quiet, almost as if Leo were a wounded animal that she wanted to avoid startling.

"She told me to get a visa, and to get my sorry ass back to the States to find your grandmother," he said with a sad smile. "But I couldn't find her. I came back to Boston in the spring of '47 — Guiliana would have been two years old at the time. I returned to Taunton, thinking perhaps now that time had passed, her family would speak to me, but they were gone as well — moved to God knows where." Leo was making a herculean effort to keep his emotions in check, but Niamh could tell by the set of his jaw and his rapid blinking that his heart was still broken after all this time. She wanted to comfort this man who already felt like family after just a few short hours, but she wasn't sure where to begin.

"I had a good life, *bellisima*." Leo shook his head as if to clear the bad memories. "A few years later, I met Isabella's grandmother, Emilia. We were happy for a time, and she gave me three wonderful boys before we split."

"You're divorced?"

He nodded, eyes filled with regret. "We stayed together for the boys, but as soon as they were grown, we could not pretend anymore. I think she knew that I never got over my *Margherita*, and it wasn't fair to her."

"When was the last time you looked for her? Maggie, that is?"

"She was gone without a trace, and once I married Emilia, I tried to put that part of my life behind me. I couldn't live in the past anymore."

Niamh nodded, every muscle in her body screaming to reach out and hug this precious man who had gone for decades without knowing what became of his child and the love of his life. She could see how much the loss had cost him, and therefore she offered the only thing she could think of that could possibly help.

"Would you like to work with me to try and find her?"

Chapter 42

Maggie — 1945

It had been four long months, and Maggie still hadn't found a way to get a message to Leo that she was alright, and that she was being kept at St. Gerard's. Her letters to her parents, of course, went unanswered, and the only telephone in the home was located in Sister Jane Regina's office. There was no way she would be able to get access to it. Finally, she decided to make what her father would call a Hail Mary Pass, and she appealed to Mairead, whose baby was due to be born any day.

"Mairead?" Maggie whispered one night after lights out. Tricia and Grace had long since had their babies, and so far, there hadn't been any more girls assigned to share the little room where they slept.

"Mmm?" came the answer through the darkness. As her due date grew closer and closer with no word from Jeffrey,

Mairead had retreated farther and farther into herself, until Maggie had trouble recognizing her as the happy-go-lucky girl who had greeted her that first morning back in March.

"I need you to do me a favor. I think the nuns are taking my mail."

"What?" Mairead's shadowy figure struggled to sit up bed — no easy feat considering the massive bump at her middle. "Why do you think that?"

"Can you promise that you're not going to get angry with me?" Maggie asked, crossing her fingers and praying that this friend, unlike Betty, wouldn't betray her confidence.

"I'll do my best," came Mairead's reply. "What is going on, doll?"

Maggie took a deep breath and let the whole story come pouring out of her — Leo, his status as a co-belligerent in the ISU, Sadie and Guillermo, her parents, Charlie, Betty, and then finally, her letters that weren't being answered and, Maggie assumed, were never even being sent. When she finally finished, there was only silence from Mairead's side of the room, until finally the other girl let out a low, long whistle.

"I didn't know you had all that in you, Maggie, my girl."

Maggie let out a heavy breath at Mairead's tone, which was surprised, but not at all angry. "When you go through the tunnel, can I give you a letter to mail to Leo after you go home? Please? It's my last chance to get word to him—" Her voice broke, and the next thing she knew, Mairead was hauling herself out of bed and coming over to sit next to her.

"Of course, I will, doll, you know that." Mairead wrapped an arm around Maggie's shoulder, playing with the ends of Maggie's long hair in the dark. "We've both certainly got ourselves into a pickle, haven't we?"

Maggie had no choice but to laugh at that, choking on tears as she sat on the edge of her bed on the second floor of St. Gerard's Home for Unwed Mothers in Dorchester, Massachusetts, next to what seemed to be her only friend in the world, both of them with no choice but to keep moving forward and see what the next few days, weeks, and months would bring for them, and for their babies.

* * *

June 23, 1945

My dearest Leo,

This is at least the one hundredth letter I have written to you since we last saw one another in February. I have reason to believe, however, that none of my letters have reached you, and that is why I'm praying with every fiber of my being that this latest attempt gets into your hands.

My parents had me sent away to a mother and baby home, St. Gerard's, in Dorchester, Massachusetts, to wait out the remainder of my pregnancy. I told them that we were to be married, but they threatened to have you arrested and brought up on charges, and since I couldn't let that happen, I agreed to come here for the present. Now that Germany has surrendered, I pray every day that you will be released, and that you can come and take me home. We can get married like we talked about before the baby is born in August, and we will be a family.

I can't imagine what you have gone through these last few months, not knowing what happened to me, but I can assure you that I am here, I am well, and I remain as in love with you today as I was the first time I saw you. I am entrusting this letter to a friend, who will see that it is sent directly to you at Camp Myles Standish. Please come soon, my love, so that we can be married before our daughter or son comes into the world. I remain,

Yours faithfully, Maggie

* * *

Mairead's waters broke on the afternoon of June 30, and when she was transported through the tunnel, she had Maggie's letter to Leo tucked safely in her bag and ready to be mailed.

"He's not here, Maggie," Mairead whispered as she waited for the orderlies to come and retrieve her. "Jeffrey isn't here. What am I going to do?"

Maggie squeezed her friend's hand tight, and wished that there was a way she could go with Mairead to support her through what must surely be a terrifying time. "You're going to have this baby, doll," she reassured Mairead with sentiments she didn't believe. "You're going to bring this beautiful little person into the world so that they will be ready to meet their daddy when he comes home."

Mairead nodded as an orderly from the hospital came into the parlor pushing a wheelchair. "We'll see each other again, won't we, Maggie?" she asked, clutching onto Maggie's hand like it was a lifeline.

"Of course we will," Maggie replied, patting her hand. "We'll look each other up once this is all behind us, and we'll meet at the park with the babies." Mairead responded with a shaky smile as the orderly helped her into the wheelchair and began pushing her towards the door without a word for either of the two women.

"Wait — Mairead," Maggie called, but the orderly just kept

walking. "You never told me your last name!"

"It's Sullivan," Mairead called back, already through the door and on her way to the tunnel.

"O'Callaghan!" Maggie yelled after her, hoping that Mairead could still hear her. "Maggie O'Callaghan from Taunton!" Her shoulders slumped when there was no reply, defeat washing over her in an exhausting wave.

"Harrumph," came a sigh of displeasure from the staircase, and Maggie turned to see one of the more dour of the St. Gerard's nuns poised on the landing. "That wasn't wise, Ethel," she admonished, but Maggie had had enough of the nuns telling her what to do and who to speak with. Now that Mairead was gone, she was really and truly alone.

Chapter 43

Maggie — 1945

Maggie's labor began in the early morning of what must have been one of the hottest days on record in New England. She'd been having contractions for weeks, the low, dull throbbing in her pelvis that warned her of what was to come, but none of them lasted long or came with any regularity. This morning, however, was different.

Maggie slept in just her thin cotton nightshirt, having folded the blankets down at the foot of her bed back in June and not touched them since. The baby kept her temperature burning like a furnace, and that combined with the August heat and humidity was enough to make Maggie feel like a human sacrifice roasting over a spit. The contractions began in the middle of the night, and by the time the sun rose that morning, they were coming steadily and growing stronger with each pass. Maggie knew she should alert someone to her situation, but fear of what would happen when she was brought through the tunnel left her paralyzed and unable to do more than lie in bed, laboring.

It was past eight o'clock by the time Maggie was missed and Sister Evangela came in to find Maggie drenched in sweat and breathing like a mare in foal, nostrils flaring with every exhalation of air.

"Saints preserve us, child, why didn't you call for help?" Sister clucked, whipping Maggie's soiled nightdress over her head and replacing it with a fresh one.

"Have I — gotten—" she paused to get her bearings, "—any mail today?"

"You have not, and I'm astounded you can ask after the mail at a moment like this. Will you be all right for a moment if I run downstairs to call over to the hospital?"

Maggie nodded and focused all her attention on breathing through the pain of the current contraction. She knew that having a baby was a painful process, but she had never imagined it would be like this. She felt as if her bones were being torn apart from the inside, as if a locomotive was being driven through her pelvis. This couldn't be normal.

"Please," she begged Sister Evangela when she came back into the room to report that the orderly would be over soon to take Maggie through the tunnel, "Leo. Please can you telephone Leo and tell him that his baby is on its way?"

"They always ask for someone," Sister Jane Regina said to Sister Evangela from the doorway. "I pity the ones who call for the men who got them into this sinful state in the first place. They never learn."

Maggie wanted to reply, wanted to scream in the Sisters' faces that Leo wasn't like all those other men they heard of, and that as soon as she went home with the baby, they would get married and build a life together, but another pain overtook her and it was all she could do to remain conscious, breathing through the agony that she had always been told was punishment for Eve's sin.

* * *

Giving birth at the Boston Bethlehem Hospital was easily the most horrific, traumatic, and transcendent moment of Maggie's entire life.

As soon as the orderly brought her up to the Labor and Delivery floor, Maggie was certain that the baby must be nearly here, and that her pain was sure to end soon. The orderly wheeled her into a standard hospital room — white walls, white linens, and bright white lights — and helped her move, groaning in agony, onto the bed. He then turned and left the room, leaving Maggie in the most excruciating pain she'd ever felt in her life, all alone.

The room was small — no more than ten feet by ten feet — and there was nothing for Maggie to focus her attention on to distract her from the torture her body was putting her through. She ground her teeth together and tried to pant and breathe through the gruesome process of being simultaneously ripped apart and torn inside out, with no one there to hold her hand or tell her how the hell to live through this inhuman torment. She was adrift in a sea of terror and pain.

After what might have been minutes, hours, or days, a young nurse with a starched uniform and ginger hair came into the room to check her vital signs. Maggie grabbed onto the young woman's arm and used her heels to dig into the mattress, trying in vain to lift herself up and away from the pain. She was beyond speech, but something about her must have touched the nurse, who looked at Maggie as if she wanted to cry for her.

"Let me find the doctor for you," the pretty redhead soothed, squeezing Maggie's hand. "I promise I'll be right back, and we'll see what we can do to ease your discomfort."

Discomfort? If Maggie had been able, she might have laughed at the idea that this bone-grinding scourge could be qualified as discomfort. But her love-starved emotions were so grateful for the nurse's compassion that she simply nodded in response and prepared for another wave of pain to crash over her.

All the doctor did was check between her legs in with a business-like authority, nod at the nurse, and mumble something about restraints.

Restraints? They couldn't mean...

...but they did. Almost before she knew what was happening, an older nurse with a black wimple and veil which marked her as a nun began tying Maggie's hands into the leather cuffs on the side of the bed. The leather cut into her skin, and Maggie fought them with the feeble strength she had left in her body, but it was no use. She was tied down, her legs bent up and placed in stirrups, and whatever tiny thread of control Maggie had managed to keep over her own body was wrenched away as the pain burned its way through both her body and her will.

"Push, girl," the older nun to her right commanded, as the nurse on her left simply held her hand and shared what strength she had. "Offer up the pain to the Lord and push."

If she was asked later to give an accurate account of the

moment of birth, Maggie wouldn't have been able to do it. Those last few minutes were a blur of effort and strength and pain, though the only sensation she could recall with any clarity was the feeling of tears streaming down her cheeks in rivulets that somehow both burned and cooled as they flowed.

And then she heard it — a thin wail — and she looked up in time to see the doctor hold up a red, shriveled, waxy, angry little monster who was the most exquisite creature Maggie had ever laid eyes on.

"Let me hold her," she begged, the words tearing at her dry throat. She was exhausted, and still not entirely sure she wasn't dying, but moved by a force that insisted she hold the baby *now*.

"How do you know it's a girl?" the redheaded nurse asked, and Maggie blinked up at her.

"I don't know," she replied, choosing her words deliberately. "I just knew it was her."

"It's not wise to hold the baby," the nun instructed her as Maggie reached out, needing to feel her daughter against her cheek. "It will just make it harder on the other end."

Rage tore through her at the implication that her child would be taken from her after this ordeal, and Maggie spoke with a force that had never before known.

"Give me my baby." Gone was the acquiescent girl who had spent a lifetime kowtowing to nuns in Catholic school, and in her place was a mother who would move heaven and earth for her child.

"She wants to hold her baby," the kind nurse said to the older one, "and surely God himself wouldn't stand in the way of that."

The old woman sniffed and muttered something about

atonement under her breath, but thankfully she left, and after the cord was cut and the baby had been checked over, she was wrapped in a hospital blanket and placed in Maggie's arms.

A calm like she had never before experienced washed over Maggie as she gazed down at the tiny little girl in her arms. Six pounds, four ounces, the nurse had said. How could such a small person wield that much power over her, Maggie wondered in awe. She counted ten perfect miniature fingers, each ending in a teeny tiny fingernail. The baby had a round face, with the tiniest little double chin, and a shock of dark curly hair, but it was her eyes that brought Maggie to a bout of fresh tears. The new arrival watched her mother with bright green eyes the color of emeralds — the color of her father's. She was so like Leo, and yet also entirely herself. "Oh, Guliana," Maggie whispered, kissing the little fingers that clung onto hers. "Your daddy is going to love you so much."

Chapter 44

Niamh — 2016

"How can one woman suddenly disappear into thin air?"

Niamh rested her forehead on the computer desk at the New York Public Library, the comforting hand of her grandfather patting her on the back. They'd been at the library when the doors opened that morning, ready to use every modern tool at their disposal to find Leo's lost love, but four hours later, the only thing they had learned was that Margaret Veronica O'Callaghan really did seem to have vanished.

"It's alright, little one," Leo soothed, rubbing circles of calm on Niamh's back. "You tried everything you could think of, and I'm so grateful." Niamh had started with the Forefathers.com database, then moved on to state and county birth and death records. Every single search had come up empty, as if the woman Leo loved, her mother's mother, had never existed at all.

"I'm sorry, Nonno." Niamh lifted her head and turned to face the man whose features were already coming to mean home and family to her. "I thought that with the internet, and all the databases in the library..." She trailed off.

"And while I'd have danced like a man half my age if you had found her, at least I know that her name was not in any of the death records."

Niamh nodded as Leo gave voice to the fear that had been curled in her belly all morning. What would she do if they unearthed a death certificate? How would she react? How would he? Would that cause the frail and scared pieces of the old man's heart to shatter anew?

"I have to believe that I will see her again soon, when I close my eyes for the final time." Leo tapped the end of Niamh's nose with the tip of a knobbed finger. "Now let me take you for lunch, Niamh. I could eat the table." But something he said gave Niamh pause.

"Do you really believe that, Nonno? That you will see her again when you die — heaven and hell and God and all that?"

Leo smiled, the lines on his face deepening, eyes shining. "I have to believe that, Niamh. If I didn't, what would be the point of dragging these old bones around anymore?"

* * *

"Raw fish? All the delicious food in this city, and you want raw fish? I will never understand your generation." Leo wrinkled his nose at the menu in front of him, looking for all the world like a toddler who had been told he was getting Brussels sprouts for dinner.

263

"Nonno, have you ever actually tried sushi?" Niamh laughed.

"Why would I try sushi? Didn't America fight the Japanese in World War II so that I would never have to eat my fish without it being cooked first?"

"I think it had more to do with Pearl Harbor, but you're the one who was alive back then, not me." Niamh leaned across the table, pointing out a section of the menu to her grandfather. "See, they have plenty of cooked options too. You could get a California roll, or an eel and avocado roll. I think there's even one with cooked lobster."

"That's my granddaughter," Leo said, a smile breaking over his face. "Lobster is one of my favorite dishes."

"It's settled then. You'll get a lobster roll, and I think you should try a California roll. It's just crab and cucumber with rice and seaweed. But," she raised an eyebrow at him over the menu, "I'm getting spicy tuna and I expect you to at least try a bite."

Leo burst out laughing, and Niamh's cheeks burned in self-conscious embarrassment.

"What's so funny?" she asked, grabbing her napkin off her lap while simultaneously checking her teeth with the tip of her tongue. Was there something there from breakfast? Had it been there all day?

"No, no, Niamh. You are fine," Leo chuckled. "But the look you gave me, telling me you expect me to try a bite of a new food — you looked just like my mama in that moment! The expression, the eyes, everything. It is as if she was speaking to me through you."

"Oh." Niamh placed the napkin back on her lap and smiled at her grandfather. "Is that a good thing? Do I look like your mother?"

"You look more like my Maggie," Leo said, his expression softening, "but you've got my mother's eyes. My eyes too, come to think of it. My mama was a wonderful woman, but she ran our house with an iron fist. In fact, up until I was shot, being in the army was easy compared to living with my mama."

"She sounds like a tough cookie."

"The toughest, but also the most loving. I still miss her, you know. Please, tell me if it is none of my business, Niamh, but do you plan to have any children?"

Niamh took a deep breath and blew it out her mouth. Her grandfather had no idea the can of worms that question opened up. Just then, the waiter appeared at their table, and Niamh gave a silent thanks for the brief reprieve and time to gather her thoughts. Once she'd placed their orders and taken a long sip of her beer, she began.

"That's a tough question, Nonno. Yes, I want to have children. I want to have children more than I want just about anything in this world, but it hasn't happened for us yet. Being queer, Christine and I can't really go about having kids in the traditional way." She broke off, realizing that she was wandering into a tough topic to discuss with her ninety-four-year-old grandfather. Leo, however, merely nodded.

"I'd imagine science can help with that," he offered.

"Well, yes. We've used donor sperm, and I want to be the one to carry the baby, but so far, I haven't had any luck getting pregnant." She took another sip of beer, finding it odd to be discussing donor sperm and fertility issues with Leo, but he seemed to be taking it in stride.

"Could your wife have the baby?"

"She could, but Nonno, you are the first blood relative I've ever met besides my mother. I just want to look into my baby's eyes and see myself, you know?"

Leo shifted in his seat, closing his eyes and not saying a word for almost a full minute. At one point, Niamh worried that he'd fallen asleep, but then he opened his eyes and looked right at her.

"Can I give you some advice from an old man?" he asked. Niamh nodded.

"Children are their own people, Niamh. After I lost Maggie and Guliana, the idea that my child, my blood, was out there in the world somewhere without me was devastating. She was a piece of me, and I couldn't make myself understand how she could exist without my knowing her. I thought she was mine, mine and Maggie's."

Niamh nodded, wondering where he was going.

"But years later, when my sons were born, I realized that they did not belong to me any more than I belonged to my own parents. They were their own entirely separate people. Sure, one had my nose, and one had his mother's temperament, but they did not exist to fulfill me at all. They were there for me to love, just like I loved Guliana without ever having met her. Do you understand?"

Niamh swallowed. "I'm not sure I do."

"We can't look for meaning or answers from our children, Niamh. As parents, it is our job to love them and to give them security. Their job is just to figure out who they are as people, so that they will do the same for their children someday. I did not love my boys any less just because their mother and I divorced. It doesn't matter who your child comes from — you or your wife. You will love them for who they are."

As their food arrived and they dug in with their chopsticks, Leo more reluctantly than her, Niamh thought about her grandfather's wisdom, hard won from years as a father. Perhaps he was right. After all, however she became a parent, Niamh was lucky enough to go through it with the love of her life. Although he hadn't said so in so many words, she had a feeling that Leo would have given his remaining arm to have been able to raise his daughter with his Maggie.

Chapter 45

Maggie — 1945

It was the afternoon of Guliana's fifth day of life, and still there was no word from Leo. The nurses had reported that Maggie's parents would be coming to pick her up that day, and it was expected that she would be leaving Guliana behind.

Maggie gazed down at her daughter in absolute awe as the little girl sucked hungrily at her mother's breast, and she gently brushed a curl off the baby's forehead with the back of one finger. She had no idea what the next few days would bring, but she was absolutely sure of one thing — she was going to keep her baby.

The door creaked open, and Maggie pulled her shirt over the baby, guarding her modesty, before looking up. A tall, pinched-looking woman stood in the doorway, a folder of papers in her hands.

"Good afternoon, Margaret." The woman strode into the

room as if she had every right to be there. Instinctively, Maggie clutched Guliana closer. "My name is Edna Marks," the woman said by way of introduction. "I'm the social worker assigned to your case through Catholic Social Services. I have all of your paperwork right here." She slapped the folder down on the table next to Maggie, and went so far as to uncap a pen and lay it on top of the documents she wanted Maggie to sign.

"Excuse me?" Maggie asked. "I think there must have been a misunderstanding. My parents will be here this afternoon, and they will be taking the baby and me home. There's no need for a social worker."

Miss Marks sighed the long-suffering exhalation of one who had heard this story countless times before and had no patience for hearing it again. She took her wire-rimmed glasses off her nose and proceeded to clean them with a pristine handkerchief from her handbag. Once they were cleaned to her satisfaction, she placed them back on her face and crossed and uncrossed her legs.

"Miss O'Callaghan—" She paused, glancing at the file. "It is *Miss*, isn't it?" she emphasized the word, and if Maggie had been doing anything other than nursing her brand-new baby, she'd have thrown something at the woman. "Miss O'Callaghan, taking the baby home will not be possible. You were sent to St. Gerard's with the intention of placing your baby for adoption with a good Catholic family. There is a family waiting for this child, and it is inconsiderate to keep them waiting any longer than necessary."

"*Inconsiderate?*" Maggie's voice rose in both pitch and volume. "Do you actually expect that I will hand over my daughter to avoid being thought *inconsiderate?*"

"Another thing for you to think about, *Miss* O'Callaghan, is just how you intend to support the baby if you do keep her. Do you have a job? A home of your own?" Maggie opened her mouth to reply that she had held a job in the past and that she was sure she could do so in the future, but Miss Marks beat her to it. "And even assuming that you were able to provide for the child, there will be nothing at all you can do to protect it from the stigma of being an Italian prisoner's bastard."

Maggie's face grew hot with rage at the woman's words, and it took everything she had not to get out of bed and slap this social worker in her ugly, ignorant face. In fact, the only thing that prevented her was the baby sleeping like an angel at her breast. "The only thing my daughter needs, Miss Marks, is her mother. This conversation is over."

* * *

"But I don't understand." Maggie took a ragged breath to steady herself. "You call yourselves a Christian organization, and—" She broke off, sobs racking her small frame as she sat across the conference table from Sister Jane Regina in one of the hospital's many conference rooms. On the table in front of her was an itemized bill from St. Gerard's totaling well over three thousand dollars for room, board, medical treatment, and even "spiritual advising." All of these costs, Sister explained, would be paid by the baby's adoptive family. If, however, Maggie chose to take Guliana home and raise her, then she would be responsible for the amount, which was due in full today. A fury she had never known before rose in her chest, and as Guliana was now sleeping in the nursery instead of being held in her mother's arms, Maggie gave herself permission to let the stoic nun know exactly what she thought of these practices.

"You are stealing babies, is what you're doing," Maggie hissed through gritted teeth. "You are taking advantage of desperate families who don't know where else to turn, and you're burying women like me so deep in debt that we have no choice but to hand over our children." A sob threatened to escape from her lips, but Maggie swallowed it down, fueling the inferno of her rage with all the sorrow and desperation she'd felt over the past six months. "How dare you?"

"We are people of God," Sister conceded, "but in order to continue offering succor to the fallen women of our flock, we must have funds with which to keep the lights on."

At the Sister's prepared and emotionless declaration, Maggie saw red. She stood, wincing at the pain from her still raw episiotomy, and leaned both hands on the table for both emphasis and support. "You say that my daughter's birth is proof of my sin, Sister, but the real sin is the one you're committing right now. The God I believe in would never seek to take a child from its mother. Mark my words — you will burn in hell for this."

Before Sister Jane Regina could respond, the door to the conference room opened, and Ambrose O'Callaghan stepped inside. Maggie's heart flew into her throat at the sight of her father — the steady, kind protector of her childhood. She wanted to run across the room and throw herself into his arms, beg him to help her find a way to keep Guliana and find Leo, but experience told her it would do no good. They weren't a family prone to displays of emotion, and tearfully begging her father to help her keep the baby he had sent her away to keep a secret would likely do more harm than good.

"Mr. O'Callaghan, I presume," Sister asked in that infuriatingly cool tone of hers. "Margaret and I were just completing the paperwork. She's free to go."

"Free to — no," Maggie interrupted. "I want to introduce my father to his granddaughter. I want him to meet Guliana." She looked back and forth between her father and Sister Jane Regina, sure that her only hope at this point lay with her stoic old dad falling instantly in love with her baby and saying that they could bring her home.

"I'm afraid that won't be possible, Margaret," Sister said as she aligned the papers on the table into a neat file and placed them inside a file folder. "The baby has already been taken by the social worker to meet her new family." She stood, tucking the folder somewhere in the depths of her flowing habit, and made to duck out of the room.

"What?" Maggie cried, pushing past her father with a rush of strength and running from the room, frantically searching for the nursery through her tears. "No! My baby! *I want my baby! Bring her to me!*" When she finally turned the corner and found herself face to face with the giant window overlooking the nursery, Maggie saw that the bassinet which had formerly belonged to her daughter was empty. Guliana was gone, all traces of her cleaned away as if she had never existed at all.

Great, racking sobs overtook her body, and Maggie crumpled to the floor as if even her legs recognized that she couldn't possibly hold up under the onslaught of grief brought on by the loss of her child.

"It's easier this way," Sister Jane Regina was saying to Mr. O'Callaghan, "if it's a clean break. She'll heal, and it will be like this never happened."

Somewhere deep within the well of grief she was drowning

under, Maggie took in the nun's matter-of-fact words. *Easier this way?* Nothing about this was easy — the physical pain of labor had been nothing in comparison to this crushing onslaught of emotional agony.

"My baby..."

Hands gripped Maggie under the arms and lifted her to her feet before depositing her into the wheelchair that had suddenly materialized in front of her. Maggie stared at the ground off which she had just been pulled as if through a fog, expecting to see pools of blood from the wound that had been cut through her heart, but there was nothing there. The chair began to move as if by its own accord, and Maggie was struck by the fact that now even her physical autonomy was being taken from her. Guliana, Leo, Sadie, her family, and now even her ability to walk on two feet.

By the time she was wheeled to her father's waiting car and deposited unceremoniously in the backseat, Maggie's shrieks and sobs had subsided to gasps, and even the occasional hiccup as her body tried to recover from the physical assault brought on by her agony. Her father reached a hand into the backseat and left an awkward pat on Maggie's knee, which was surely meant to be comforting, before turning the key in the ignition and pulling the car out of the hospital lot.

As they pulled away, Maggie turned and placed her palms over the back window of the car, watching the main doors of the hospital grow smaller and smaller.

She had never gotten to say goodbye.

Chapter 46

Niamh — 2016

"I want to see the camp, Niamh. Will you take me?"

Leo, who had been staying with Niamh and Christine over Niamh's school vacation week, looked at his granddaughter over the rim of his coffee cup and raised one eyebrow in a question. Niamh had been waiting for— and dreading — this question all week. She was excited to see the sight of the old camp where her grandparents had met and fallen in love, but anxious that the trip would be too emotionally taxing on her nonno.

"Are you sure, Nonno? It's a few hours' drive, and there isn't much still standing from the forties. It's an industrial park now." Niamh scooped eggs onto her grandfather's plate as Christine breezed into the kitchen wearing a business suit and smelling of Vera Wang perfume.

"I am sure, *mi patatino*. I may be old, but I will not break.

Tell her, Christine."

"He won't break, honey," Christine echoed, looking around the kitchen in confusion and breaking into a grin as Niamh pressed a travel mug of coffee into her hand.

"Traitor," Niamh muttered, but she melted as she watched her wife drop a kiss on her nonno's head before grabbing her laptop bag and her keys.

"I'll be in court all day, but just text me if you're not going to be home for dinner." Christine came around the island to kiss Niamh before leaving.

"Have a good day, and do whatever Leo tells you to do."

"You're ridiculous," Niamh exclaimed to Christine's retreating back. "Nonno, be honest. You like her more than me, don't you?"

"Your Christine is a wonderful woman. You are my blood, and she makes you happy." Leo shrugged before digging into his breakfast with gusto.

"You still didn't answer my question," Niamh teased.

"And you did not answer mine. Will you take me to the camp?"

Niamh looked at the clock — accounting for traffic, they could be in southeastern Massachusetts in just over an hour. The forecast promised sunny weather. There was really no reason she could think of *not* to agree to the trip. Even Christine thought she should go.

"Fine," she agreed with a sigh. "Finish your breakfast and we'll go. But if it's too much for you, we're getting a hotel down there and staying overnight."

Leo chuckled. "You have been talking to your cousin Bella too much — you're starting to sound like her. Why must you both treat me like an old man?"

"Nonno, you're ninety-four!"

"Exactly — I'm ninety-four. I'm not one hundred." He winked at her. "I think you're afraid you won't be able to keep up with me."

"That must be it." Niamh smiled and rolled her eyes. Her nonno was frustrating, but he was *hers*, and if he wanted to drive three hours round trip to see an industrial park, then she'd drive him three hours round trip to see an industrial park.

* * *

Google hadn't lied — there really was almost no evidence that an enormous military embarkation camp had stood on this spot over seventy years ago. A cursory drive through of the area had revealed an innumerable array of warehouses, office buildings, and trucking depots. Leo was dismayed that it looked nothing like his memories, and Niamh's heart ached for him.

"Why don't we go get some lunch, Nonno?"

"No." Leo was firm. Decided. "I spent three years of my life here. It may look different, but I want to feel the ground under my feet again." They were parked in the lot outside of a PepsiCo plant, and before Niamh could register what was happening, Leo had opened the car door and was striding across the parking lot so quickly that Niamh had to jog to catch up with him.

They walked in silence for several minutes, across two parking lots and through a patch of scrubby-looking trees, before Leo stopped so abruptly that Niamh had to sidestep to avoid walking into him.

"The main gate is down the road a bit, further away from where we got off the highway. There's a lake." Niamh nodded, and after a moment, Leo continued. "That's where she'd come through every morning. First her father brought her, and then eventually she took the bus. I can still remember seeing her step off that bus in the morning, eyes searching for me." Leo sighed, and Niamh looped her arm through his for support. "The laundry she worked in — they called it Midway after the island in the Pacific — it was always so damn hot, but she never broke a sweat, at least not that I could see. She was perfect." Leo stared off into the middle distance, and Niamh knew that he was seeing places and people who had been gone for more than seven decades.

"And where did you live, Nonno?"

Leo turned somewhere between ninety and one hundred and eighty degrees to the right, although Niamh had no concept whether it was east or west, north or south. "That way," he said, pointing his arm through the trees. "All the ISU boys were in a barracks down there a ways. We had our own canteen, our own hospital, and even a gymnasium. That's where..." he trailed off.

"That's where, Nonno?" Niamh asked after a moment, peering up at her grandfather, this man who had lived through so much. He was silent, staring through the trees, and Niamh was beginning to worry that she had been correct, that this was too much for him, when he said in barely more than a whisper, "That's where Maggie told me we were going to have a baby."

"My mother."

"Yes, *mi nipotina*. Your mother." The strength of Leo's voice

277

never faltered, but Niamh could see the tears welling in his green eyes, and she was torn between a desire to lighten the mood and the knowledge that her nonno needed to grieve.

"Was this the last place you saw her?" Niamh asked, her voice no more than a whisper in the wind.

"No." He shook his head with a sad smile. "I walked her to the front of the camp, to the main gate, and I put her on the bus as the snow fell around us. That was the last time I saw my *Margherita*." Niamh nodded and searched her brain for something she could say that would ease this man's suffering. She had all but given up, when she heard him whisper, "And every night when I go to sleep, I put her on that bus, and I watch her ride away from me. Every night for seventy-one years, *Margherita*."

* * *

"We need food," Niamh declared as they walked back to the car. "Siri, show me restaurants in the area."

"That's the Italian in you, my girl," Leo said with a grin. "When in doubt, find food."

Niamh snorted, scrolling through the results on her phone. "There's a generic American restaurant, looks like pub food, a bunch of chain places, pizza, pizza, pizza... Oh! How do you feel about Mexican food?"

"I've never met a tamale I didn't like," Leo replied, opening the car door and settling himself into his seat. "Before we leave, though, there is one more place we must go."

After a few wrong turns and several dead ends, they found the location Leo wanted — the Grotto.

"This was built by the first Italian POWs to arrive in the

States," Leo explained, directing Niamh to park along the side of the road. "It was something of our own in this world that was so foreign to us; I can't tell you what it means to me that it is still here."

Niamh followed her grandfather off the road and into a clearing, pine needles and sticks crunching under their feet. The Grotto, just off the road, was built almost entirely of field stone — gray rocks stacked in neat rows to form a wall built into the side of a hill. At the foot of the wall stood a simple stone cross, and further up, in a small alcove, was a statue of the Virgin Mary. The air around the Grotto was still and silent, save for the call of one warbler to another in the trees above. They couldn't be more than an eighth of a mile from the busy main road, but as far as Niamh could see, they were in a world unto themselves. She turned, startled, at the soft grunt emitted by her grandfather as he dropped to his knees in front of the Grotto and made the sign of the Cross.

His prayer was in Latin, and Niamh couldn't understand a word of it. She hadn't been raised with religion, and the representation of Catholics in the news was usually limited to those arguing against causes she believed in — like her own marriage. Niamh stood to the side, legs crossed, hands behind her back, and tried to unobtrusively study her grandfather at prayer. Her eyes must have been burning a hole through his back, because after a moment, he spoke.

"Your thoughts are so loud I can hear them, Niamh."

"I don't want to interrupt."

"You could never. Come kneel by me." Leo shifted over a few inches to make room, and Niamh lowered herself to her knees beside him.

"How can you pray to a God who has taken so much from

you?"

Leo kept his eyes trained on the statue, which was stained with acid rain and showed signs of the decades spent in the forest. "God hasn't taken anything from me, child. People have. People have used God as an excuse to take my Maggie from me, to take our Guliana from her, and even to take Guliana from you. But that was not God. God brought you back into my life, and for that I am grateful."

"How—" Niamh asked, half to her grandfather and half to the universe itself, "how can you be so calm about it?"

Leo turned, slowly and carefully, until he was sitting on the stones in front of the Grotto, looking back towards the car. "You think that I am not angry over all that I have lost?"

Niamh nodded.

"If I allowed the anger over everything that has been taken from me to flow freely, it would destroy me and everything in my path. When I was twenty-three years old, I met the love of my life. We were together for less than six months, but we loved more in that time than most people ever get to love in their whole lives. And then we were ripped apart by people who thought they were doing the right thing. Your great-grandparents, Niamh."

Leo took her hands in his own, and Niamh could feel his bones through the papery skin. "They were not bad people. They made a bad choice, but they did it because they loved their daughter. Even the people who took Guliana from her mother — they thought that they were doing the right thing by giving her to two parents instead of an unwed girl who claimed to be in love with the enemy. I promised myself long ago that I would accept the good in my life and forgive those who had wronged me. Life took your mother and your grandmother away from me, but it brought me my sons and my grandchildren. It brought me you, Niamh. And so, I choose to be grateful, and leave no room for hate in my life."

Niamh expected to see tears in her nonno's eyes after such a speech, but there were none. Instead, Leo looked as if he had unburdened himself somehow. His shoulders were straighter, his eyes were brighter, and he was able to pull himself up to a standing position with very little help from Niamh.

"I came to the Grotto not to complain or demand vengeance, Niamh. I came to thank my creator for all that he has given me, no matter the cost. Now, where is this Mexican restaurant you found with your phone?"

Chapter 47

Maggie — 1945

The first few days at home passed in a fog. Maggie left her bedroom only to use the bathroom, refusing even to eat until her mother finally sent Frankie up with a tray of sandwiches and strict instructions not to leave until he had personally witnessed Maggie eat at least a few bites.

The doctor came by with a binder and Epsom salts to staunch the flow of her milk, but the throbbing ache from her engorged breasts mirrored the bruised feeling in her heart. When Maggie dreamed of Guliana, as she did every time she closed her eyes, her breasts would leak, soaking her through her nightgown and the bed linens down to the mattress, as if her entire body was weeping for the child it had lost.

Finally, it was Sunday, and Maggie had an hour's reprieve from the whispering stares of her family as they all packed off to Mass at eight o'clock in the morning. It was the opportunity she had been waiting for. As soon as the door clicked shut behind her mother, Maggie stepped out of bed and into a dress from the previous summer. The fit was tight and uncomfortable, but for a woman whose very skin felt like a burden, an ill-fitting dress was hardly something to keep her home. She borrowed one of Frankie's cardigans, which came down to her knees, and before she could lose her nerve, she rushed down the street to the bus stop.

On the surface, nothing in Taunton had changed since the summer before. The war in Germany was over, but most of the men had yet to return home and were simply redirected towards crushing the Japanese. The sun shone in Maggie's eyes as she hurried down the sidewalk, a harsh reminder that she hadn't been outside in the fresh air more than a handful of times since the previous February.

She wished she'd brought sunglasses.

Maggie hugged the sweater around her thin shoulders like a cape, wishing she could disappear inside of it. So far, no one had recognized her, but she knew the day was coming when she wouldn't be able to avoid the knowing eyes and the *Maggie, where have you been*'s. The official story was that she'd been sent to live with her mother's great aunt in Blackstone, caring for the old woman in her final days, and that now that poor dear Aunt Veronica had passed on, Maggie had been allowed to come home. She was sure no one believed the lie, but she dreaded having to look people in the eyes and pretend that she hadn't just been through the most agonizing ordeal of her life.

The bus was on time, and as Maggie stepped aboard and found her seat, she was brought back to all the other times she had ridden the same route, driving down Broadway to Bay Street, passing the Mayflower cemetery, Holy Rosary Catholic

Church, and the Polish American Citizens' Club. *It should look different*, she thought, *after everything*, but she recognized that although her surroundings were much the same as they had always been, it was she who was different. She'd been to hell and back, and nothing would ever look the same.

When she exited the bus at the front gate of the camp, Maggie approached the guard shack with trepidation. Would they call down to the Italian barracks and let them know she was here? Or should she ask for one of the soldiers who managed the civilian workers, someone she had worked with before who might get her into the camp and take her to Leo?

She chose to be direct, and when the private working at the gate asked how he could help her, Maggie stated that she was there to see and deliver an important message to *Caporale* Leonardo Castiglione, Italian Service Unit. The private's eyebrows rose in surprise at her request, and Maggie prayed she had heard him wrong when he told her that all the Italian co-belligerents had been shipped back to Italy the month prior, per order of President Truman.

"Pardon me," she stumbled over her words, hoping against hope that this time the private would say something different. "Can you repeat that?"

"I'm sorry, Miss." The young man's eyes were kind, and Maggie wondered if she wasn't the first young American woman to show up at the gates, asking for a man who had left her far behind. "The ISU boys were shipped home last month."

Maggie wanted to rage, wanted to scream and tear her hair and burn the whole goddamned camp to the ground. But she didn't. She couldn't. She had been knocked down one time too many, and she just didn't have it in her to get up again.

"Thank you," she muttered, and turning, stumbled back towards her bus. Where could she go but home, where they had to keep her and the only price she had to pay came in the form of silence? Everything would return to normal, Mam had promised. She could move on with her life.

What no one seemed to understand, however, was that without Guliana and Leo, there was nothing to move on to.

Chapter 48

Niamh — 2016

"What if, instead of insemination, we do in vitro?"

Niamh, who had been in the process of lifting a forkful of fettuccine carbonara to her mouth, froze. They were out to dinner at their favorite Italian restaurant, celebrating Christine winning a case and Niamh's newly discovered heritage. She stared across the table at Christine, who looked back at her with a nervous smile.

"Come again?"

Christine took a delicate sip of her pinot noir before placing the glass gently back onto the white tablecloth. She toyed with the stem of the wineglass for a moment before continuing.

"I've been thinking. You know I'd love to carry a baby — *our* baby." She reached across the table and took the fork from Niamh's hand before threading her own fingers through her wife's. "And I know how important it is to you that the egg be yours. So, we could harvest your eggs, inseminate them with donor sperm, and have the fertilized embryos implanted in my uterus."

Niamh simply stared at Christine, who looked at her with wide, expectant eyes. The restaurant around them went quiet, as if they were the only two people in the room. If this were a movie, Niamh thought, then this is when the whole place would go dark and a spotlight would shine directly onto them. This could work, she realized. Her egg and Christine's uterus — they could make a baby together and both get to play an integral part. A grin broke across Niamh's face, continuing to spread until she feared she might burst from the size of it. She squeezed Christine's hand. "They can do that?"

"They can." Christine took another sip of wine before admitting, "I went to see Dr. Bennett yesterday so I could get all the information before I talked to you." Niamh watched in awe as Christine reached into her purse and retrieved a handful of pamphlets. *Egg Retrieval. In Vitro Fertilization. Fertility Over 35.*

"You went without me?" Niamh's excitement dimmed a little at the idea that Christine had gone behind her back, but before she could sink too far, Christine shook her head.

"No! I mean, yes, I did go without you, but only so I could see if this is even a possibility before I brought it up to you. I didn't want to get your hopes up for nothing."

"Then... it's possible?" Niamh felt lightheaded with excitement. Christine could have their baby — Niamh could watch the woman she loved grow and give birth to a baby that might have her own eyes or her own nose.

"It's possible." Christine grinned, doing a little happy dance in her seat. "Do you want me to make an appointment? I told the doctor I needed to talk to you before we move forward, but if you're on board, they can see us next week. Unless you need time. Do you need time?"

"Damnit, Christine, we've been waiting how many years at this point? Can we go to the fertility clinic right now?"

Christine laughed. "I wish we could. It's going to be a process — there are shots for you, and I don't think the egg retrieval process is exactly easy, and we'll need to buy more donor sperm. And Niamh," she said, her expression turning serious as she reached across the table to wrap her hand around Niamh's again, "there's still a chance it won't work."

"There's always a chance it won't work," Niamh replied, wondering for the millionth time what she had done to deserve Christine. "If we were straight and one of us could make our own sperm the old-fashioned way, there's a chance it wouldn't work. Things can always go to shit; that doesn't mean we shouldn't try."

Christine sat back in her chair, looking like a woman who'd had the weight of the world lifted off her shoulders. To Niamh, she had never looked so beautiful. "When did you get so philosophical?" she asked. "What happened to my wife, the pessimist?"

Niamh thought of all she'd discovered in the last few months — her own inability to get pregnant, the DNA test, learning about and meeting Leo and her cousin Bella, hearing Leo's tragic story about her grandmother Maggie and how they lost their baby, her mother... "You never know what's going to happen or where life's going to take you, Chris. It's the strange arithmetic of the universe. But we're here now, and we have this chance, so it would be stupid not to take it."

Christine nodded and lifted her wine glass. "To the strange

arithmetic of the universe."

"And science," Niamh added, lifting her own glass and touching it to her wife's.

"And to us."

Chapter 49

Maggie — 1945

"I don't know what I can say that she'll want to hear. She hates me."

"Just try. We can't think of anyone else. Mam said to leave her be, but it's been over a month."

Maggie heard the whispering outside her bedroom door, and from her cave underneath her pink dotted swiss comforter she could make out the voices of Frankie, Beansie, and... oh no.

Betty.

"Mags?" The door creaked open, and the sound of footsteps on the carpet alerted Maggie to the imminent demise of her solitude. "Mags? Betty's here. I thought you might like to see a friend." Frankie really was trying, bless him.

"She's not my friend," Maggie replied through the covers. "I have nothing to say to her."

"Maggie, you're being an imbecile," came Paul's decidedly less compassionate voice. "Get out here."

"Boys, out. Leave us girls together to talk," Betty stated with authority, and Maggie could hear her shooing the boys out of the bedroom before she came back to take a seat at the bottom of the bed. "You can hate me all you want, Maggie, but I'm on your side."

Six months of unexpressed betrayal bubbled to the surface, and Maggie threw back the comforter to face the person who had been her best friend, the same person who had told her parents that she was pregnant and gotten her sent off to a maternity home that had ultimately stolen her baby.

"How. Dare. You?" She spat the question in a venomous staccato. "You were my *friend*. I *trusted* you." Maggie stared at Betty with pure hatred, and it took less than the space of a hiccup for Betty to break down.

"God, Mags, I haven't slept well since you went away. I thought they'd make it better. I thought they'd take care of you."

"By sending me away and taking my baby from me?" Maggie's voice rose with each word, until she was yelling. What did it matter? She didn't care who heard her.

"No!" Betty cried. "I swear, Maggie, I swear on my life that I never thought that. I've been sick—" Maggie opened her mouth to tell Betty to stuff it, but Betty backpedaled. "I know it can't hold a candle to what you've been through, Mags, but I've been sick at the thought that I had something to do with it."

Maggie was silent, taking in the sniffling girl at the end of her bed. She hadn't expected Betty to be contrite. Betty had never admitted she was wrong in her life. Maggie didn't think she knew how.

"I'm sorry, Mags. I'm so sorry, and I know that doesn't change anything, and it won't bring anything back or take away what I did, but I'm sorry and I need you to know that."

There was a scrambling outside the door, and Beansie grumbled from the hallway, "We asked ya to come over to cheer her up, Betty, not snot all over her."

"Go away," both girls yelled in unison, as they had done countless times before when Maggie's brothers had tried to listen in at the door. The tension between them eased for the smallest of seconds, but all Maggie could manage in response was a shrug.

"I can accept your apology, but I can't move on, Betty. I can't pretend it's OK. I just — I want to die, Betty. I can't live like this."

Before Maggie had time to register it, Betty had moved to her side and taken her in her arms, rocking her friend like she was the baby in need of comfort. This expression of empathy was so unexpected, and so utterly the opposite of the way everyone had treated her since she had left Leo standing in the snow, that it caused something inside Maggie to break open, and all the tears came rushing out.

Maggie clung to her friend and cried for over an hour, and Betty did nothing but simply hold her, rubbing her back and occasionally emitting comforting noises from the back of her throat. These tears weren't born from fury or frustration, but they were simply the tears of a young woman who had lost her daughter and the love of her life, and who had absolutely no idea how she was supposed to live the rest of her life without them.

Chapter 50

Niamh — 2016

"I found her."

"What?" Niamh scrambled up in her bed, grasping through the sleep-induced fog in her brain to reach the voice on the other end of the phone. Who found whom?

"Oh, God, I woke you up, didn't I? Niamh, it's Bella."

Bella. Her cousin. Leo's other granddaughter. They hadn't spoken in a few months.

"S'OK," Niamh mumbled, stretching her arms over her head while holding the phone between her shoulder and her ear. "I'm up, just — I'm getting there."

"Who is it?" Christine's muffled, sleep-filled voice came from under the duvet, and Niamh put her hand over the mouthpiece of the landline.

"It's my cousin Bella — go back to sleep." She leaned back against the pillows and turned her attention back to the caller, making an effort to keep her voice down so as not to disturb Christine any further. "What's up, Bella?"

"I found your grandmother."

Niamh reacted with stunned silence. After a few seconds, she held the phone receiver out in front of her and stared at it, turning it first one way, then another, as if somehow an explanation would fall right out of it. It had been months since they'd stopped looking, giving up hope that Maggie was out there somewhere.

"Niamh? Are you there?" Bella's tinny voice asked through the landline. "I'm here." Niamh returned the phone to her ear, asking the question that burned in her chest. "Is she... alive?"

"As far as I know she is. Are you OK, Niamh? Is your wife home?" Bella's concern was warm and comforting, and Niamh realized with surprise that Christine was now sitting up next to her against the pillows, leaning over to hear Bella's far-away voice as well as she could.

"She's right here." Niamh shot Christine a grateful smile, and Christine responded by taking Niamh's free hand in both of hers and squeezing it. "How did you find her? Does Nonno know?"

"I haven't told him yet. That seemed like something that should come from you. Anyway, I was digging through records, and I found the purchase and sale on a house in Dennis, Massachusetts under the name of Margaret O'Callaghan, born April 13, 1925. Then I checked the tax records for the town, and as of last year, Ms. O'Callaghan is still the owner and only resident of the home. The name and the birth date add up, Niamh. She's alive."

Tears fell unchecked down Niamh's face, dripping off her chin and making tiny wet circles on her t-shirt. "We need to tell Nonno. He's lived long enough without her."

"I already checked the flights." Bella's voice was all business; she had switched into event planner mode. "Can you be at the airport in an hour? There's a Delta flight leaving for LaGuardia at eleven."

"Hell yes, I can!" Niamh swung her legs over the side of the bed; Christine was already up and grabbing a small suitcase from under the bed.

"Great. I'll pick you up at twelve-thirty. We can get lunch, and then go tell Nonno together."

When the call disconnected, Niamh simply sat for a moment, watching Christine toss deodorant, an extra set of clothes, and a book she'd been meaning to read into the suitcase in a flurry of activity. "My grandmother is alive, Chris..."

"I know, love. I heard." Christine's voice was as warm and rich as melted chocolate as she paused her packing to come around the side of the bed, pull Niamh to her feet, and take her in her arms. "She's alive, and it sounds like you're about to make Leo a very happy man."

"What if she doesn't want to meet me?" A ball of ice descended into Niamh's gut, freezing everything around it and causing her to choke on her own words. "What if she doesn't want to see him again and she breaks his heart?"

"Do you really think that's what's going to happen?"

"No — I don't know," Niamh whispered, suddenly frozen with fear.

"You don't, but the woman Leo described to you doesn't sound like someone who would turn away her own flesh and blood granddaughter, nor would she forget the love of her life."

"You're right..." Niamh trailed off.

"Of course I am. I'm always right. Now let's go — I need to drop my wife at the airport before I go to work."

* * *

"Bella didn't give up looking for Maggie, Nonno. She's alive, and she lives on Cape Cod."

Every doubt or worry Niamh had dissipated when she saw her grandfather take in the news. His emerald eyes widened, and even his pupils dilated, almost entirely obscuring his irises in their need to open up and let in as much of this miraculous news as possible.

"This is not a joke, girls? This old heart can't take a joke like that." His voice broke, revealing the depth of emotion within, and Niamh nearly cried herself when his face broke into a wide grin that would give any child on Christmas morning a run for their money.

"It's not a joke, Nonno," Niamh heard herself say, before reaching out and brushing the tears from his cheek with the back of one hand.

"I—" he hesitated, searching the right words. "I need to see her now, please. When can we go to her?"

"We thought perhaps tomorrow," Bella soothed, looking at Niamh for confirmation. "Niamh can stay here overnight, and then I'll take you both to the airport in the morning. You can fly from LaGuardia to Cape Cod in just over an hour."

Niamh nodded, confirming that she also thought this a good plan, when Leo reached for his cane and stood, unassisted, to his feet.

"No."

"No?" Niamh was confused — hadn't Leo just said that he wanted to see Maggie?

"We. Go. Now." Leo punctuated each word by stomping his cane onto the floor. "I have waited seventy-one years for my Maggie, and I will not wait another second. Isabella, use that blasted iPhone and get us a reservation on an airplane to the Cape."

Bella looked over at Niamh, eyes twinkling, and Niamh had the distinct feeling that this animated version of her grandfather was one Bella had seen before.

"Looks like you're going back to the airport," Bella chuckled.

"Niamh! Isabella!" Leo called from the front entryway of the brownstone. "I have the keys, and if you're not in the car in three minutes, I will leave without you. Driver's license be damned!"

Chapter 51

Niamh — 2016

"I came here with my mother once," Niamh recalled as she navigated along Route 28 in Hyannis in their rented SUV. Leo had insisted on paying for the flight and the rental car, telling Niamh it was for all the Christmases and birthdays he'd missed in her life — and besides, he wanted to upgrade for more legroom. "I was very little, and we rented a house on the beach with some friends of hers who had kids my age. I wonder whatever happened to them."

"You don't remember their family name?" Leo asked, leaning forward to adjust the height of his window. It was spring, and the Cape was adorned in varying shades of gray and brown, but it was warm enough to turn off the heat in the car and crack the windows, letting in a breeze that was tinged with salt.

"I don't. I don't think I was more than four or five years old at the time. I remember playing in the waves with my mom for hours." A smile played on her lips, and Leo kept her talking.

"Tell me about how my daughter played at the beach."

"She was so much fun." Niamh allowed herself to laugh. "She taught me how to jump in the waves and let them carry me back towards the shore. She let me dive into the surf on my own, but she was always right there to grab me if it became too much." Niamh snuck a glance at her grandfather, who was watching her intently. "We'd have a competition at night to see who'd collected the most sand in their bathing suits. I said that it wasn't fair that she always won, because her bathing suit was bigger than mine and could hold more sand.'

Leo threw back his head and laughed.

"Well, it wasn't fair," Niamh argued with a grin. "Whoever lost had to pay for the ice cream that night."

"And how many times did you have to pay for the ice cream, my girl?"

"None." She took her eyes off the road just long enough to wink at him. "I was probably in kindergarten. I didn't have a job."

"And what was your favorite flavor?" Leo asked, seemingly enjoying Niamh's trip down memory lane as much or even more than she did.

"Lime sherbet with chocolate jimmies," she replied, laughing at the horrified and disgusted look that crossed the old man's face. "Have I offended your taste buds, Nonno?"

"You have offended taste buds everywhere, Niamh." He shuddered. "You're lucky that I love you. And what was Guliana's favorite?" Leo still insisted on calling his daughter by the name he and Maggie had given to her, rather than the name she was more commonly known by. He said it like a blessing — a benediction for the daughter he'd loved for seventy-one years but had never gotten to hold.

"Black raspberry," Niamh replied, taking a left at the prompting of her GPS.

"That's my daughter," Leo chuckled. "You must have gotten your taste in ice cream from your father."

"Seeing as I've never met the man," Niamh said with a concerted effort at appearing breezy, "I wouldn't know." She kept her eyes trained on the road, a residential street lined with scrubby trees and shingled, colonial-era homes, but she didn't need to see Leo to know that his mouth had set into a thin line and his eyes had darkened like the ethereal sea before a storm. They had discussed the man who fathered Niamh the week before, and Leo had been disgusted by the man who knew he had a daughter, knew where she was and how to contact her, and yet had never bothered to try. The word *bastardo* had growled from between Leo's lips at least three times.

"What are you doing?" Niamh asked suddenly, noticing that Leo had turned off the GPS and was fiddling around with the touch screen on the car's dashboard.

"I think there is a way to search for restaurants on this thing," he muttered. "Do you know how to do it?"

"I do, but I can't do it when the car's moving. And now I don't know where I'm going anyway." Niamh turned on her blinker and coasted as far onto the side of the road as was safe. When they stopped, she turned to her grandfather with a raised eyebrow. "Why are you looking for restaurants? Are you hungry?"

"Can't an old man want to take his granddaughter out for ice cream?" Leo grinned, eyes twinkling. Niamh laughed, typing "ice cream" into the search bar and tapping on the first and closest option.

"Captain Frosty's is on Route 6A in Dennis — it's about a ten-minute drive. Will that work?"

"*Perfecto.* I have only one thing to insist, Niamh."

She paused, about to pull back onto the main road, and looked at her grandfather. "Yes?"

"You will not order that disgusting lime and chocolate concoction."

* * *

Leo hadn't said a word since they'd gotten back into the car at the ice cream stand, and Niamh could practically see the tension in the old man's body as he fiddled with his seat belt, put the window up and down several times, and finally began clutching the cloth of his pant leg in his right hand.

Just after the car turned onto Mayflower Avenue in Dennis, Niamh pulled over to the side of the road and pressed the triangular button next to the steering wheel to turn on her hazard lights.

"Are you OK, Nonno?" she asked, her own excitement over meeting her grandmother paling in comparison with her concern for the man sitting next to her.

"Am I that obvious?" Leo asked, raising an eyebrow with a wry smirk.

"Well, you are making me wonder if the insurance we took out on the rental car covers vomit stains. How's the ice cream sitting?"

"Like lead," he replied, features grim. And then, "Do you want to go on alone? Introduce yourself to Maggie and have some time for yourselves?"

Niamh turned in her seat, tucking her right leg up under-neath her to show her grandfather that she'd sit with him here on the side of the road as long as he needed her to.

"What are you afraid of, Nonno?" Leo looked chagrined, and Niamh knew she had gotten it right. He was scared to see the love of his life after all these years. "I'm not going over there without you, so spill it."

"Your wife is a prosecutor, no?" Leo asked. "I see she has taught you some of her tricks."

"I'm also a teacher, don't forget." Niamh fixed Leo with her best elementary school teacher scowl.

"So you are, so you are..." Leo sighed, leaned his head back against the headrest, and closed his eyes. "What if she doesn't want to see me? What if it brings up too many memories that she doesn't want to relive?"

Niamh sighed, letting the breath escape her lips in short bursts while she considered. "Nonno, every time you speak of her, the joy in your face is palpable. It's clear you love her; you said your time together was the happiest of your life. Wouldn't she feel the same?"

Leo's lips curled into a sad smile, and his eyes remained closed. "Yes, my girl. But losing her, and then not knowing what happened to our daughter, was the most painful experi-ence I've ever had to withstand." He cracked one eyelid and fixed one piercing green eye on his granddaughter. "And I had my arm lopped off in a field hospital in Morocco, so when I talk about pain..." he trailed off. "As hard as that was for me, I'm sure it was nothing compared to what *Margherita* went through. A mother..." He swallowed, and Niamh felt the familiar clutch in her heart. She didn't know what it felt like to be a mother; perhaps she never would. "I saw Emilia when she gave birth to our boys. The love a mother has for her child — there's nothing like it. How can I ask Maggie to remember giving up Guliana?"

The car was silent except for the *clack-clack-clack* of the hazard lights, and Niamh could feel waves of anxiety crashing into her grandfather and threatening to drag him under. She stayed quiet for a few minutes, willing Leo to understand that she took his concerns seriously before responding.

"I've never had a child, Nonno," she whispered, "but I know what it is to lose someone I love. The same someone that you and Maggie lost — my mother." Niamh held her breath, and when Leo nodded, she continued. "Nothing will replace her, for any of us, but even though meeting you has reminded me of what I lost, that can't possibly compare to what I've gained in knowing you. I wouldn't trade it for anything. The loss will always be there, but if I had let my grief for my mother prevent me from meeting you..." A nervous laugh bubbled to the surface. "I don't know. But I'm glad I didn't, and I'm glad I have you. And Maggie will be too."

Leo sat up, adjusting himself in the seat, and offered Niamh a tentative smile. "And I'm bringing her you."

Niamh reached out for Leo's hand, which he happily gave. "We're in no hurry. We can sit here as long as you need to," she said, squeezing his fingers in hers.

"You're a wise woman, Niamh. You remind me of your grandmother." Leo winked at her, and then pointed to her seat belt. "Better get that back on, love. I've got a girl to go see."

Chapter 52

Maggie — 2016

Maggie loved the rough, pencil-sketch texture of the cedar shingles that made up her home, and how they stood out in harsh relief against the smudged impressionist pastels of the beach sunset.

That was one thing that hadn't changed in the fifty or so years since she'd bought the little cottage on Cape Cod.

Maggie sighed. It was almost time for her to meet her friend Betty for dinner. It wasn't that she didn't like Betty — the woman had been her friend for almost a century — it's just that all Betty ever talked about was her grandchildren. Where they were, what they were doing, who they were dating. The way she talked about them, one would think that no one else had ever had a family before in the history of the world, and certainly no one had a family as brilliant as Betty's.

Maggie rolled her eyes, set her book down on the table in her front garden, and with the help of her cane, rose to her feet. She loathed the cane — said that it made her feel old — but she had been using it faithfully ever since her niece pointed out that if she fell and broke a hip, she might not be able to live on her own anymore. Maggie would be damned if she'd go into a nursing home — they reminded her entirely too much of her time at St. Gerard's. So if using a cane meant that Maggie could remain in her own home at ninety, then use a cane she would.

The sound of a car pulling into the driveway caught her attention, and Maggie turned on the steps leading up to her porch. Who could possibly be here now? She didn't recognize the blue SUV.

Maggie watched as an attractive young woman with a dark pixie cut got out of the driver's seat. *Probably lost*, she thought, though she couldn't imagine anyone getting lost in the age of those GPS things her nieces were always going on about. "Hello?" Maggie called to the young woman. "Can I help you with something?"

There was movement on the passenger side of the car, and when the tall man who emerged turned to look at her with an emerald-green gaze, Maggie felt all the blood drain from her body. The cane fell to the ground, and Maggie brought both hands to her mouth to catch the sob she heard herself emit as if through a tunnel.

"It's her," Leo said to the young woman at his side, and without taking his eyes from Maggie's for a second, he strode across the driveway and through the gate with the strength of a man sixty years his junior.

"Leo—?" Maggie managed to choke out before he reached her and grasped her around the waist with his arm, pulling her to him with a combination of care and desperation. She gazed up at him, eyes shining. "Leo, how—?" But before she could continue, he leaned down, cupping the papery skin of her cheek in one hand.

"I've waited more than half a century, *Margherita*. May I kiss you now?"

Not wanting to waste a moment for fear that this was a dream, one that she could wake from at any second, Maggie settled her arms around his neck and reached her lips up to his, kissing him with an intensity she hadn't felt since, well, since the last time she'd seen him. Leo responded in kind, and she delighted in the sensation of being held by him again after so many years. For a moment, the lifetimes since they'd last seen one another melted away, and it was as if no time had passed at all. She was nineteen, in love, expecting a baby, and Leo was going to take care of them both.

As the kiss ended, they still remained pressed together, lost in the moment, and Maggie gradually became aware of reality again. She was crying and so was he, hot tears mingling on their cheeks as they talked over one another, trying to make sense of the enormity and impossibility of the two of them, here, together after all this time.

The moment was broken by the sound of someone clearing her throat behind them, and Leo stepped aside, chuckling. Maggie immediately missed the contact, the heat of him, and she instinctively reached out to pull him back to her when she caught sight of the young woman who had come with him, standing in the gateway to the garden and staring with intensity at her purple-painted toes.

"Maggie, love." Leo gestured to the young woman, who stepped forward slowly and raised her eyes to meet Maggie's. A jolt of recognition ran through her, a lightning bolt of *knowing*. Maggie felt little surprise when Leo continued, "I'd like to introduce you to our granddaughter, Niamh Reilly." Niamh took another hesitant step forward, and Maggie gasped. The hair, so dark brown that it looked black, cropped short against Niamh's head, was the exact shade that her own had been until the silver began to streak through it. Her eyes, a vivid green that shone through thick, dark-rimmed glasses, matched Leo's perfectly. The tattoos decorating her arms were all her own, though, and Maggie had a feeling that they told a remarkable story of who this young woman was, and how she had come to be here.

Lightheaded from the waves of emotion crashing over her, Maggie reached out to take hold of the railing, but she found Leo's arm waiting for her, steadying her just as he had when they were young. She leaned into him, allowing him to snake an arm around her waist. "Well, then. Hello, Niamh. Would you like to come in?"

Chapter 53

Niamh — 2016

The first thing Niamh noticed about her grandparents was that they could not stop touching one another. It was nothing inappropriate; rather a constant reassurance that the other was truly there, physically present, and that they weren't going to disappear as quickly as they'd arrived.

"We don't want to trouble you," Leo said, rubbing his thumb along the back of Maggie's hand. She looked up at him, eyes shining, and managed to convey *are you fucking kidding me* with her eyes better than Niamh would ever have imagined a ninety-year-old woman could.

"Come in and I'll make us all some coffee," Maggie said, moving towards the door and tugging Leo behind her. She was taller than Niamh had imagined she'd be; her snow-white hair floated around her shoulders like a cloud, and her eyes, the color of the ocean out of her front window, showed no signs of the milky film that comes with age. She was beautiful, and based on the besotted expression on Leo's face, he thought so too.

Later, when they were seated on Maggie's sky-blue sofa and appropriately caffeinated, Maggie finally asked, "How did you find me?"

"Property records," Niamh replied. "My cousin Bella found a purchase and sale on your house, and we went from there."

"You're a hard woman to track down." Leo grinned down at Maggie, the corners of his eyes crinkling in pure joy. "I looked. After they shipped me back to Italy, I sent so many letters, but I never heard a word."

Niamh watched as her grandmother squeezed her eyes shut, and she recognized the look of a woman willing the tears not to fall.

"I was able to get a visa and come back in '47, but your family had moved by then. No one would tell me where they had gone, and there was no record of a Margaret O'Callaghan anywhere. I looked for you, Maggie. Please believe me." The pleading look on the old man's face made Niamh want to reach across the couch and comfort him, but one look at her grandmother told her that she didn't need to.

"And I looked for you," she whispered. "I sent letters to everyone I could think of. I made transatlantic phone calls. I couldn't find you, so I assumed you didn't want to be found. By '47, my name wasn't O'Callaghan anymore. It was Morris."

"You're *married*?" Niamh yelped. How was this even possible? No, her grandfather deserved a happy ending to this love story. Hell, she deserved a happy ending to this love story.

"Widowed." Maggie turned to her granddaughter with a sad smile. "Charlie and I were married less than four years before he was killed in Korea. I thought if I was married and respectable, then they would tell me where Guliana was and give her back to me." Seventy plus years of grief had done nothing to ease Maggie's pain, and Niamh could hear it in the way her voice shook when she said her daughter's name.

"But they didn't." Niamh completed the thought for her.

"No. They did not."

Leo shifted on the couch, clearly uncomfortable with delivering the news he had to share. Niamh did it for him.

"Guliana — Julie — was my mother. She passed when I was twelve in a car accident."

Maggie's hands flew to her mouth. The tears she'd been fighting to keep in broke through their dam, and her shoulders shook with silent sobs. Niamh was ripped in two at the pain her grandmother felt — it was like losing her mother all over again, but from her grandmother's perspective.

"I'm so, so sorry... Ms. O'Callaghan... Maggie..." Niamh didn't know what to say; she knew there was nothing she could say that would help to stanch the flow of emotion erupting from the woman in front of her. Maggie fell to the side, and there was Leo, ready to catch her and hold on for dear life while she grieved the daughter she had lost all those years ago.

"I'll give you a minute," Niamh mumbled, awkwardly rising from the couch and fumbling for her key. "You two should — I'll be right back." She ran for the door, pushing it blindly open in her rush to get to the car. She needed to breathe, needed to ride this tide of emotion before it dragged her under. She needed to come to terms with the fact that any joy her existence brought to her family was tempered by the worst loss anyone can experience. She needed Christine.

Chapter 54

Maggie — 2016

Maggie had invited Leo and Niamh to stay for dinner, but Niamh insisted on leaving to check into her hotel. After making her promise to return in the morning, Maggie acquiesced to her leaving, and she and Leo watched from the window as their granddaughter backed down the driveway and onto the street.

There was never a question of Leo leaving for the hotel.

"I don't even know where to start asking questions about your life," she began, suddenly shy in the absence of Niamh. "I've thought of you every day for seventy years, and now that you're right in front of me..." she trailed off.

"Let's start here," Leo said, eyes twinkling as he sat down in Maggie's comfiest armchair and pulled her onto his lap. "I want to talk about everything and not leave anything out, but I need to touch you. I need to prove to myself that you're not a dream."

Maggie giggled, a sound she hadn't made in decades, and settled herself in the crook of Leo's arm, her ear against his chest. "Aren't we a little old for this?"

"Never," Leo declared, and held her tighter to him.

"You said you have another granddaughter. You were married, then?" Maggie asked, posing the question with all the delicacy of an unexploded grenade.

"Divorced. I couldn't love her the way she needed to be loved. We had three handsome boys, though, and my granddaughter Isabella. And you, *Margherita*? Did you ever have more children?"

Maggie sighed, reveling in the rumbling of words in Leo's chest before answering.

"No. I married for…" She paused, considering how best to put her twenties into words. "I married for the wrong reasons. I was a shell of a person, and Charlie wanted to take care of me. I couldn't forgive my parents for what they'd stolen from me, and when my brother Owen came home, he could barely look at me, so when Charlie came home and proposed, I jumped at the chance to leave my parents' house." The memories were hazy, as though they'd been lost in the dark for the better part of a century. "We never had children. I couldn't…" Maggie trailed off, comforted by Leo's strength beneath her and his steadfast ability to simply let her *be*. She had never needed to pretend with him. He just understood.

"You are going to adore Niamh," Leo finally said. "She's so much like you, it frightens me sometimes." Maggie responded by swatting him in the arm, settling into their old rhythm as if they had seen each other only yesterday.

"The poor girl lost her mother," she sighed. "Does she have any other family?"

"She's married." Leo's voice hummed in Maggie's ear. "Her wife is wonderful — a lawyer — and they're trying to have a family. That's what prompted Niamh to look for us; she wanted a connection with someone whose blood ran in her veins."

"Well, she certainly found that," Maggie said with a smile. Nothing could replace Guliana, but having a piece of her in Niamh soothed the jagged edges of Maggie's grief.

* * *

After a light supper of BLTs and lemonade, and after fielding several calls from a panicked Betty — *No, no, everything's fine, but I won't be joining you for dinner. Something came up* — Maggie invited Leo to sit on the deck with her and watch the tide come in over the sand.

"Is it always this breathtaking?" he asked, after a moment of watching the Atlantic Ocean slowly progressing up the beach, licking up inch after inch of terra firma with each passing minute.

"It always has been for me," Maggie replied with a sly look toward Leo, aware that neither of them were talking entirely about the view. "When I bought this place, it was mainly because of how far the tide goes out. I got myself a dog after Charlie died, a setter I called Seamus, and she'd run on the flats for hours until I called her in. Then she'd collapse in a heap of fur and snore loud enough to wake the dead." She smiled at the memory. She'd had other dogs since, but none that compared with Seamus.

"Isn't Seamus a boy's name?" Leo asked, scrunching his forehead in confusion.

"Are you going to begrudge me the name of my beloved companion, who has been dead for over fifty years?" Maggie raised an eyebrow before rising unsteadily to her feet and crossing the deck to lean on the railing.

"I wouldn't dream of it," Leo replied. "My God, Maggie, I don't know how, but being around you makes me feel like I'm twenty years old." She heard him stand from his chair and come up behind her, wrapping his arm around her waist and pulling her back into the warmth of his body. She closed her eyes and inhaled the scent of him, still a tantalizing combination of tobacco and Old Spice, and only opened her eyes again when she felt a slight pressure from Leo's embrace.

Maggie gasped. In Leo's hand was a delicate velvet box, and nestled inside was a magnificent art deco-style emerald ring.

"Leo..." Maggie turned in his embrace to face him, this man who had held her heart for the better part of a century. "What—"

"Marry me, Maggie. Please? I asked you once before, and you said yes, but then life got in the way. I swore to myself a long time ago that if I ever again got the chance to put a ring on your finger, I wouldn't waste it. Say you'll marry me."

Maggie looked down at the ring, which was now nestled between them, and then back up to Leo. "How soon can we do it?"

"Most courthouses open at nine... so that's what, fourteen hours?"

Maggie grinned, rising up on her tiptoes to kiss the man who had only been back in her life for a few hours, but whom she had loved for a lifetime.

Chapter 55

"You're sure?" Niamh asked for the sixth time, staring at her phone in incredulity. "You're like, sure sure?"

"I'm sure." Christine's grinning face came into focus, and Niamh had to resist the urge to jump up and down on her hotel bed. Instead she squealed with the most incandescent joy she had ever felt, kicking at the sheets on her bed in a strange rendition of a happy dance.

"I took three tests," Christine reported. "All positive. We're pregnant."

Niamh had called Christine at the crack of dawn, aware that today was the first day that Christine could take a pregnancy test to see if the in vitro had been successful. Christine had wanted to wait a few days for Niamh to return home before testing, but Niamh had insisted that Christine pee on the stick while she waited on FaceTime, chewing her fingernails to the

316

quick as they waited for the results.

"My God, it's killing me not to be there right now," Niamh whined, wanting nothing more in the world than to press her face to her wife's belly and to know that their baby was growing in there at this very moment, cells dividing and multiplying, creating this miracle child who would be born in roughly thirty-six weeks.

"You're the one who couldn't wait," Christine teased. Niamh could see her walking through their home in her sweats and tank top, hair piled on top of her head like a crown in an enormous messy bun. She had never loved Christine more fiercely than she did right now.

"I think pregnancy has made you hotter," Niamh mused, a smile playing at the corners of her mouth.

"Remember that when the morning sickness hits and you're cleaning up my vomit."

"There's no one else's vomit I'd rather clean up."

"You, Niamh Reilly, are a stone-cold weirdo." Christine laughed, turning the corner into their bedroom and climbing back under the covers of their bed.

"Yes, but you love me, so I'm not sure what that says about you."

"Not sure," Christine mused thoughtfully. "Something to bring up in therapy. So, what's going on with your grandparents today?" Niamh had filled Christine in on everything the night before — the romance of it, the agony of telling her grandmother that her only child was dead, and then the looks they exchanged that made Niamh feel very much like a third wheel. "Do you think they... you know..."

"Ew, Christine. They're my grandparents. And they're in their nineties." Niamh rolled onto her side, imagining that she was home and that Christine was right next to her.

"I don't know." Christine waggled her eyebrows suggestively. "Leo doesn't seem as old as he is. And he could have gotten some Viagra in anticipation of the reunion."

"I do not want to think about that!" Niamh shrieked, sending her wife into gales of laughter. God, it felt so good to be happy, if a little grossed out. She'd found her grandparents, they had found each other, and now she and Christine were going to be moms. She wasn't sure she had enough room in her heart for all this good news.

"Really, though," Christine continued, "what's the plan for today?"

"I thought I'd bring over some breakfast. My grandmother said that there's a place called Grumpy's on 6A that has great muffins. I figure I'll pick some up and head over around ten to see what they want to do today."

"Just make sure you knock first when you get there."

"Oh my God, is this what you're going to be like for the next nine months?" Niamh scrunched up her nose.

"If you're lucky."

* * *

By the time Niamh arrived back at the cottage on the beach, she found her grandparents dressed and waiting for her in the garden. Leo wore his usual slacks and button-down with a sweater vest, and Maggie wore a pretty tea-length dress in cerulean blue that brought out the color of her eyes. "You look beautiful," Niamh greeted her with a kiss on the cheek before reaching up to give Leo a hug.

"I always knew she'd be a beautiful bride." Leo winked at Maggie before turning to Niamh, a grin spread across his whole face.

"Come again?" Niamh stared at the couple, just then noticing the ring on her grandmother's finger and the bouquet of hydrangeas in her hand.

"We're off to the courthouse to make it official," Leo replied. "It's time this little lady made an honest man out of me."

Niamh watched in amazement as her grandfather winked at her grand- mother, and Maggie responded by blushing an adorable shade of pink. She racked her brain for something to say, but came up empty. This was — it was amazing.

"Niamh, I know we haven't known each other long, but will you be my maid of honor?" Maggie asked, reaching out a hand and placing it on Niamh's wrist.

Words still wouldn't come, so Niamh simply nodded, a familiar ache rising in the back of her throat. "I'm emoting. I hate emoting."

Maggie laughed, eyes shining. "You get that from me."

"OK then. I've waited long enough," Leo declared. "To the courthouse!"

"To the courthouse," Maggie and Niamh echoed, and they all climbed into the rented SUV.

Niamh was tempted to tell her grandparents about Christine's pregnancy, but she didn't want anything to take the attention away from these two people who had waited a literal lifetime for this day. There would be plenty of time to tell them tomorrow, she thought. There was so much good news to share that Niamh thought her heart might burst, and as she settled into the backseat of the SUV, she was touched by the sight of Maggie resting her head on Leo's shoulder as he drove, and Leo pausing at a stop sign to drop a kiss on top of her head.

Her grandfather had been right, Niamh realized with a quiet smile. Family isn't about blood, not at the core. Family is about finding the people you love and holding on tight, sharing experiences, raising children, and promising a lifetime of shoulders to lean on. Family was what Leo and Maggie created seven decades ago, and what they found in each other. It was what Niamh already had with Christine, what they would have with their children, and what she now couldn't wait to share with her grandparents.

About the Author

Kerrin Willis writes historical fiction with a romantic twist. She is a high school English teacher who prides herself on being a feminist and a strong protagonist in her own story, and she would probably have been burned as a witch in colonial New England. Kerrin can usually be found pausing *The Little Mermaid* and subjecting her two daughters to a lecture on the dangers of giving up their voices.

Kerrin has a BA in English from Stonehill College, and an MA in English from Simmons College, and is currently working on her MFA in Fiction from Southern New Hampshire University. She lives in Taunton, MA.

You can connect with me on:

🌐 http://www.kerrinwillis.com

Also by Kerrin Willis

Iron & Fire

1675 — Plymouth Colony — Verity Parker promised to look after her family.

Raised among the bookshops and turmoil of Reformation London, Verity now finds herself in Puritan New England, where she must learn to keep her head down and her mouth shut, or risk dire consequences. The only person who values her tenacity is Kit, the heretical ironworker she has been forbidden to see. When King Philip's War breaks out, Verity must stay silent as the Puritan elders spread hateful rhetoric about the "savages" in the forest. When she witnesses a young girl die in childbirth, Verity must stand by as neighbors blame God's vengeance. But when tragedy strikes her own home, Verity must choose between her duty to her family and her love for Kit. Will she choose to keep the peace, or will she defy the leaders of the colony for a chance at happiness?

Printed in the USA
CPSIA information can be obtained
at www.ICGtesting.com
LVHW010239090823
754563LV00006B/120